CABAL

CAL ROGAN MYSTERIES BOOK 5

ROBERT P. FRENCH

FOREWORD

Thank you for purchasing *Cabal* the fifth Cal Rogan Mystery. At the end of the book there is information about the other books and contact information.

In the story you will see references to the Canadian Security Intelligence Service. It is usually abbreviated as CSIS and pronounced see-sus. Also the Royal Canadian Mounted Police or RCMP or 'Mounties' are mentioned. These organizations help keep Canada safe, helping to make it one of the best countries in the world which to live.

ACKNOWLEDGMENTS

So many people go into the writing of a book and I would like to thank those who helped me with *Cabal*.

A special thank you to Andrew McKay of the Royal Canadian Airforce for pointing me in the right direction for information on the RCAF and for his service to our country.

A thousand thanks to every single member of my Launch Team for your support. You guy's rock!! I would like especially to thank the following members of the team who helped me hone the plot and whose eagle eyes found errors missed in the proofread. I made some critical changes based on your feedback. You all made this a better book. Alphabetically by first name, I would like to thank: Adele Knight, Alice Campbell, Andrew Tucker, Barry Thomas, Beverley Canuel, Bob Watson, Cindy Warrick, Colleen Beson, Dave McColeman, Deborah Andrew, Diane Griffin, Donna Bordage, Ed Campbell, Eva Beaton, Gillian Romain, Gloria Cardey, Grant Coull, Holly Stolarski, James Philips, Jamie DeAvilla, Janet Cline, Jeffrey Benham, Jim Bolger, John Mylett, Judith Baxter, Ken Pitman, Kenny Fraley, Krystle

Huwyler, Larry Branson, Linda DiMezza, Linda Harbour, Lisa Mauk, Lorraine Garant, Mary Clare Scully, Mel Calaby, Natoshia Avery, Patti Flanagan, Peter Lighthall, Rhiannon Cooper, Richard Pollack, Rod Marsh, Roz Wood, Sheryl Korljan, Siobhan Allen, Susan Oswalt, Terry Cochrane, Toni Keating, Valerie Hykawy and Vicky Sampson. If I missed anyone, my apologies. All errors are mine, not theirs.

As always, I would also like to thank the Vancouver Public Library for providing the perfect working location for any writer. Every word of *Cabal* was written here.

Dedication

To my wonderful wife Penny who believed in me when I had stopped believing in myself.

ALSO BY ROBERT P. FRENCH

Junkie (Cal Rogan Mysteries Book 1)

Oboe (Cal Rogan Mysteries Book 2)

Lockstep (Cal Rogan Mysteries Book 3)

Three (Cal Rogan Mysteries Book 4)

Captive (Cal Rogan Mysteries Book 6)

Jailed (Cal Rogan Mysteries Book 7)

All are available in paperback from Amazon.

1

ANNALISE

Thursday, Ottawa

Why is she late? She's never late. Ever since I've known her she's always been on time. I check my watch again. Over ten minutes. Maybe I should call or text. I clutch my purse closer. It doesn't feel any different, despite the explosive nature of the contents. How did I get mixed up in this? I'm in so far over my head. I should have told Sally days ago.

I'm sure the security guard sensed something was wrong when I left the building. Sure, he smiled at me when I passed his desk but maybe he knows. Maybe someone checked Neil's emails.

If only I hadn't— Oh, it's no use rehashing the whole thing and playing the blame game.

Where is she?

A text! I remove my glove and feel the bite of the Ottawa winter as I rummage in my purse. Because of my hat, sunglasses and scarf, the phone doesn't recognize my face, which is kind of the point. My hands tremble as I enter my passcode. Her text reads, *I'm just parking.* It's her second text. I must have missed the first one. It says, *Got delayed by a call from my boss. Had to take it.*

Thank God. I need to get the papers into her hands. She'll know what to do. She always knows what to do. A problem shared and all that. It was a crazy idea sending them to Denis. How could he possibly be of any use? What was I thinking? I should have come to her in the first place.

There are a few people walking along the canal—all bundled up against the cold and on their way to an early lunch, no doubt—but I'm the only one sitting on a bench. I turn to look towards the ramp leading into the Rideau Centre parking; no sign of her yet. Then I see the young man. His face seems vaguely familiar. He sits on the next bench over from me and shuffles off his heavy backpack. There is a length of string protruding from the middle compartment. His jacket is definitely not made for a Canadian December and he seems to be trembling. I can't help feeling sorry for him. He looks like he's a new immigrant and it's likely his first encounter with our snowy winters. He looks middle-eastern. Maybe he was a refugee. Who knows what he may have gone through to get to the safety of Canada.

He cuts a look at me and gives me a shy smile. No, not shy. Embarrassed maybe. I give him a smile back. I want to reach out to him. Say something welcoming; tell him the winters aren't so bad once you get used to them. Maybe I should tell him where he can get a good winter jacket, without paying an arm and a leg for it.

But before I can say anything, I see her; she's crossing the street towards me. Relief floods in and, with a quick smile to the young man, I stand and walk to her. She wraps me in a big hug and for the first time in five days, I feel safe.

Thank God she's here. We just stand hugging in the middle of the sidewalk, people passing on either side of us.

Suddenly she tenses.

I pull back and look at her face.

She's scared.

I turn and follow her gaze.

Five meters away the young man is on his feet clutching his backpack to his chest and holding the string sticking out of it.

Sally pushes me aside and shouts "NOOOO!" as she runs at him.

He yells, "ALLĀHU AKBAR."

He looks at me, his lips say one word, 'Sorry.'

As she is about to barrel into him he pulls the string.

2

CAL

Monday, Vancouver, four days later

Hey Rocky." The name from the past brings a flood of memories, most of them bad. It's a voice from the past too. I turn. He's standing right beside me; it's like he appeared from nowhere. It's how he got his street name. He's aged a decade in the three years since Roy's death. Living on the streets in the downtown east side will do that to a person.

"Hey Ghost, how's it going?"

He shuffles from one foot to the other. Undecided. "Yeah," is all he says. A pause, then, "Yeah, I'm OK I guess. You?"

"I'm good," I lie. If I were good, would I be here right now at Wastings and Pain—as this junction of Hastings and Main Street is often called—looking for a dealer in the winter rain? I hope this encounter is quick. He does his shuffle again and pulls at the arm of his raggedy jacket. Come on Ghost, spit it out.

"You're a cop now eh?" he says, equal parts of hope and worry written across his bearded face.

"Private Investigator." That seems to wash away some of the worry. "Why?"

He worries his lip with what remain of his bottom teeth. "Dj'a remember Wily?" The image of a short, skinny alcoholic, with a tinder-spark temper, springs into my mind. I have a nasty premonition of what's coming. I just nod. "Stupid bastard got hisself killed last week." He looks at me expectantly but I don't rise to the bait. Here it comes. "Only I was wondering if you could, y'know, like, uh, look into it."

There it is.

A trickle of rain finds its way under my collar and down the back of my neck. I don't have a lot of time. I need to make this buy, use it and get back to work. I should just say 'sorry' and move on. But I don't. "How'd he die?" It comes out as a sigh.

"'S a long story. Could we go somewhere out of this goddamn rain?"

All my instincts scream, 'no, no, NO.' "Sure. Meet me in forty-five minutes at the Ovaltine; I'll buy you lunch." It's what Roy would have wanted me to do for his friend.

I wonder what Roy would have thought about what I'm going to do next.

———

THE GUY AT THE CHECK-IN DESK LOCKS EYES WITH ME AND smiles. He seems like a nice guy. He must be to work here. We go through the sign-in process and he waves me on to the main room. The nurse behind the desk gives me the talk and the kit and I turn around. There's a row of booths, each one with a tabletop and a chair. The chair faces a mirror. The chairs are filled with addicts in various stages of fixing up. A guy in a red hoodie is inserting a needle into a vein. He tries twice before succeeding. I hear a woman sighing "Oooooooooh, yes," as the drug hits her system. Some of them are on the nod, enjoying the afterglow of the hit. A guy in a long black overcoat, covered in stains, pushes himself to his feet and wanders off. I walk over to take his place in booth number seven. I look in the mirror. It's there for two reasons: one, so that the nurse can have a front view of the addicts in order to spot any onset of problems; and two, so that the addicts can watch themselves shooting up. This will sometimes affect the addict so strongly that she or he will be given a motivation to seek the counselling that's available here.

Welcome to Insite, Vancouver's safe injection site. This place has saved hundreds of lives. Maybe mine will be one they save today. I sit down and lay out the kit and start. Remove my jacket and roll up a sleeve. Tie the surgical rubber around my bicep. Pull out the flap of heroin from my pocket, unable to stifle the worry that it may contain dangerous, even fatal, amounts of fentanyl. Into the cooker it goes with the sterilized water. When it bubbles, I turn off the cooker and drop in the gauze ball then rip the protective wrapper off the syringe and insert the needle and fill it. Ready. I look at myself in the mirror and in my mind's eye, I see them all staring at me: Sam, Stammo, Roy and even Em is there. Worst of all is Ellie. I imagine her reaction to watching.

Then a knife of pain hits me. They all disappear as I insert the needle and push the plunger. I free my bicep from the elastic and it hits.

"Oh... Oooooh... Oooooooooooooooh."

THE OVALTINE CAFÉ IS A TIME CAPSULE. WALK THROUGH THE doors and you are back in a bygone era. I doubt it's been renovated since the day it opened in 1942, which incidentally, makes it the oldest, continuously-running restaurant in the city. But it's clean, with good food, served in big portions and is probably the only place in Vancouver where you can still get a good, filling breakfast, any time of day, for less than ten bucks.

Ghost is tucking into his corned beef hash like there's no tomorrow. Between mouthfuls, his story unfurls.

"So, like I was saying, last Tuesday night was bitter cold, so me and Wily and Tommy Connor—you remember him, he was Freddy's younger brother—so we all stayed the night at the Catholic shelter downtown. 'S an OK place if you can put up with the praying part. Not that I'm complaining, they treat you alright there." He scoops up another mouthful of egg and hash. "Anyhoo, next morning, we came back and it was still pretty cold so we picked up our welfare and went off to the Balmoral Pub." I smile. The Balmoral Pub bears not the least semblance to the Queen of England's country estate of the same name. "So, we'd had a couple of beers," a 'couple' in this context is anywhere between two and a lot, "when this guy walks in. Big mother but well dressed, well... he was dressed well enough that he looked out of place in the Balmoral anyways. He looks around and he spots Wily and walks over to our table. He leans down and whispers something to Wily, who goes as white as a sheet. Looked like he'd seen a ghost. Next thing we know, Wily's grabbed his stuff and he's walking out with the guy and we never seen him again."

"You mean he went missing?"

"At first, yeah. We was worried 'cause we din't see him for a couple of days. We all live in Oppenheimer Park, we got a big tent we all share. He never showed up and all his stuff was gone. Then on Friday morning the cops show up looking for us and told us he was found dead on Thursday. Then they ask me and Tommy to come and identify the body. They drive us over to the morgue at VGH and sure enough, it's him."

"Did they tell you the cause of death?" I ask.

"Din't have to. Someone had beaten the snot out of him. We figured it was the big guy but the police wasn't that interested in what we thought."

He goes quiet and scrapes the last remnants of his hash off the plate then starts spreading strawberry jelly on his toast. "So you want me to find out if this big guy killed him?"

"Yeah," he answers. "Except that there's something more urgent. Me and Tommy want him to have a proper burial, in a cemetery with a gravestone and all, like you gave old Roy. Wily's got a sister, she lives in Ottawa, got a big job with the Feds, name of Annie. If you could track her down, she'd wanna know about Wily and pay for him to have a decent funeral. Wily was real fond of her; said she was good people. Do you think you could track her down, Rocky?"

"Sure. We could give it a try. What's her last name?"

"We don't really know."

"What was Wily's name?"

"Dunno that either."

Great. Half of the people who live in Ottawa work for the federal government and I have to find the one named Annie. I look at the hope written on Ghost's face and can't bring myself to tell him it's mission impossible. I just say, "I'll see what I can do."

"Oh thanks Rocky, you don't know how good that makes me feel. When do you think you'll know?"

I take out a business card and hand it to him. "Give me a call on Wednesday."

It's a long shot but I might be able to find something out. But right now, I need to pay the bill and get back to the office before Stammo starts wondering why I've been gone so long.

———

"YOU TAKING BANKER'S LUNCH HOURS NOW?" STAMMO GROWLS as I walk into the main office. "You're only just in time for the meeting."

"What meeting?"

"Jeez, Rogan where's your mind at? We've got a meeting with that guy Etienne Grey. The one who thinks his wife is cheating on him. It's a good that he's late, otherwise we wouldn't have looked very professional if you'd shown up halfway through. Why'd you take so long anyway?"

I can feel a flush rising in my cheeks. I'm only using three times a day, I've got it under control, but I can't let anyone know. I say the first thing that comes into my head. "I ran into an old friend and we got talking. Turns out he's got a problem we can help with."

"Oh," comes the reply, "Good." He seems mollified. "Is he one of your buddy Arnold's friends? I like *them* for sure. They're all loaded."

I skip over the worry that this will be a *pro bono* job and simply say, "It's tracking down a next of kin."

"Good. Easy work. What's the name?"

He's not going to like this. "Well—"

I'm saved the embarrassment of admitting I don't have a

clue by the sound of the front door opening, followed by Adry's greeting. Our three o'clock meeting is here.

Stammo rolls back from his desk and wheels out of the office into the reception area. I follow. The client is handing an expensive looking coat to Adry. He's in his thirties, tall, basketball-player tall, with blond hair, blue eyes and a serious expression. Nick extends his hand and the client has to lean forward a bit in order to shake it.

"I'm Nick Stammo and this is my partner, Cal Rogan."

"Etienne Grey. Pleased to meet you." His shake is firm and his serious expression softens a little. I have the unusual experience of having to look up to make eye contact. It strikes me that Stammo has to do this all the time now. Before the incident that put him in that wheelchair he was fairly tall too. It's one of the many things that he's had to adjust to and, as always, I feel the twinge of guilt that maybe I could have done differently on that day three years ago.

I lead the way to our tiny conference room and hold the door open for Grey and Stammo.

Once we've taken our seats, Stammo leads off, "How can we be of service Mr. Grey?"

"It's a bit embarrassing really." I've lost count of the number of times a client has started with those words, or a variation thereof. "It's my wife." That's the next most common phrase heard in this room; actually it's usually 'It's my husband.' Stammo and I stay silent and let him go at his own speed. He sighs before continuing, "We've always been honest and open with each other but recently Susan has been going out in the evenings and coming home late, often at two or three in the morning and she refuses to tell me where she's been. When I've questioned her, she swears she's not having an affair but just point blank won't tell me what she's been doing. It's driving me crazy; I just have to know what's happening."

On the face of it, he seems like a really nice guy whose wife is almost certainly cheating on him, but something tells me otherwise. I need to watch him for anything out of place.

"Is it specific days?" I ask.

"Not really, though she's often out on Wednesdays."

"Does your wife work?" asks Stammo.

"Yes. Like me she's a lawyer. She's at a different firm and she specializes in corporate law. It's quite a high pressure job. I don't know how she does it; on the nights where she's out she's wrecked the next morning and then she's sometimes out again the following night. And when she gets back home, she often has difficulty getting to sleep. I swear sometimes she only gets a couple of hours sleep a night. I'm worried sick."

Stammo glances at me then asks, "How are your marital relations?"

"Normal, I guess."

Neither Stammo nor I speak. We know he'll fill the silence. But he doesn't. Just as he's about to open his mouth, Adry enters with coffee and Stammo's favourite cookies. She puts them on the table. "You guys remember I'm leaving early today?" she says quietly, probably aware that she has broken the flow of the interview. I'd forgotten that her new boyfriend is coming over at four o'clock to take her out for an early meal and a hockey game but I nod in time with Stammo and she leaves quietly.

Grey takes a sip of coffee and nibbles a piece of chocolate cookie.

"You were saying..." Stammo prompts.

"Yes. I suppose it's normal. We have a date night every

Friday. She never seems to go out on a Friday night or at weekends."

"What do you mean 'seems'?" I ask. Either she does or she doesn't; surely he must know. That suspicious antenna is twitching again.

"I travel on business quite a lot. Sometimes I don't get back until Saturday morning or I'll leave on a Sunday afternoon. I wouldn't know whether or not she goes out on the nights I'm away."

I nod. Maybe I'm being overly wary.

"When you say you suppose it's normal, what exactly do you mean?" Stammo asks.

Grey looks uncomfortable. "We, uh, make love most Friday nights and at least once on Saturday and on Sunday." I feel a tug of jealousy. "And she's still as affectionate as always." The tug becomes a yank. "But it's clear that something's bothering her. She just won't tell me what it is."

I'm starting to get the feeling that maybe this isn't the case of a wayward wife.

Stammo slips the notepad off his lap and onto the desk. "We'll need some details about your wife," he says.

As Stammo takes down the information on Susan Grey, I wonder what is taking her out on weeknights. Assuming it's not a lover, what might it be? I'm drawing a blank.

As I watch Stammo scribbling notes, I'm aware of a certain twitchiness coming over me and I know exactly what it means. And it is nothing good. Although it's only a couple of hours since my last hit, my body is starting to crave heroin again. When I fell back into using after Em's death and Sam's defection with Ellie, I was able to cope on a once-a-day hit. Then it became twice a day. A couple of months ago I went to three times a day but now the cravings are becoming more insistent. I can hear the siren call of the Beast urging me on to take just one more hit.

"Can you email me a current picture of your wife?" Stammo's question pulls me out of the pit of my thoughts.

"I thought you might want a picture," he pulls his slim briefcase onto his lap and takes out an eight by ten. "This was taken last month to post on her firm's website. It's a very good likeness."

An intelligent face smiles out of the photograph at me. Susan Grey looks competent, kind and stunning all at the same time.

And I know her.

Or more precisely knew her. I knew her very well.

———

"SHE'S FOOLING AROUND ON HIM," STAMMO ASSERTS.

"I've got a hundred bucks says she's not."

"You're on! Make it two hundred, if you've got the stomach for it." I nod. "Let's see your money." He pulls out his wallet and slides ten twenties on to the table. I do the same. "Adry," he calls.

She comes in wearing her big smile. "What are you boys bickering about now?"

"A bet. Here," he hands her the cash. "Hold on to the stakes for us."

"OK," she chuckles. "What's the bet?"

"I reckon his wife's having an affair and Rogan says she's not."

"Oh I'm with Cal. Did you *see* that guy? He's drop-dead gorgeous. No woman would cheat on him, believe me."

"I didn't think he was that hot," Stammo says, with a rare reference to his own orientation.

She shrugs and takes the cash. "We shall see."

As she gets back to the reception desk, she says, "Oh, hi sweetie. You're early. Come and meet my other guys."

She walks back in with another face I know. Jason from Insite. He booked me in today. He knows I'm a user. Adry told us that her new boyfriend was a drug counsellor but not where he worked. "Guys, this is Jason. Jason this is Nick." He walks over and shakes Nick's hand. "And this is Cal."

He turns and we lock eyes for the second time today. He recognizes me and does an OK job in hiding the shock on his face. But not OK enough to fool Nick. "Do you guys know each other?" he asks.

Jason: "No." Me: "Yes."

Crap, I should have known he'd say no. I cover with, "We met once a few years ago. Back when I was using."

"Oh yes, I remember." He's not much of a liar either. I hazard a glance at Stammo and I'd bet another couple of hundred that he's guessed I'm using again.

Jason shakes my hand. "Nice to meet you both," he says. "We've got to get going if we want to get a bite to eat before the game."

"See you in the morning guys," Adry says and they leave, both excited by the prospect of watching the Canucks maybe blow another game.

Stammo turns to his screen. "I'm gonna watch CBC News. See what's the latest on the terrorist bombing last week." He pulls on his headphones and plugs them into his computer. He's cutting me out. He read Jason like a book. He knows I'm using again.

I need to tell him how I know Susan Grey but now's not the time.

"*Hi Dad. Only nineteen days.*" Ellie's face beams at me from my phone. Since her age hit double digits, she's stopped calling me Daddy and moved to Dad. It's OK but I must admit to a little sadness that she's growing up so fast and so far away. Over the last few months, little by little, Sam has let me back in. I now know they live in Toronto and I know the name of Ellie's school but their actual home address has not yet been shared. I have even got Sam to agree that I can see Ellie over Christmas. I booked my flight two months ago and Ellie and I are counting the days.

"Hi my lovely girl. How was school today?"

"*You always ask that. It was OK. Ethan was funny; he made me laugh during French class. Madame D'Artois was angry with him.*" Instant switch of subject: "*What cases are you working on?*"

Now that she's asserted that she 'wants to be a police-woman for sure, for sure,' she always wants to know about our cases.

"We got a new case today. It's a man worried about his wife. She keeps going out late at night and she won't tell him where she goes."

"*Maybe she goes shopping?*" she giggles. "*Or maybe she's a vampire.*"

"Do you even know what a vampire is?"

"*Yes. Ethan told me. He was one for Halloween. He kept saying 'I want to suck your blood' in a funny voice. He's hilarious.*"

I sense the dawning of a pre-teen crush.

"I don't think she's a vampire El."

"*Well if she is you'll know what a good detective I am.*"

We chat on for a while until I hear Sam's voice in the

background. *"Bedtime, sweetie."* Her voice brings so many emotions sweeping in but I crush them down. El and I say our goodnights and I'm left alone with my thoughts. I think about Sam and Ellie and about whether Stammo has really guessed I'm using again and about how in hell I'm going to track down the late Wily's sister, Annie.

But most of all, I think about our new client's wife, Susan Grey, née Beckett.

And I think about my heroin.

3
CAL

Tuesday

As I turn off the ignition, the sound of the radio fades. It's five days since the Ottawa bombing and it's still the only thing on the news, which is fair enough, it is after all the first real terrorist attack to happen in Canada. It's one area where we didn't want to catch up with the rest of the world. Eleven people killed. They have been able to use DNA to identify most of the bodies, the names and backgrounds have been released to the press.

As I get out of my beloved Austin Healey 3000, Adry pulls up beside me in her little grey Mazda. "How was the game?" I ask as she gets out and locks the doors.

"We won, four to two," she grins.

"Great." I'm not a big hockey fan; I don't even know who they were playing. We walk to the elevator. "Jason seems like a great guy." I say.

"He is." She goes silent for a moment. "How is it you know him Cal? He wouldn't talk about it to me."

I can feel a flush in my cheeks and she sees it too. "I'll tell you when we get up to the office."

The elevator ride is a bit awkward. A foreshadowing of things to come?

As we walk into the office, Stammo says, "About time you guys got in. I've made coffee and it's time for morning prayers." That's Stammo's new term for our morning meeting where we review cases and plan the day. He picked it up from an English ex-cop he met in a pub.

We go through the workload, which is all pretty vanilla-flavoured cases, until we get to our newest case: the odd behaviour of Susan Grey. "The obvious thing to do is to stake out their place and follow her when she goes on one of her little expeditions," Stammo suggests.

Before I can speak, Adry chimes in, "Listen guys, I know you hired me to be the office manager and all but I'd kinda like to be involved in the detective work too. Any chance I could come along on the stake out?"

"Sounds good to me," Stammo says. He looks at me for agreement.

I don't want to burst her bubble so I say. "I think it's a great idea for you to get involved in the investigation side of the business." I get rewarded with a big smile. "But in this case, I don't think we need to do a stake out. I didn't get the chance to tell you yesterday but I know Susan Grey."

"How?" they ask in unison.

"She was my first serious girlfriend. We met at UBC. First year. I was doing Lit and she was doing pre-law."

"And you didn't think to let the client know?" Stammo gives me his disapproving frown.

"I thought about it for a second or two but then I thought maybe I could just go and talk to her, see if she would confide in an old friend."

The disapproval turns to sarcasm. "Oh great. What are you gonna say? 'Your husband's hired me to check up on you. Are you fooling around on him?' Yeah, that'll work, no problem." He snorts.

I know why Stammo's angry and I don't blame him. "No. I thought I'd just run into her and invite her for coffee, let it drop that I'm a private investigator and see if she reacts. Maybe she needs a friend she can talk to, other than her husband."

"Hmm. Might work." He's only partly mollified.

"If it doesn't fly, I'll hand it over to you guys and you can stake her out."

He nods and looks back at his project spreadsheet. "You said you had a next-of-kin case," he says.

"Oh yeah." I'd almost forgotten about the job of trying to find Wily's sister in Ottawa. I tell them about my meeting with Ghost.

When I finish, the first words out of Stammo's mouth are, "So, I'm guessing it's *pro bono*." Then comes the real question. "Did this Ghost character come to the office?" He knows the answer. It's time.

"No. I ran into him at Hastings and Main. And before you ask, I was down there to buy heroin."

For a couple of seconds the silence is profound. I hear the ping of an elevator arriving at our floor then voices in the corridor. Then Stammo speaks.

"When did you start?"

"Six months ago."

Stammo does the math. "After Em?" His voice is gentler.

I just nod.

Adry steps over, kisses me on the cheek and rubs my arm, then turns around and goes back to her desk.

Stammo just nods and goes back to his spreadsheet.

Their silent acceptance is harder to bear than any anger.

———

THE LOBBY OF THE TELUS GARDEN OFFICE TOWER IS IMPOSING to say the least. I'm sitting in one of the expensive white chairs which resemble opening buds and are as elegant as they are uncomfortable. The curved wooden beams which support the glass roof are like the ribs of some giant whale, in which, like Jonah, I am sitting. From the fifty foot water-fall behind the glass security desk to the granite planters—each containing a tree surrounded by a profusion of white orchids—to the baby grand piano being beautifully played by a slim young man in a plaid shirt, it is corporate opulence gone wildly overboard.

While waiting for my target at one end of the social spectrum, I'm working for my client at the other end.

"Can I speak to Doctor Marcus, please?" I say into my mobile.

"Speaking."

"Kaye, it's Cal Rogan." Then I remember. "Rocky." She only knew me by my erstwhile nickname; it makes me think of Roy.

"Oh yes. Hi, how are you? I haven't seen you in years."

We do the catching up thing, then I ask, "You have the body of a homeless man there. He was beaten to death last week."

"Yes. Very nasty. He was tortured before he was killed. Who would do that to a homeless man?"

Tortured? That makes no sense at all.

"One of his friends has asked me to track down his sister but the problem is they only know him by his street name, Wily. Do you have an ID for him?"

"Just hang on." I hear the soft click of her typing. I'm holding my breath. I realize that this matters to me. Wily was a good friend of Roy and it gives me an... I dunno... a kind of... well... kinship. I make a quick decision. *"Sorry, Rocky. He's listed as a John Doe."*

"OK, thanks Kaye. Listen, when you're ready to release the body, let me know. If I can't find his next of kin, I want to make sure he gets a decent funeral."

"Will do."

We say our goodbyes and I go back to watching the elevators.

The twitchiness is getting worse but I'm determined to miss my lunchtime fix. See if I can get through until night-time. All I have to do is miss this one. They say one day at a time but with heroin it's more like one hour at a time. A lot of detective work is just waiting but it's a hell of a lot more difficult to just sit and wait when you are literally itching for a fix.

Then I see her. She's stepping out of an elevator with a young woman who looks about twenty. They turn and head towards the door. I get up and head in the same direction, trying to time it just right. We converge on the doors at the same time and as they glide open, I make the universal 'after you' gesture to Susan and her companion.

Perfect timing.

Our eyes meet.

"Susan?"

She pauses for a second and then beams. And in that smile I am transported back almost a quarter of a century. I can feel my heart skipping. "Cal?" She looks at me then wraps me in a hug which lasts longer than I would have expected. When she finally lets go she slides her hands down my arms until she is holding both of my hands in hers. She turns to her younger companion and says, "Why don't you go ahead and get us a table Abigail, I'll be there in a couple of minutes."

She squeezes my hands. "It is *so* good to see you. What are you doing here?"

The worm of duplicity starts to squirm in my gut. "I have a client in this building."

"A client? I always imagined you would become a prof and teach your beloved Shakespeare to eager students. What is it you do?"

"I'm a private investigator."

"Wow."

"I assume you became a lawyer," I say. The worm squirms more firmly.

She gives a grin. "Well, duh."

We both laugh.

"I really want to catch up with you. I'm going to be in the building all day," I lie, "how about we meet for a quick drink after work at the Kingston next door."

She thinks for a second and I can see her inner debate. Finally, she reaches a decision and it's not the one I want. "Well actually Cal, I..." Her voice trails off. It hangs in the balance. I'm holding my breath again. New decision. "Sure, why not? The Kingston at six."

"You're on," I smile, wondering what changed her mind; I'm not convinced it's just my boyish charm.

She kisses me on the cheek. "I'd better go," she grins. She steps forward, the door opens for her and, as I enjoy watching her walk briskly along Georgia, I feel the twitchiness return.

My phone buzzes in my pocket. I pull it out. I don't recognize the number. "Cal Rogan."

"Hey Cal, it's me Ghost."

"Hey. What's up?"

"*Can you come over to the east side. I wanna show you something.*"

There's stuff I have to do on another case, one with a big fee attached. We've been asked to track down the scion of a prominent Vancouver family: a youngest son with a drinking problem. "Can it wait?"

"*Yeah...*" the reply comes out as a sigh. "*I suppose so... It's just that...*" He clears his throat. "*So when do you think you can come?*"

There's a disappointment in his voice verging on pain. I cave. "Sure, I'll be right over. Where do you want to meet?"

"*How about the Balmoral?*"

"Sure. See you there in twenty minutes."

I hang up and wonder if I caved in sympathy or because the Balmoral is a three minute walk from the alley where my dealer hangs out.

————

I'M DRINKING MY BEER FROM A BOTTLE; I'D RATHER NOT TRUST the cleanliness of the glasses here. Ghost and Tommy Connor have big glasses of draft in front of them, being more persuaded by volume than by clean. On the table is a plastic Safeway bag.

Ghost takes in half his glass in three big swallows and gives a contented "Ahhhh. That's the stuff." He wipes his lips on his sleeve and pushes the plastic bag over to me. "We found this," he says.

"It was under the tent," Tommy says. He is a skinny alcoholic who closely resembles his late older brother Freddy, who was Roy's best friend. "We was all sleeping in a big tent in Oppenheimer," he explains. Oppenheimer Park has become Vancouver's biggest tent city: a sad symbol of government's inability to deal with the city's homelessness problem. "Anyways," he continues, "'cos it's so damn cold, me and Ghost decides we can't sleep there overnight no more. So we took the tent down and here's what we found."

"Yeah," Ghost adds, "we thought you'd wanna take a look at it. It was hidden under the tent. Like Wily didn't want no one to see it." He pushes it an inch or two closer to me.

The bag is pretty grubby. I open it and inside is another plastic bag wrapped around what looks like a small box. It's tied up with string. "What is it?" I ask.

"Dunno," offers Tommy. "We figured it might be evidence, eh. So we didn't want to touch it in case we did something wrong."

Evidence for what, I cannot imagine.

They both sit looking at me expectantly. I untie the string, unwrap the second, and then a third plastic bag. "He certainly wanted to protect whatever it is," I say.

"Is it a clue?" Ghost asks.

"No. It's a box." I take it out of the innermost bag.

It's a pink box a little smaller than a shoe box; maybe a box for a little girl's shoes. It is held closed by a white ribbon, the bow on top crushed by the tightly wrapped plastic bags which encased it. As I take it out something rattles inside.

I untie the bow and lift the lid. There are two items inside and they could not be more different.

I remove the larger item.

"A book." The disappointment in Ghost's voice is evident.

But it's not just a book. It has a rich, dark-brown, leather cover, soft to the touch. On the front, in gold filigree, is written *La Bible*. Beneath the title is *Louis Segond*, and beneath that is the chi-rho symbol inside a golden circle. It feels old in my hands and, although I'm far from being an expert bibliophile, it feels very valuable to me. It must have been valuable to Wily too. Most alcoholics, as far-gone as he was, would have sold this off long ago to buy booze.

I open it gently. On the first page, scribbled in French, in block capitals is: PROPRIETÉ DE DENIS LAMARCHE. The writing looks like it was done by a kid. I turn the page; in contrast, is a beautifully penned note. It is written in fountain pen, the ink slightly faded. I translate it for my companions, "To Denis, on the Occasion of his Confirmation, from his Loving Parents, Samuel and Clarisse. January 27, 1980. Sainte-Foy, Québec."

"Huh, confirmation," says Tommy. "I never knew Wily was religious."

"He wasn't," says Ghost. "Not now anyways. But I always noticed when we were in the Catholic shelter he knew the words to all the prayers." Tommy nods in agreement. "He sometimes even said something in Latin to the priests." He finishes his beer and looks at me expectantly. I pull a twenty from my wallet and hand it over. "Get another round for you and Tommy," I tell him.

"Thanks, Rocky. D'ja want another one yerself?" I shake my head and he makes his way to the bar.

Gently, I place the Bible back in the box and take out the other item. It's a memory card, identical to the one in my camera. I wonder why this was so valuable to Wily that it's in the same box as his Bible. I'll take a look at it later. Maybe there'll be some photographs which might give a clue to his death. I can feel the tingle that goes with a new case and that old desire to solve it before my former colleagues in VPD can. Stammo wouldn't approve.

When Ghost gets back with the refills, I ask them both, "What did you guys know about Wily's life before you met him?"

"Not much," says Tommy.

"You know what it's like on the streets, Rocky," adds Ghost. "You don't ask too many questions. But I can tell you this: Wily was a very clever guy. He never made a big deal of it but he'd read a lot in his time. Knew a lot of stuff about a lot of stuff if you know what I mean."

"Yeah, and he was great at math," chimes in Tommy. "I think he knew a lot about computers too. Sometimes when he'd had a few drinks he'd talk about artificial intelligence and stuff like that. None of us could understand what he was saying but he'd go on about it for hours." He smiles fondly at the memory.

"Is it OK with you guys if I hold onto this stuff for a while? Now we know his name, assuming he's the Denis Lamarche whose name's on the front page, I should be able to track down his sister Annie and at least I can give her his Bible. I'm sure she'll want to give him a decent funeral too. There can't be that many Annie Larmaches working for the Federal government in Ottawa." As I say the name, it rings a bell, I'm just not sure where from but it gives me an uneasy feeling.

THE KINGSTON IS AN ANOMALY. IT IS A PINK, FOUR-FLOOR, boutique hotel which has been handed down through generations of the same Irish family for a hundred years. It is surrounded on three sides by the Telus Garden development, to whom the family stubbornly refused to sell out—much to the great pleasure of many Vancouverites who are watching the face of our downtown core changing, not always for the better.

The Kingston's Taphouse could not be more different from the Balmoral. The carved wooden bar is elegant without being pretentious, spoiled only by the television screens—broadcasting talking heads still going on about the Ottawa terrorist attack—which cover up some of the ornate carving. The planks on the floor are rough, the clientele are smooth and, with its fine selection of beer, it is a favourite hangout of mine.

I'm enjoying an excellent Four Winds IPA at the bar while I wait for Susan Grey to arrive. The good news is that I was able to avoid the lure of the downtown east side's heroin dealers and I have been able to push down the pangs of my heroin-yearning; the bad news is that since my meeting with Ghost and Tommy, I've spent the afternoon having no luck in tracking down my missing rich guy. I've talked to his two closest friends and visited a number of his favourite haunts, all to no avail.

"Hello stranger, can I take this seat?" There is laughter in Susan's voice that lightens my crushing mood.

She sits and orders a Martini, brought quickly by a barman who really knows his stuff.

After the initial banter, I ask the question I hope will start the ball rolling. "So, tell me what's been happening with you for the last quarter century."

"Oh my God. Is it that long? I feel so old."

"You look fantastic," I say, the words coming out of my mouth without thought.

She grins. "You look pretty good yourself."

I gesture towards her left hand. "I see you're married now."

"Yes. Ten years. He's a wonderful guy." She seems sincere

and I'm feeling pretty sure in my bet with Stammo that she is not being unfaithful to Etienne Grey.

"Great husband, great job, still looking twenty years old. Seems like you have the perfect life," I say.

For an instant, there is a flicker of uncertainty in her face but she pushes it away with another smile. "Pretty much," she says.

"For a moment there you looked uncertain," I say.

"No, no. I was just thinking about something at the office," she lies. I know it. And she knows I know it. She changes the subject and asks about my life.

As I tell her, I know that I'm not going to learn her secret this evening.

I'm going to have to put plan B into action. Starting tomorrow night. Wednesday. The night her husband says she's often out.

4

NICK

Wednesday

The pain is hammering away in my head. I don't know if it's lack of sleep, too much Jim Beam or the dread of what I have to do next. But a promise is a promise. Especially one you make with yourself. The chat with my lawyer yesterday afternoon helped. It all seemed easy then but now that I'm faced with having to do it, it's not going to be easy at all. I hope he gets in before Adry; I don't want her to see it if it gets nasty.

I hear the office door open and he walks in. He looks like hell on wheels. "Are you OK?"

"Yes and no. I haven't had a hit since midday on Monday and the pain is pretty bad."

"I've got some Extra Strength Tylenol in my desk. Will that help?"

"Can't hurt."

He follows me into the main office and to my desk. He dry-swallows three of the pills. "It's going to be bad for a few days," he says, "but I'll get through it somehow. I'm sorry, Nick."

"Yeah... well..." I bite my lip for a bit. "I'll tell you the truth Rogan. When we started this business, I made a promise to myself that if you ever started using again, I'd close the business down and start up on my own. I talked to my lawyer yesterday and told him to prepare the papers."

We lock eyes. The silence is so deep you could hear a mosquito fart. He doesn't say a word. I feel like a judge about to pass sentence. I take a deep breath. "I'll hold off, just so long as you stay clean and start going to meetings."

He breathes out a deep sigh. "Thanks Nick," I can see tears forming in his eyes. "I won't let you down. I promise."

"Good," I grunt. I can feel my own eyes prickling. "Good." I look away and open up my computer.

"'Morning men." Adry's in.

She walks into the main office with a Tim Horton's bag. "Doughnuts," she says, dropping them on my desk. "I'll get the coffees." She breezes through into the little kitchen area and returns with three steaming cups.

Time for 'morning prayers'.

5

CAL

I've been a bit distracted during the morning meeting. I can't keep out of my head the thought that Stammo was about to shut down the business. A part of me is angry about it but, in the main, I am just awash in shame. I can't stand the thought that I might have destroyed the company I've come to love. Stammo glared at me in the early part of the meeting because I was on my phone but I was searching for a meeting; there's one at twelve fifteen today and I'm going to be there, not just for the sake of the business but for Ellie. I can't get the image from Insite out of my mind, the image of her watching me fix up, and if Sam knew, she'd probably—

"Cal!"

"Sorry, what?"

"Your update on the Susan Grey case?"

I tell them about my meeting at the Kingston Taphouse and my plans for this evening.

"Right. Meeting over, let's get after it." This is Nick's new end-of-meeting phrase; he picked it up from CNN, I think.

"There's one other thing," I say. "The homeless guy who

was beaten to death. I found out his name. It was Denis Lamarche. I want to track down his sister Annie. She works for the Feds in Ottawa. Could you see if you can get a phone number for her Adry?"

"Sure, no prob."

"Just don't spend too much time on it," Stammo growls, "it's a *pro bono* job."

Adry chuckles at him. "OK Mr. Grumpy. I'll check for Anne, both spellings, and Anna too. How do you spell the last name?"

"It's Lamarche. L-A-M—"

"What did you say?" Stammo interrupts. "Lamarche?"

"Yeah, Ann—"

"There was an Annalise Lamarche who was one of the victims of that terrorist attack in Ottawa last week."

Stunned silence reigns for a moment.

"Denis Lamarche's body was found on Thursday," I say.

"If it's the sister, what are the chances they'd both die violent deaths on the same day?" Adry asks quietly.

"Slim to none," I reply.

This time it's Stammo who breaks the second silence.

"I don't believe in coincidences."

Over the twitchiness and pain of withdrawal, I feel that tingle in my gut: the special thrill that comes when you get a break in a case.

"I'll be right back," I say as I rush from the office.

———

STILL OUT OF BREATH FROM MY DASH DOWN TO THE CAR AND back, I place the box on my desk. I take out the memory card. "Denis Lamarche hid this under the tent he lived in at

Oppenheimer Park. I was wondering if there were any pictures on it that might give a clue as to how he died."

Stammo takes it. "Well let's take a look."

He opens a drawer in his desk and takes out the company's camera: an item that we thought would be essential to running a private investigation firm; an item which, until now, we've never used. He powers it up and slides in the memory card. He taps a few buttons. "Huh," he grunts.

"What is it?" Adry and I say in unison.

He taps a few more buttons. And a few more.

He turns the camera around so we can see what's on the screen.

It's blank.

"So there's nothing on it," I can't keep the disappointment out of my voice.

"I wouldn't say that."

"What do you mean?" I ask.

"There are no pictures on it," he says.

"That's what I said. There's nothing on it."

"No. There may be no *pictures* on it but that's not nothing," he's using his annoying, patronizing voice.

"It's a camera's memory card," I'm using my annoyed, exasperated voice. "What else could be on it?"

"Watch and learn," he says, a favourite expression of his.

He slides the card out of the camera, slowly puts the camera back in its bag and, equally slowly, puts the bag back in his desk. He's doing it to annoy me and succeeding admirably.

He wheels over to the cabinet where we keep our office supplies; on the bottom shelf are the computer supplies and a bunch of accessories and cables. He calls Adry over. "Behind that box of ink cartridges there's a small yellow box. Can you get it for me please?" Again I think about the frustration he must feel at being unable to do some of the simplest things. And I think about the guilt I feel because he's in that chair.

He wheels back to the desk with the yellow box in hand. He takes out a white plastic gizmo with slots of various sizes on the top and a cable coming out the side. He plugs the cable into his computer and slides the memory card into one of the slots.

Adry and I move around behind his desk and each of us peers over one of his shoulders. In a couple of clicks, we are looking at a folder with two files in it. One is named 'docs' and the other is 'hint'. Stammo double-clicks on the 'docs' file. A window pops open and it is filled with gobbledegook. There are letters and numbers but mainly it is a bunch of squiggles and odd characters.

"What the hell is that?" I ask.

"I don't know. It's some sort of file. Maybe a WORD doc."

He tries to open the file with WORD but that doesn't work either.

"What about the other file, 'hint'," Adry suggests.

Stammo double clicks the other file.

Ten words appear on the screen: 'garter is the key. you'll know what it means annie'.

Stammo snorts. "Well Annie may know what that means but I don't."

"Garter?" says Adry. "Well the obvious thing is a little snake you find in the garden. The other is a garter belt, you know, one of those elastic things women used to wear to hold their stockings up."

"Yeah," says Stammo, "but what we've gotta remember is that Denis Lamarche was an alcoholic living on the streets. This might all be nothing, just a bunch of raving."

"Just because he was an alcoholic doesn't mean it's all nonsense," Adry says.

"Doesn't mean it makes sense though..."

As they bicker on like the old married couple they're not, I stare at the words on the screen: 'garter is the key. you'll know what it means annie'. I say it over in my mind. I say it different ways, putting different emphases on different words. Nothing. Denis and Annalise were from Québec. I'd say it in French except that I don't know the French word for garter, neither snake nor belt. Nothing. I look at each word individually. The. Key. Is. Garter. Hmmm. Key? Then it comes: the memory of another case.

"Can you copy those files onto a thumb drive?" I ask.

"Sure." He pulls a thumb drive out of his desk and pops it in his computer. After a few clicks, he pulls it out and hands it to me.

"I'll be back later," I say as I head to the door.

"Wait a minute, Rogan." Stammo's voice stops me in my stride. "You've just discovered that the brother of a terror-attack victim was killed on the same day as she was. Don't you think we should, I dunno... what?... maybe call it in to the RCMP?"

I ignore the sarcasm dripping from his jaws. "Good idea. Call it in to their counter-terrorism unit. Just don't send them the files yet."

I'm out the door before he can object.

————

DAMIEN CROTTY AND I WERE UNLIKELY FRIENDS IN HIGH school. He was a Goth and I was a nerd but we bonded over a book we both loved. Now he's a millionaire techie and I'm a thousandaire PI. He runs a very successful computer security company that does, among other things, testing the computer security of his clients by trying to hack into their systems.

He's wearing jeans and a t-shirt which says, *Free will: the persistent illusion that we have any control over the choices we make.* Somehow he is one of those people who can make jeans and a t-shirt look like a fashion statement.

"Thanks for seeing me on such short notice, I really appreciate it."

"No prob. It's great to see you. What's up?"

I hand him the thumb drive. "There's a file on that drive that I think might be encrypted. I was wondering if you could find out what's in it."

He grins as he plugs it into the laptop on his desk. "You're not asking much." He stares at the screen. "Well first thing, there's no malware on the thumb drive. That's a good start." He does a couple of clicks. "I'd say you're probably right that it's encrypted. Do you have the key?"

"Look in the file called 'hint'," I say.

"Hmm. 'Garter is the key.' Not too likely." He taps away for about twenty seconds. "Nope. As I thought, the word garter is not the encryption key for this file."

"The guy who I think encrypted it was québécois, maybe it's the French word for garter."

He types away for a bit longer. "Garter is jarretière." Type, type. "Garter snake is couleuvre." Type, type. "Nope. Neither of those work. Normally, keys are a lot longer than six letters. You should ask the 'annie' mentioned in the 'hint' file. She may know."

"I wish I could but she's dead."

"Oh... Sorry to hear that."

"Is there any way that you could decrypt it without the key?" I ask.

"Brute force decryption? I could try but don't hold your breath." He types away for a minute or so. In the silence, I feel the withdrawal pains in my body biting down. "OK. I've sent it to one of our servers to try but as I say..." He shrugs his shoulders.

He pulls the thumb drive out of his computer and hands it to me. "I was planning an early lunch. Do you want to join me?"

"I'd really love to but I've got an appointment I dare not miss."

He promises to let his computers keep working on the decryption and that he'll call me if they succeed, then we say our goodbyes and I think ruefully of the lunch I'm missing. It would be infinitely preferable to where I'm heading right now.

———

"MY NAME'S CAL AND I'M AN ADDICT." IT'S A WHILE SINCE I've said those words. They make me feel bad and good at the same time. I look at my watch. "It's forty-seven and a half hours since my last fix." As I tell them my story, I look across the crowd. They are typical of the usual crowd at an NA meeting: there are a couple of well-dressed businessmen; a group of three younger guys who look like they might be in some high-tech company; a handful of homeless men, one of whom I can smell from where I'm standing. There are only two women: one is a short blonde who looks like she's someone's much-beloved grandma and the other is a striking south asian woman, casually well-dressed. The crowd may be diverse but this room is special. We are all exactly equal here. We are all addicts. For some reason, I think of Damien's t-shirt. *Free will: the persistent illusion that we have any control over the choices we make.* How can that be true? It starts to bug me and I fumble over what I was saying. I apologize and continue with my story, telling the part about when I started using again after Em's death. As I speak, I notice the south asian woman is looking at me intently. She has one of those stares that seems to look into one's soul. Yet there is both sympathy and humour in her eyes.

I manage to get to the end of my story without any further fumbles.

"Thanks Cal," says the chairman. "That about wraps it up for today. There's coffee and snacks at the back to compensate you for missing lunch to come to a meeting."

He winds up the meeting in usual fashion and I start to head out. I want to check in with Stammo and find out what he's learned about Annalise Lamarche and I need to find out if Damien has got anywhere with that encrypted file. Plus I need to—

"Excuse me, Cal." I turn and face the speaker. It's the woman who looked into my soul. Up close, I see how beautiful she is. She's almost as tall as me and she emanates an aura of calm and warmth. She extends a slim hand elegantly. "My name's Tina. Do you have a second to answer a question?"

I really don't. "Yes, of course."

We are both still shaking hands. Her hand feels almost insubstantial yet her grip is firm. I feel a little pang of regret as we unclasp our hands; I wonder if she felt the same.

"Full disclosure," she grins. "I'm a journalist and I know we're not the favourite profession of cops and ex-cops." She's right but I find myself making reassuring noises. "I just got back from Ottawa; I was covering the bombing. But I'm also working on a long-term project about unusual killings in

Canada and I was wondering if I might interview you about the case you mentioned. It can be on or off the record; your choice."

The thought of rehashing all of the case that culminated in Em's death churns uncomfortably in my gut. It really is absolutely the last thing I want to talk about ever again. I shake my head as I look into her eyes but say, "Sure, *but if I help, what do you promise me?*" Did I just say that? She looks taken aback. "Sorry," I say, feeling myself flush. "It's a line from *All's Well that Ends Well.* It just popped into my head. I'm really sorry, I didn't mean to imply..."

She comes to my aid by bursting into laughter. *"I as free forgive you, As I would be forgiven,"* she says. "Any cop who quotes Shakespeare gets a pass from me."

I am too amazed at her quotation to speak, but she fills in the silence. "I promise you a good dinner for your help, Master Constable. How does that sound?" She hands me her business card.

"How about this evening?" Oh my God, I'm sounding too eager.

"It's a deal. Seven o'clock at the Lift?"

"'Tis in my memory lock'd." I say, but then my memory catches up with the instant attraction I have to this woman. "Oh, wait a minute, I have to do a surveillance this evening."

"Oh." She looks disappointed.

Awkward silence.

She says, "Maybe some—"

"You could come with me." I *am* the eager beaver today. "Surveillance is usually a lot of sitting about in cars waiting for something to happen. You could ask me about the case and we could maybe have hotdogs or something."

"Sounds like a plan. You could pick me up from the address on my card. What time works?"

"I'm going to follow her from work. I doubt that she's likely to leave work much before six but to be on the safe side, I need to be at her office by five." I look at her card. It's an address in Coal Harbour. "If I pick you up at four forty-five that should work."

"Done." She shakes my hand again.

Without letting go I say, "I'd better get going. See you at four forty-five."

"I look forward to it."

"Me too."

As I leave, I think of Em and the sting is not as sharp.

The withdrawal pain however is as sharp; in fact, sharper.

———

I FEEL TWITCHY AND SHIVERY SITTING OPPOSITE GHOST. I'M not too optimistic that I'll get much out of this meeting, he's had more booze than usual for two in the afternoon and he's a step or two away from full coherence. His sidekick Tommy is not with him.

The withdrawal pains are bad and I need to stay away from the downtown east side in case I succumb to the lure of the dealers there. Ghost feels out of his element in the Railway Club and he's getting some odd looks from the clientèle.

"Tha's a good beer, Rock," he slurs. "Tommy'll be pissed he didn't get any, eh."

"Listen, man. You remember that memory card we found in that box of Wily's?"

"Yeah. Little plastic thing with photos on it, right?"

"Yeah. Except it wasn't photos on it, it was computer files. There were two of them."

"Makes sense. Wily knew all about computers. I dunno nothin' about computers but he was a fuckin' genius. He used to go to the library every day and use 'em for email an' stuff like that."

He finishes his beer and looks at me expectantly. It's a fine line: I buy him another one and his dwindling *compos mentis* disappears; refuse and he clams up. I wave our server over.

"Listen Ghost. I've been looking into Wily and I tracked down his sister, Annie."

"Fuckin' great, Rock. I knew you could do it. Roy always said you was the best. She gonna pay for his funeral and all?"

"Thing is... she was killed in the bombing in Ottawa last week."

His eyes do a pretty good imitation of saucers.

"You're kiddin' me." he slurs. He misses the significance of the fact that they both died on the same day. "Fuck!! I don't wanna see him go without a funeral." A big tear forms in his eye and trickles down his aged-beyond-his-years face.

"Don't worry, man," I say. "I'll see he gets a good send-off. I promise you."

He switches to maudlin. "You're a good man, Rocky. Roy always thought the world of you, you know that. He loved you, man. I love you too, you know that, right Rocky, right?"

The server saves me from having to answer by bringing our beer. She's nice. She gives Ghost his beer without any judgement in her manner. Again, out of the blue, I think of Damien Crotty's t-shirt. Does old Ghost have any control over the choices he has made in his hard life?

Ghost takes a deep draft of his beer to relieve the reality of his life as a homeless man. I take a deep draft of mine to help numb the physical pain.

"So Ghost, what do you know about Wily's life before he came to live on the streets?"

"I dunno. He was kinda private. I'm pretty sure he had something to do with computers. Like Tommy said the other day, he talked about all sorts'a stuff we din't un'er-stand." His coherence is slip-sliding away.

"What about his family? Did he ever talk about them?"

"Fambly, yeah. He loved his sister, Annie. Wot'j'a say happened to her Rock?" He doesn't wait for an answer; he just shakes his head and continues, "She was the only one gave a fuck about him. His parents disowned him. They was upper-class pricks. His Ma was French, from Québec, a real old fambly, datin' back to the sixteen hundreds. And his ole man was some Limey, Sir somethin' somethin'."

That doesn't sound right. His last name was Lamarche; that's more a québécois name than an English one.

"Are you sure about that Ghost?"

He drains the last of his beer in three big swallows. "Yeah man," he says and lays his head down on the table. "Yeah."

———

THIS IS GOING TO BE TRICKY. STAMMO IS NOT A FAN OF THE *pro bono* cases I take on from time to time but I really need his help with this one.

"So Nick," I say in my most humble tone. "I need your help with something."

"Oh yeah?" Not too encouraging.

"It's the Denis Lamarche thing."

"Huh-uh."

"I'd really appreciate it if you could take a look at his family background. There's something doesn't make sense."

"You *do* realize that's a *pro bono* case. We're getting paid diddly-squat for it. Right?" His face is set in a frowning mask.

"Yeah. It's just that... well... you're good at researching stuff and I—"

He bursts into laughter. "Your face. Priceless. What do you think I am? A money-grabbing business guy? I'm a cop for Chris'sake. I may not be ready to call in the Mounties yet, but there is no way that it's a coincidence Denis Lamarche and his sister died on the same day. I may have had an attack of sarcasm this morning but I've been looking into it for sure."

He looks at my face and starts laughing again. The relief is so great, I join in and we are soon in hysterics.

Adry walks into the main office. "OK, boys. Settle down. What's so funny anyway?"

If I say, 'We're laughing because Annalise and Denis Lamarche died on the same day,' she'll think we've lost it. So I just wipe the tears from my eyes and say, "It's nothing."

Adry shrugs and turns back towards the reception area.

"Hang on Adry," Stammo says. "You should sit in on this."

He wipes the tears from his eyes and I think that since we started Stammo Rogan Investigations he has laughed more than he ever did as a cop. "After you left this morning Adry and I decided that this whole Denis and Annie thing was just too weird to leave alone. So we did some digging. And do you know what we found?"

I just shake my head.

"A big fat nothing."

"What do you mean?"

"She's a cipher. She was a middle level manager in the Department of National Defence. She did procurement administration or some such stuff. Not married. Had a handful of friends on Facebook but as far as I could find out she wasn't active on any other social media. Her Facebook posts didn't indicate any romantic attachments and she never mentioned her brother. She didn't have a lot of Facebook friends but she had a lot of interactions with a Sally Hyde who also worked for the Feds. We called her personal assistant at the DND but she said Annalise had no family, said her parents were dead. I specifically mentioned her brother but she said they had no record of him. It just felt wrong. So I thought I'd try and contact her friend Sally. I called the Public Service Commission to see if they could tell me where I could find her. They said they had no record of her.

"But what I can't shake is that both brother and sister were killed on the same day, three and a half thousand kilometres apart. That is *not* just a weird coincidence. So I called Steve at VPD. Asked him about Denis' murder and it just doesn't feel right either. He'd been tortured before he was killed. Who the fuck tortures a homeless man before killing him? Steve just put it down to someone with a grudge but I don't buy it. Something just doesn't add up. And it's driving me nuts."

"You're right, Nick," I say. "Something's not right. I took those files over to my old school pal, Damien, and he says that the one named 'docs' is probably an encrypted file. You remember what it said in the hint file? 'garter is the key. you'll know what it means annie.' That tells me that Denis was the one who encrypted the file."

"So what's in the file?" The frustration is plain in Stammo's voice.

"Dunno. Damien said he'd try and decrypt it with what

he called brute force decryption, whatever that is, but without the key he's not too optimistic."

"Did you come up with anything else, Cal?" Adry asks.

"Just one thing. Denis' friend, Ghost, said something that didn't make sense. He said that Denis' and Annalise's father was from England, some sort of an aristocrat or something, and that their mother was from Québec. But Lamarche is a French name. Why would they use the mother's name? Maybe it's nothing; maybe Ghost was too drunk to be thinking right, but I don't know."

A depressed silence settles on the office. It's the more-questions-than-answers depression that occurs in some cases. I like it. It means that we're about to make a breakthrough. What can I say? I'm an optimist.

————

THIS FEELS WEIRD. IT'S JUST A LITTLE TOO INTIMATE FOR A first date. Is this even a date? We are sitting, just inches apart, in the seats of the Healey in the Telus Garden car park. We are illegally parked in the spot designated for someone called Royce Hill. It gives us a good view of the blue BMW M3 owned by Susan Grey. Her husband said that she often took her nocturnal excursions on Wednesdays, so here I am with my new friend, Tina, about whom I know only two facts: one, like me, she's an addict and, two, she's a journalist; and if I reflect on the nature of knowledge, she may be neither. However, I have no reason not to believe her. We have done the family-background-where-were-you-born-do-you-have-any-brothers-or-sisters thing and are on to the serious stuff. She got into coke at Carleton, where she was studying journalism. A friend said it would help her study through the night before exams. And it worked, she graduated top of her class. Problem was: she graduated, the coke didn't.

I've told her the story of Roy and my descent into the world of heroin. We each listened to the other's story without judgment which was nice. More than nice. Maybe only an addict can view someone else's addiction without judgment.

Being with her is helping me cope with the increasingly insistent need for a fix.

"So, who do you journal for?" I ask, proud of my cute turn of phrase, if not the actual grammar.

"I'm the Canadian reporter for the Daily News Hound dot com."

I'm impressed. They are a force to be reckoned with in the world of new media. The suspicious side of me makes a mental note to check that out... except...

"I don't even know your last name." I say.

"It's Johal." She grins. "Yours is Rogan." She examines the puzzlement on my face and says, "I googled the details of your case back in the summer and found Stammo Rogan Investigations and, hence... you."

"You should be—" I stop in mid-sentence. Susan Grey is getting into the blue M3. "Game on!" I growl.

Tina laughs. "I like a man who loves his work."

The Healey starts on the first turn of the key, not a given in fifty-something-year-old English sports cars in winter. A random thought intrudes: I wonder if Denis Lamarche's English father also had a predilection for sports cars of the 1960's.

Susan's M3 pulls out of its parking spot and I follow, glad that Tina is sitting beside me. A man and a woman in a car look less like a surveillance team. But that's not the only reason I'm glad. We follow Susan's M3 out of the Telus Garden parking and on to Richards.

"Where do you think she's going?" Tina asks.

"Not a clue. My partner thinks she's having an affair but I don't. I've got a two hundred dollar bet with him."

"How come you're so sure? Or do you guys gamble over everything?"

"I used to date her, when we were in first year at UBC. I just don't think cheating's her style."

Susan's car turns right on Davie. We stop two cars behind her at the lights at Granville. I point to the Two Parrots, one of the places cops like to hang out for a good, cheap meal. "Have you ever eaten there?" I ask.

"I have," she says. "I interviewed a couple of cops there one time."

"We should go there sometime." I say it without thinking.

"You're on." She says it without any hesitation.

Suddenly, I find myself tongue-tied.

The lights change and we follow Susan west on Davie. We cross Burrard and the only place she can be going is the West End. I'm guessing she's heading for a restaurant. Maybe Stammo's right; maybe she's going to meet a lover for dinner. I feel a deep sense of disappointment... right up until she does a right turn and starts to weave her way through the residential streets. As I follow I'm right behind her. I've lost the cover of having another car between her and me. If she looks in the mirror she might well recognize me. I can't really slow down to put distance between us because, like all cars driving in this part of the West End, she is crawling along at less than twenty klicks. After several turns, she parks outside a large, three-floor house; it's the last parking place on the street. I drive past her, pushing myself back in the seat so that if she looks at my car as we pass, the only one she'll see is Tina. I have to turn left at the end of the block because of the weird way the streets are blocked off to discourage people from driving through the residential areas. I stop immediately and, leaving the car double-parked, I jog the ten paces to the street corner. I slide my head forward and look down the street. Susan Grey is walking up the front steps of the house outside of which she parked.

With a long sigh, I turn and walk back to the car. I start to shiver. For a moment the thrill of the chase drove away the rising pain of withdrawal.

"Did you see where she went?" Tina asks.

"Yes."

"Are you going to try and find somewhere to park."

"No need. I know what her problem is." A sadness settles on my shoulders. When Stammo and I were still cops, I went undercover into the house I just saw Susan entering. Nothing good can come of her being there. I don't even feel good about winning my bet with my partner.

"What is it?" Tina turns in her seat to face me as I get back in the Healey. "Are you OK?" She touches my arm.

I shiver again. The need has gone from insistent to screaming. "No. The withdrawal pains are getting bad."

She squeezes my arm. "Don't worry. We'll get you through this."

6

NICK

Thursday

There's a lot of things I like doing that I never knew I'd like when I was still a cop. Running meetings is one of them. I was never that ambitious when I was on the job. My ex pushed me to try for a sergeant's job but I never wanted to do it myself. But I kind of like running a company and chairing meetings is a part of it.

"So Cal, what's new with the Susan Grey case?"

He purses his lips. Uh-oh. I can tell this is not going to be good news. He kind of flexes his shoulders. I wonder if that's something to do with the withdrawal pains he's getting. Or has he dealt with them by taking a fix. I'll never know again whether he's clean or not. The thought churns my gut.

"Do you remember Dominique Dufresne?" he says.

Searching... "I remember the name but..." I shrug.

"The last case you and I did at VPD..."

Searching... Got it. "Oh Yeah, the Oboe thing. Didn't he

run an illegal gambling joint in the West End? What's-his-face was laundering money for him."

"Bingo. Guess where I saw Susan Grey going last night."

"Oh crap." I don't know whether Etienne Grey would rather have his wife gambling their money away or being unfaithful. Except... "Wait a minute. Surely he must have been shut down. Steve knew about it and it was in the notes on the case. Maybe it's not a gambling joint any more."

He looks relieved. "I didn't think of that. You're right. Except that I don't remember there being any prosecution."

"Why would you? We'd left the Department by then. Do you want me to call Steve and check it out?" I ask.

"Good idea, but we should hold off telling her husband until we've got something definite to tell him. I'm going to check it out myself."

Adry says, "Is that the right thing to do, Cal? Shouldn't we tell the client everything? Nick, you're the one who's so keen on daily reporting to the clients."

"She's right, Rogan," I say.

"We don't have anything to report," he says. "She went into a house in the West End. Just hold off until this evening. I'll know more then."

"OK. But just 'til this evening. What's next?" I look at my spreadsheet. "Oh, right. It's the missing person. The rich kid with the drinking problem."

I look up at Rogan.

But it's the person standing behind him that gets my attention. Rogan and Adry swivel around in their chairs, following my gaze.

It's a woman. Late thirties. Quite tall. Smartly dressed in a navy blue suit with a white silk blouse. She's good-looking but she's looking at us coldly. She doesn't say anything. We all just stare at each other.

Adry is the first to speak. She stands up. "Can I help you?" she says.

The woman smiles, almost warmly but not quite.

"I'm here to see a Mr. Stammo." She looks like a lawyer.

"I'm Nick Stammo." I wheel out from behind my desk and over towards her. "And you are?" I extend my hand.

She doesn't take it. Not acceptable.

"Is there somewhere we can talk privately?" she says.

I hold her stare. "Not until you tell me who the hell *you* are." Out of the corner of my eye I see Rogan get up and stand beside me. Solidarity brother.

Her face softens. She smiles and it seems genuine. Seems. "I'm sorry," she says. "I flew out here on the red-eye. My name's Jennifer Halley." She reaches into the pocket of her suit jacket and takes out a business card.

I take it. The logo is a Canadian maple leaf with what look like blue sword blades sticking out of it and with a crown on top. It says, 'Canadian Security Intelligence Service. Jennifer Halley.' No title beneath, just a phone number and an address in Ottawa. I'm not going to just take her word for it.

"Adry," I say, without taking my eyes off our visitor.

"Yes Nick." Her voice is right beside me.

"Look up CSIS online and call their office in Ottawa." I hand her the business card. "See if this is genuine."

"Don't do that." There is a tone of command in her voice. Adry stops in her tracks and looks at me. I look back at Jennifer Halley. "Please," she says. There is something else in her voice now. I'm thinking fear. But of what? If she's really with CSIS why wouldn't she want us to verify that?

I look into her eyes. Time stops.

She speaks first. "I'll tell you why later. Just hear me out first."

I'm getting a bad feeling about it but Rogan says, "OK."

We exchange glances and I say, "OK. Leave it for now, Adry." She hands me back the card. "Come in and sit down," I say and wheel back to my desk. Agent, or whatever, Halley follows and sits down at the guest chair beside my desk. I gesture towards Rogan. "This is Cal Rogan. He's my partner. Anything you have to say to me you can say to him."

She stands up. "I'm sorry. That was a pretty crappy way to introduce myself. Let's start over." She extends her hand and smiles. "Hi, I'm Jennifer Halley." *This* smile is genuine. I shake her hand and she turns to Rogan and does the same with him.

She sits back down and Rogan sits at his desk.

"So what can we do for you Agent Halley?" I ask.

"First thing is, we don't have agents; I'm an intelligence officer." Then why doesn't it say so on your card, I wonder. She continues, "You called the Public Service Commission in Ottawa yesterday. I was wondering why."

In the second I take to gather my thoughts, Rogan says, "You flew three and a half thousand kilometres, overnight from Ottawa, to ask us that?" It's a damn good question.

"I did," is all she says.

I mull that over. It's crap.

"Why?" Rogan asks. "You could have sent one of your local people or you could have asked someone from the RCMP to come and see us. Hell, you could have picked up the phone. And anyway, why would you care."

"I could have done, yes. But I wanted to talk to Mr. Stammo face-to-face." She turns to me. "So, Mr. Stammo, why did you call the Public Service Commission?"

I look at Rogan and he gives a slight shrug of the shoulders. I turn back to her. "We're trying to find the next-of-kin of Annalise Lamarche. I tried calling her personal assistant at the Department of National Defence but she said her parents were deceased and they had no next-of-kin information. I saw on her Facebook page that she was friends with a Sally Hyde who works for the federal government, so I thought I'd talk to Sally and see if she could help. I called the Public Service Commission to try and track her down but they said they had no record of her. That's about it."

"Why were you trying to find the next-of-kin of Annie Lamarche?"

"Her brother was killed in Vancouver on the same day she was killed in the bombing in Ottawa."

She doesn't try and hide her surprise. "Denis is dead?"

"Yes. He was tortured and beaten to death."

Her eyes narrow as she processes that. "How is your firm involved?"

"Denis Lamarche was an alcoholic and homeless," Rogan answers. "He was a friend of a friend of mine. My friend asked us to track down his next-of-kin so that Denis could have a decent burial."

"You called her Annie," I say. "You must have known her too."

"I did. Not well, but I knew her through Sally."

"So why *are* you here Ms. Halley?" I ask.

She's silent for a moment. She looks from me... to Rogan... to Adry... then stands and walks to the door. She turns back towards us. "I'll get back to you."

She walks out the door and down the corridor and I notice that she doesn't have a briefcase, or even a purse. I have an odd feeling we're never going to see her again.

I'm still puzzling over the odd appearance of Intelligence Officer Halley. Stammo thought we should call CSIS and try to verify she was who she said she was, but something tells me she's genuine and has a good reason for us not doing that. Despite what he says, I'm sure we are going to see her again and soon too. I hope so because I have a very interesting question to ask her. However, time to put all that out of my mind right now. I need all my faculties front and centre for my next task.

I press the doorbell and hear it chime inside the house. There is no other sound except the background hum of the traffic on Davie, two blocks away. I look up and around. There is one... no, two... no, there are *three* cameras trained on me. I wave at the one above the door and press the doorbell a second time. This time I'm rewarded by the sound of a door opening.

The last time I was at this door, almost three years ago now, it was opened by gambling boss Dominique Dufresne's bodyguard, who was built like a Mack truck. I wonder if he's still on duty. I'm hoping not, I remember, without a lot of enthusiasm, him escorting me from the premises. I hear two bolts sliding back and the turning of the latch. The house Susan Grey entered last night has very thorough security.

The door swings open.

"We're closed."

The speaker is eighty-five if she's a day. She is dressed in the clothes of a Victorian maid—all black and white and frills—and looks like she could blow away in a brisk wind.

"I was wondering if I could make an appointment."

She looks at me like I've recently escaped from Riverview Hospital. I said the wrong thing. I focus in on her. I remember a psychology teacher in one of my UBC classes, too many years ago, saying, *'In any interaction, remember that the other person wants to understand you as much as, or even more than, you want to understand them.'*

"Could I come in, please," I ask. "I really need your help."

I don't know where those words came from. They came out of my mouth but where did they arise from? I don't know and will probably never know.

She looks uncertain for a second, two seconds max, then she opens the door wide and ushers me inside. As it was three years ago, the front door leads into a small, square entrance area, except that it's changed. It is wood panelled below with expensive cut-glass panels above, which obscure the view into the rooms beyond. She closes the front door and for an instant we are in an airlock between the outer world and the unknown interior of the mansion. She presses a button beside the door which leads inside.

Silence descends.

I look at her.

She looks at me.

Time progresses, as indeed it always does.

A shadow flits across the cut glass and the inner door opens.

It's not the same muscle but it might just as well be. A good two metres tall and half as wide, he gestures me to step inside. Being a man of wisdom, I do as I'm told but can't help wondering if I will step out with such facility.

The room I enter is not the room I entered three years ago. It has been renovated into a circular foyer of epic proportions. To the extreme right and left are staircases curving to the upper levels. There are sofas of fluid design which look simultaneously both inviting and forbidding. It's like I want to go sit on them but don't dare to, in case I somehow profane them. The decor is predominantly red plush yet starkly modern—no mean feat of the designer— and the artwork on the walls is both expensive-looking and erotic.

In a flash of intuition I realize where I am.

In seven hours these sofas will be draped with the bodies of gorgeous young women, dressed simultaneously both demurely and seductively, on display for the pleasure of Vancouver's wealthiest sybarites.

Etienne Grey's likely worst dread has been multiplied many-fold: his wife is not having an affair with a man but with a whole legion of us. My two hundred dollar bet with Stammo has been exponentially magnified.

"How can I help you, sir." The voice of the muscle snaps me back to my current situation. There is a politeness in his tone with an underlay of menace. Through my confusion, Hamlet's voice comes to my aid: *'Let the doors be shut upon him, that he may play the fool; nowhere but in's own house. Farewell.'* If I play the fool here I might just get to say farewell to this house.

"Sorry," I say, slurring the word in a feint of drunkenness. "I think I'm in the wrong place. I came here to play the craps tables." Silence from the muscle and the 'maid'. "I've been out of town for a while. I'm an old buddy of Dominique." More silence. "Y'know... Dominique Dufresne."

A soupçon of understanding flows across the face of the 'maid'. She yammers a few words in a language alien to me.

"Mr. Dufresne's gone," says the muscle, mispronouncing the last name.

I decide, for my own safety, it's better to keep up the subterfuge. "Do you know where he moved to?"

The muscle gives a nasty little chuckle. "Millhaven," he says. The 'maid' cackles; it's not a pretty sound.

Millhaven is Canada's max-security prison, an institution so evil that it gives the lie to this country's liberal values. I pretend to be confused. "Is that on the east side?" I ask.

"Show the gentleman out, Mariana," he says.

Taking my elbow, 'the maid' leads me into the 'airlock' and opens the outer door.

I give everyone an imbecilic smile and head out, glad to have left without having any bones broken, or worse.

———

"I'M AFRAID MS. GREY ISN'T AVAILABLE RIGHT NOW."

Those eight words fire up the anger I'm feeling deep in my gut. I lean forward and speak quietly, so the other denizens of the lobby can't hear me. "If you don't have Susan Grey in front of me in the next sixty seconds, I am going to walk through your offices and hassle the hell out of everybody, and I mean everybody, until I find her. Your choice."

She reads the truth in my face and redials the number. "Susan," she says, "I think you need to come out to reception, like right now." She listens and grunts at the response. "She'll be right out, sir," she says, clearly unsure that I have earned the last word.

I'm so agitated I don't give a devil's curse for her words. I look at my watch. If Susan's not here in those sixty seconds, I'm going to... Well, I don't actually know what I'm going to do but it's not going to be pretty. For no particular reason, I think about Damien Crotty's t-shirt. *Free will: the persistent illusion that we have any control over the choices we make.* I feel compelled to be here. I don't feel I had any control over that choice. And I can't help musing on the fact that the slogan came into my head without any exercise of free will on my part.

"Cal? What are you doing here?"

Susan's words drag me up from my mental meanderings. "I need to talk to you." I say.

"I'm in the middle of a—"

"Susan," I say, *sotto voce*, "we need to talk *now*."

She does an accurate read of my mood. "Come with me."

She leads me into the main office area, past a cluster of conservative cubicles and into a cramped conference closet; it's too small to be considered a room. "Wait here," she says in a voice that brooks no disagreement.

I sit and wait, my aggression deflated.

She's back before I can ruminate any further on the nature of free will.

She closes the door and before sitting down, she demands, "Cal, what the *fuck* are you doing here?"

"To ask you what the *fuck* you're doing going into a high-class brothel in the West End on a Wednesday night?"

It's like I slapped her in the face. She slumps back in her chair and stares at the ceiling. A whole herd of emotions stampede across her face ending in puzzlement.

"How did you...?" Now it's anger. "Have you been stalking me?"

"Stalking? No. Following, yes."

"What the hell, Cal. We have one drink together and you start *following* me? Why would you do that? We're long over. I'm married now. I told you that."

"It wasn't personal," I say, knowing I'm going to have to make a choice.

"It wasn't *personal*?" she is close to shouting now. "Then what—?" I can almost see the gearwheels in her mind meshing together. "Were you being paid to follow me?"

I nod. "Yes." I say it as gently as I can.

"Who?" she asks.

"You know I can't tell you that."

"You're a private detective, not a cop. Who says you can't tell me?"

"Client confidentiality. A lawyer should understand that."

She gives me a look which I interpret as unwilling acceptance. I lean forward. "What were you doing there, Sooze?" The gentle use of her nickname, from all those years ago, calms her and a deeper acceptance settles onto her face.

"It had to come out sooner or later. Maybe it's better that it's you who saw me going in there. If my husband had seen me..." She shakes her head. *Now* I'm on the horns of the dilemma. If I tell her who my client is, I will probably kill their marriage and almost certainly get sued by Etienne Grey in the process. If I don't tell her, she'll likely tell me stuff that I'll then have to report to her husband, which is a betrayal of her I cannot live with.

She breaks into my discomfort with, "Here's the deal. Your client is either my firm, a rival firm, a company whom we are suing that's looking for dirt on me, a company that wants to check up on me before trying to hire me or the firm, or, it's my husband." I hope I managed to keep my poker face intact and didn't give her any tells when she mentioned the last option. "Whichever, I'm going to tell you the truth and trust you have the integrity to use the knowledge wisely."

"I'll do everything I can, I promise you."

"I'll meet you tonight, after work. Maybe a problem shared will be a problem halved, who knows." She stands. "And Cal, I need you to know, it's not what it seems."

I've been in this business long enough to know that it almost always is exactly what it seems.

———

A QUICK SANDWICH, AN NA MEETING—I WAS DISAPPOINTED Tina wasn't there—two Tylenols and two Advil later and I'm back at the office. As I walk in the door, CSIS intelligence officer Jennifer Halley gets out of the guest chair in reception. Rogan 1, Stammo 0. Not that I'm keeping score.

She walks with me into the main office where Adry and Nick are looking at something on his screen.

"OK, Mr. Stammo. Your partner is back. Can we talk *now*?" She's all business and clearly frustrated at being kept waiting for my arrival.

"Sure. What'ja got?" Nick says, indicating the guest chair beside his desk. She takes it and I perch on the edge of my desk looking down at her. She is a striking woman, both beautiful and sexy. And although she is still showing some irritation there is a subtle change in her attitude from this morning. She seems less combative and warmer.

"I'm running the investigation into the bombing in Ottawa, which is why I'm here talking to you. I should warn you that anything I tell you must be kept in strictest confidence and if you divulge anything to any third party, you will be subject to—"

"Bullshit!" I say.

All three of them look at me. "You don't have jurisdiction," I say. "If Nick's call to Ottawa, to try and find Sally Hyde had raised any red flags, it would be the Mounties knocking on our door, not you. Am I right?"

"Yes," is all she says.

A flash of intuition hits.

"And you're here off the books aren't you? That was why you didn't want us to call your office this morning and confirm your identity."

"Correct again."

"I think you'd better come clean and tell us what this is all about."

She purses her lips and looks very vulnerable. Finally, she says, "OK. But I am dying for a cup of coffee."

"I'll get some for all of us," says Adry and goes to the little kitchen area at the back of the office.

Having made her decision, Jennifer Halley looks a lot more relaxed. "Yesterday afternoon, I told my boss I had a bad migraine and wouldn't be in work today. I took the red-eye flight here from Ottawa and after I talked to you guys this morning, I was all set to get a flight back and be home in time for work tomorrow morning. But the more I thought about the fact that Annie's brother was murdered on the same day as her, the more I knew that it was another coincidence I couldn't swallow. So here I am again."

"I was sure you didn't intend to come back, so I was right, Rogan."

"Except that she did come back," says Adry as she sets the coffee cups down.

Halley takes a couple of sips and sighs. She sits straight in her chair. "I meant what I said before: this information must never be discussed outside this room, OK?" She looks around and we all nod. "Let's start over. It was Mr. Stammo's attempt to track down Sally Hyde that got me here."

"If we're partners in crime, you might as well use our first names," I say.

"Thanks, Cal. You guys can call me Jen."

"So what's the story on Sally Hyde?" Nick asks.

"She was a CSIS intelligence officer and a good friend of mine. As I said this morning, I met Annie through her."

"Was?" I ask.

"Yes she was also killed by the bomber. She was meeting Annie for lunch. We got some CCTV footage from a security camera on a building on the other side of the Rideau Canal from where they were killed. Sally must have realized what was happening, she ran at the bomber but just wasn't quick enough. Her name was never released to the public." She wipes away a tear from her left eye. "The thing is, I was due to have lunch with Sally that day. She told me she had to cancel, that she was having lunch with Annie. She said Annie wanted to talk to her about a national security issue she was very worried about; she said it was terrorist related and that she had documents to prove it. I asked Sally if she wanted me to come but she thought it would be better one-on-one. If I had gone..."

She takes some more coffee.

"I thought it was just too big a coincidence that they were meeting about a terrorist threat and then were both killed by a terrorist. I was interviewed by the team investigating the bombing and they were all over it for about a day and a half. Apparently, they were told by the Department of National Defence that they knew what it was that Annie was concerned about and it wasn't related to the bombing. The team dropped it and I was told not to talk about it.

"I thought it was bullshit. It feels like a big cover up by DND. Sally was my best friend in the world. I promised myself I'd find out what Annie was going to tell Sally, even if it cost me my job. Your call to the Public Service Commission to try and find Sally was flagged and the details came across my desk. In addition, I checked with Annie's personal assistant at DND; I asked her if there had been any unusual calls to Annie just before or anytime after her death. She told me of your call. That was too big to ignore; I thought, who is this Stammo guy in Vancouver who's called for both Sally and Annie? It was what made me decide to come out here and ask you why. This morning, I was convinced you didn't know anything but when you told me about Denis being killed on the same day, it was just one coincidence too far. I can't go to the Vancouver Police Department to inquire about his murder because my bosses in Ottawa might learn about it and then I'd be in real trouble. I was hoping you guys could help me out."

A silence settles on us. Adry looks like she wants to say something but she keeps quiet. Finally Nick says, "The Denis Lamarche case was a *pro bono*. Who's going to pay our bill?"

Without missing a beat, Jen says, "I have some savings put by. I'll cover your fees and expenses."

He looks at her long and hard. "S'OK," he says. "We won't take your money, right Rogan?"

"Right," I agree, too stunned by his unexpected offer.

"Adry?" he says.

Adry looks pleased to be included in the decision making. "Sure, right," she says.

Stammo extends his hand towards Jen. "Deal," he says.

She leans over and shakes his hand. "Deal," she says, then gets up, shakes my hand and gives Adry a hug.

"OK, Rogan," Stammo says. "Tell her everything we know about Denis Lamarche."

I give her a full briefing on the case. As I speak, I can see she is taking in every detail of what I say and weighing it against what she knows. Nothing seems to surprise her until I get to the part about the discovery of the files on the memory card and the word garter. I tell her about my meeting with Damien and his attempts to decrypt the file.

"So 'garter' wasn't the decryption key?"

"No. We tried it in French too but neither of the translations worked. He said he'd get back to me if they cracked it. Damien's pretty good. If he can't crack it I doubt anyone can." My words stir a memory. "I don't know why it's bugging me but Annalise's father was British and yet her last name was French. Do you know what that's about?"

Jen nods. "Yes I do. Her mother divorced her father when Annalise was about ten and she changed all their names back to Lamarche, which was the mother's maiden name. But after her mother's death she contacted her father and he got involved in her's and Denis' lives for a few years, until *he* died suddenly of a heart attack a few years ago."

"Was she close to her father?"

"Not really, but apparently Denis was quite close to him until his schizophrenia got so bad that he lost his job and started living on the streets. Annie tried to help him but he refused to take his meds because he felt they blunted his intellect. Denis was very bright; he had two Ph.Ds, one in math and the other in philosophy. Before he went over the top he was working on developing artificial intelligence at UBC."

"Tell us what you know about Annie," says Stammo.

Jen smiles fondly. "Annie was lovely. I didn't know her that well, but she and Sally and I would often hang out together. Although her job title wouldn't have indicated it, she was in a fairly senior position with the Ministry of Defence and was involved in the purchase of armaments, specifically guns. She didn't have two Ph.Ds like her brother, but she was as smart as a whip."

"Was she married?"

"No."

"Boyfriend?"

Jen bites her lip. "Not as such." She takes a deep breath. "One night we were all out for dinner and after a glass of Chardonnay too many, she let it slip that she was having an affair with someone at work. I don't know who. She never told us his name but said that he was married. She made us swear to keep it a secret." She shakes her head. "It doesn't matter now of course but I feel like I'm betraying a confidence by sharing it with you guys."

"Don't worry," says Stammo. "We're good at keeping secrets. Anyway, I don't see how it could have any bearing on the case."

Jen shrugs. "You said that the last time Denis' friends saw him, he was leaving with someone?"

"Yes, they said he was a big, well-dressed guy."

"Well, if we're going to try and find a connection between the two deaths, the big guy's the place to start. Why don't we go and interview his friends."

"We can give it a try but these guys are... *drunk many times a day, if not many days entirely drunk.*"

Jen gives me a puzzled frown.

"Don't mind him," says Stammo. "If he doesn't quote Shakespeare three times a day, I call the ambulance for him."

As I start to dial Ghost's mobile, I wonder just how sober he and Tommy are going to be.

––––––––

It must have been one of those entirely drunk days. Ghost was incoherent on the phone and when I asked him to give the phone to Tommy, he slurred, "Ole Tommy's too pisshed to talk," and hung up with an unholy cackle.

As I enter the apartment, the withdrawal pains mesh with the frustration of not being able to interrogate Ghost. Not only that, in one hour I'm meeting Susan Grey and not looking forward to what I'm going to hear. The more I think of it, the more I fear I'm going to learn something that, ethically, I'll have to report back to her husband, thus betraying the trust of a woman I once loved and still like. It's all knotting in my gut. However, I know there is one thing that *hath charms to sooth the savage breast* and it's not music; and that's not even Shakespeare. I haven't done it in three long days and I need it right now.

I head to the kitchen. There it is, the one thing that can give me some joy for a while.

I press my thumb on it and tap the FaceTime icon.

"Hi Dad!" The happiness on her face smooths the knots away.

"Hi Sweetie. How was your day?"

"Great!! Ethan's here, do you want to say 'Hi'?"

Before I can respond. The image wobbles and a young man's face appears. He looks as surprised as I am. *"Oh, hello Mr. Cullen, how are you?"* He gives me a cheeky smile and I instantly like him.

"I'm fine Ethan. Are you having dinner with Ellie?"

"Yes, but we already ate. My parents are coming over to pick

me up in a minute. Nice to meet you Mr. Cullen." The image wobbles again and Ellie is back. *"I've got to go Dad. We're playing a game and I want to beat Ethan before his mom and dad get here."*

I try and keep the disappointment from my face. "OK sweetie. I'll call you on Saturday. And tell Ethan my name's Rogan, like yours."

Her smile slips and she bites her lip. She looks like she's about to say something and my stomach knots itself back up again. Before I can ask her the question, she forces a smile onto her face and says, *"OK. 'Bye Dad."* She waves and hangs up.

The savage breast is not soothed. If anything it's worse than it was five minutes ago.

———

MY TYLENOL AND ADVIL COCKTAIL IS DOING LITTLE TO STAVE off the withdrawal pains. It's going to be a bad night. I remember detox. The pains reached a climax after about four to five days and then slowly started to ease. I'm praying that this is the climax but I'm not hopeful.

Being here in the Hotel Vancouver is not helping matters. I am plagued with the memory of Em's death in room six-thirteen of this very hotel. Susan's law firm keeps a suite here and she suggested we meet there; I'm not sure why. I can think of a couple of reasons that don't exactly thrill me.

I knock on the door of the suite and I can't help reliving that terrible night six months ago. No it was seven months ago, seven months to the day.

The door opens.

It's Susan. I expect her to say, 'Why Cal Rogan, I do

declare. What are *you* doing here?' But she doesn't; she just opens the door and lets me in.

The suite is beautiful, with all the charm of the bygone era in which the Hotel Van was built. She walks to the minibar. There is a half-full glass bearing a lipstick stain and two empty minibar bottles of scotch. "Don't make me drink alone," she says, the pleading in her voice palpable.

"A black Russian would be great." In truth I'd prefer a beer but hotel minibars have yet to catch up to the craft beer revolution.

She takes out two vodka bottles and one Kahlua and mixes them in a glass. Without a word she hands it to me. I take a sip and a swallow and wonder how it's going to react with the painkillers.

She has moved two chairs so that they face the window, she takes the one on the left, I take the right. And we sit in silence. I drink some more and the warmth feels good. I know there's no point in rushing her; she needs to get there by herself.

So we sit.

"Do you remember Cat Lake?" she says.

The *non sequitur* catches me by surprise.

"How could I forget?" I say. She doesn't reply and in the silence I remember the spring weekend, just before the end of term, when we borrowed a friend's car, an elderly Volvo station wagon, and went camping on the shores of the little lake just off the Sea-to-Sky highway. We were the only campers there and didn't see another soul from Friday afternoon until we headed home late on Sunday night. We cooked over an open campfire, drank lots of wine, walked around naked, made love beside the lake, in the lake and in the surrounding woods. We had not a care in the world. I have thought of that weekend with happiness, and passion, many times over the years. I wonder why she mentioned it.

She empties her glass, stands up and moves over to my chair. Without a word she sits on my lap, puts her arms around my neck and buries her face between my face and her arms; and she sobs. I hold her tightly and gently stroke her hair.

I know that if the weight of her body on mine wasn't exacerbating the withdrawal pains, my body would be wildly reacting to the closeness of hers.

Finally she stops. She is still for a minute or two and then stands up. She rummages in her purse, which is on the coffee table in front of us, pulls out a package of tissues, wipes her tears and blows her nose.

She gives me a wan smile and says. "Thank you Cal."

She sits back down on the chair on my left.

"I'm going to tell you everything. Just don't look at me while I'm talking. OK?"

"OK."

She takes a big breath in and the words tumble out. "I love my husband. You were my first love, Cal, and there have been many in between, but he is my last love. I'll never love anyone the way I love him. I would die rather than see him hurt."

I just nod, he's a lucky man.

"A few months ago, a friend from law school called me up. She has her own practice in Toronto and said she had a client whose partner in Vancouver was looking for a good lawyer. When I asked who the client was, she just said, 'He'll contact you and mention my name.' I should have smelled a rat but I was just intrigued. My friend told me he would be a very lucrative client and you know how we lawyers love that." The words drip with bitterness and I have difficulty in following her wish not to look at her.

"Three days later I received a phone call from the client, he said his name was David Fox and would I meet him for dinner. I agreed and we met at the Yew restaurant."

She pauses and I fill the silence. "I had a first meeting with a client there. Her daughter was missing. It didn't work out that well for everybody concerned." I wonder how young Ariel Bradbury is faring now, nine months after her ordeal?

Susan grunts. "Well... I felt uncomfortable with him from the get-go. He was very charming but I could sense an undercurrent of, I don't know, if I had to put it into words, I would say sexual menace. The first thing he did was take a ten dollar bill and push it across the table. 'Put this in your purse,' he said. I wondered what the hell he was doing but before I could question him he said, 'Go on, put it in your purse.' I felt mesmerized by him and took the money. 'Good,' he said. 'That's your retainer. You're now my lawyer and this conversation is covered by lawyer-client confidentiality.'

"I should have handed him back his ten dollars and walked away right then. But I didn't and, in any event, it didn't matter. Although I didn't know it, he had his hooks into me. Despite the client confidentiality thing he was very vague about his business. He said he wanted me to set up a network of companies in Canada, the US and several offshore tax havens: Panama, the Caymans, Luxembourg. He said he wanted me to be the designated shareholder in some of the companies and arrange banking facilities. All my instincts were screaming for me to get out of there as fast as possible. He said that all this was for import/export transactions but to me it felt like money laundering. At the end of the meal, I left as soon as I could and told him I would think it over and get back to him.

"I immediately went back to the office and wrote down every detail of the meeting I could remember. I saved it in an encrypted file on the firm's servers and went home."

"Did you tell your husband about the meeting?" I ask.

"No. We make a point of not discussing each other's clients. Anyway, the next day I called the client at the number he had called me from and there was no reply, not even voice mail. Then later in the day he called me from a different number. I told him that I didn't think we were the right firm for him, that our offshore experience was limited —which definitely isn't true—and that the senior partners didn't approve of us taking shareholder positions in client companies. He just said, 'I see,' and hung up on me. The next morning I got an envelope addressed to me personally, marked *Highly confidential to be opened only by Susan Grey*."

Out of the corner of my eye, I see her squirm in her seat and hear her take a gulp of scotch. "This is the part where I don't want you to look at me," she says. "You remember why we had to break up?"

I don't reply, wondering why the change in subject.

"Because I decided to switch to U of T to do my law degree," she says.

I remember that her parents, who lived in Toronto, wanted her to move back there. I was so in love with her back then, I would have followed in a heart beat if I'd been able to. Although my mother had sacrificed so much to save thirty-five thousand dollars for my education, I still had to work part-time to make ends meet. There was no way I could have afforded to go and study in Toronto.

"I remember." I struggle to keep my voice even as the memory of my anguish washes through me.

"Right at the end of my first year at U of T both my parents died in a car crash on the Gardiner Expressway."

"I had no idea. I am *so* sorry." I turn towards her but she signals me to look away. I turn back and feel my sympathy turning to a growing anger. Why didn't she come back to Vancouver? I would have helped her through her loss. Her parents were well off, she could have afforded it. Then it all deflates, it's all water under the bridge.

"When it came to settling the estate, I got a nasty surprise. I discovered that my father had gambled away everything. I'd had absolutely no idea. The house was mortgaged to the hilt and when it was sold, it yielded just enough money to pay off the bank loans he'd taken out. He'd even cashed in his insurance policies. There was nothing. When the dust settled, I was left with an inheritance of seven thousand, three hundred and twenty-one dollars.

"I was devastated. There was no way I'd be able to afford to go back to U of T or anywhere else for that matter. I called my best friend from class and told her the whole story. To my amazement, she said she thought she might be able to help me out. She told me to meet her for dinner in an expensive restaurant in Yorkville, her treat. So I did.

"Melissa was one of the cool girls on campus and she was as sharp as a whip. She drove a Mercedes and was always amazingly dressed. Over dinner she told me that she knew what I was going through because her parents had never had the funds to send her to school but that she had paid her own way. When I asked her how, she told me about this agency she worked for. She told me that she earned eight thousand dollars a month, which was a small fortune for a university student in nineteen-ninety-seven. When I wanted to know more she told me that it was a 'very discreet, very respectable' agency for rich men who liked to date intelligent, beautiful, young women. She told me that all she had to do was go on three or four dates a week. She said she wasn't forced to sleep with anyone but if she wanted to she could and that would increase her revenue per date a lot. What was strange was that I wasn't even shocked. It was probably a measure of my desperation.

"Long story short, I put myself through U of T's law school as an escort. It was, as Melissa said, all very discreet and I was never once pressured to sleep with anyone but most of the men were nice and a lot of them were attractive, so I, well... made a lot of money." She takes another drink. "I sold my body then so that I can sell my brain now." There is a certain defiance in her tone of voice.

"Can I look at you now?" I ask.

"Sure."

I turn towards her. "I've never told *anyone* this. My mother swindled landlords out of thousands of dollars so she could put me though university, so I'm not about to criticize anyone for doing what they had to do."

She smiles and the defiance is gone. "Thank you, Cal. You were pretty much a law-and-order kind of guy in first year, I wasn't sure you'd understand."

"So. Let me make a couple of guesses, one: Melissa was the one who introduced you to this new client and two: the envelope David Fox sent you was full of comprising photographs of you."

"Two for two." She gets up and heads for the minibar and opens the door. "Another?' she asks. I shake my head. She looks at the glittering display of liquor and overpriced snacks, then looks back at me. After a moment, she closes the door with an air of finality and comes to sit beside me again.

"The photos were accompanied by a note. It said simply.

*Here's the deal. I pay you $1,000 an hour for your legal services
and your husband and the partners at your law firm never get to
see these pictures.*

"And what did he want you to do for him?"

She tells me every detail.

It's worse than I ever could have imagined.

———

"THIRTY-ONE HOURS," I SAY.

"What?"

"I've known you for thirty-one hours and here I am in
your home being served lamb vindaloo which, by the way,
smells fantastic."

"Yes, well, helping someone through a withdrawal crisis,
you learn more about each other than in a month of small
talk."

"Indeed. Thank you for that. Last night, it was so bad I
couldn't have got through it without you."

"No prob," Tina says it casually. But it was no small
thing. She sat with me, talking me through some sort of
meditation process that got me through the horrors of withdrawal. She stayed until I finally fell asleep. When I woke up
this morning she was gone.

As she serves the food, I watch the litheness with which
she moves. "Do you do yoga?" I ask.

She laughs. "Can't get by without *some* small talk can
we?" She serves the curry beside the rice on my plate and
says, "No, I've tried it but it's not really my thing. Why do
you ask?"

"Last night you were talking me through that meditation, I just thought…"

"That was a mindfulness meditation. It's very effective in

giving people the tools to overcome addiction." She sits down opposite me and lifts her wine glass. "Welcome to my home and thanks for the wine." We clink glasses and drink. The pinot noir is more expensive than I usually buy but it's wonderful and worth every penny.

"How about some more small talk," I say. "Tell me what it's like working for the Daily News Hound dot com."

"Oh, the Hound is great." As she tells me about her job I see something that I haven't seen in a woman since I first met Sam. She has joy in what she does; digging for the truth is as big a passion for her as tracking down a criminal is for me.

Shock, pleasure, anticipation and a touch of fear all combine, as I realize that she could easily become a big part of my life.

8

CAL

Friday

Ghost seems no worse for wear from yesterday's drunkenness and Tommy Connor is positively chipper. It may be because of the large Ovaltine Café breakfasts I've bought them, which they are scarfing down with relish. They are sober, happy and co-operative. Jen Halley and I are sitting opposite them with coffee and Jen has a laptop open in front of her. She is using composite sketch software to create an image of the 'big guy' who came into the Balmoral and left with Wily a.k.a. Denis Lamarche. As she questions them, I am struck by how the human mind is able to recognize and remember faces so easily, yet we don't have adequate language to describe them.

She turns the screen around so that they can see the latest iteration of the image.

"Yeah," says Tommy. "That's more like him."

"Except he was fatter and a bit more squinty," adds Ghost.

Jen rotates the laptop and fiddles away some more. I

would normally be interested in how she uses the software but other women are on my mind: Susan Grey and Tina Johal. The shock of Susan's revelation, about what she is doing for the crook who calls himself David Fox, is weighing on my mind. I mull over various ways by which I might extricate her from her predicament without her husband learning about her past.

And Tina—

"That's him," Tommy yells. "That's him for sure, eh Ghost?"

"Fuckin' A!" Ghost agrees.

Jen gives me a big grin. She spins the laptop back. The hard face staring out from the screen sends an unpleasant shiver down my spine. Jen taps away. "I'm sending it to a friend at CSIS. We've got some software that tries to match composite sketch images to photos. It's leading edge but still not that good. It only gives a decent result about twenty-five percent of the time but it's worth a shot. She'll do it without telling anyone it was from me. Now we just have to wait."

An idea hits me.

"I don't like waiting," I say as I grab my phone. "You guys want to earn some cash?" I ask.

Their mouths full of food, Ghost and Tommy just nod enthusiastically.

————

STAMMO IS NOT A HAPPY CAMPER. "WE'VE GOT TO TELL HIM, *he's* our client, not her."

I wash my painkillers down with a cup of Adry's coffee. "How can we do that? It will kill their marriage but won't get Susan out of the problem she's in."

"She can go tell the police." His voice echos his exasperation. "She must have enough evidence to put that sack of crap behind bars."

"She can't do that. He said that if she goes to the cops, he will make sure she and her husband die horrible deaths. On top of that she would have to give evidence. She's committed crimes by working with him. Sure, she'd get immunity from prosecution, but almost certainly she'd lose her licence to practice law." I'm almost shouting at him.

"Guys, guys. Calm down. You're smart enough to find a way out of this," Adry chimes in. We look at her, then at each other and the anger deflates; blessed are the peace-makers, indeed.

She continues, "Susan's been blackmailed into working for this guy David Fox, who's a dealer in illegal weapons. He's made her set up and manage an international network of companies to hide the transactions and launder the money he makes, right?"

"Good summary," I say. Stammo just grunts.

She smiles. "Sooooo, there must be some way a couple of clever guys, like you, can use information she feeds you to catch this guy out, without him knowing she was the one who gave you the info in the first place."

Silence.

More silence as we mentally kick it about.

I frown. "I like the idea but how the heck would we do that?"

"Tell me everything she told you," says Stammo, "and don't leave anything out."

I do as he asks.

After I finish there are long seconds of silence; then Stammo laughs. "The trouble with you Rogan, is you've just got no imagination." Then he starts humming the one Scott Joplin tune that every movie buff knows.

My attempt at a question is interrupted by Jen Halley walking into the office. There's no smile on her face. "There was no match between the sketch images and anyone in the system. It was only a one-in-four chance but I was hoping... Anyway Cal, our only hope now is that your Plan B works."

"There might be a Plan C," says Stammo, face serious again. "And maybe it should be Plan A."

I know what's coming.

"I'm all ears," says Jen.

"When you phoned me from the Ovaltine, I did what you asked. But then I got to thinking. We've probably got a good likeness of a killer. Don't you think we should hand it over to VPD and let them take it from here?"

"No," Jen and I say in unison.

Stammo fixes his best stare on her. "I know why Rogan doesn't want to do it; he wants to be the one to find the killer and show he's better than Vancouver's finest. What's *your* objection?"

"National security," she says. "If Denis Lamarche's murder is connected to his sister's death in the bombing, we don't want the local police muddying the waters."

"Huh!" Stammo grunts. He masticates her response for a bit. "OK, Rogan. I guess we can't stand in the way of the nation's security can we."

He's acting grumpily but I know him. He wants us to find the killer before VPD does, every bit as much as I do. Jen just gave him the excuse he needed.

———

THE NEW SANDWICH SHOP IN OUR BUILDING HAS DONE IT again. Stammo and I are enjoying eight-inch-long meatball subs and Adry and Jen are eating something healthy. "Let's brainstorm for a few minutes," Jen says. "Denis and Annalise die on the same day. We're assuming they are connected, right?" We all nod. "We can't do any investigation of her death because it's under a national security blanket. But let's look some more at his death. Cal, you said he was beaten to death?"

"Yes and he was tortured first. I couldn't figure why a homeless man would be tortured by anyone but when we found the memory card in his box of stuff, I guessed he was being tortured to make him give up the memory card."

"What box of stuff?" she asks. "You told me about the memory card but never mentioned the box."

"It was in a box he kept buried underneath the tent he shared with Ghost and Tommy."

"What else was in it?"

"Just an old bible in French. It might have been valuable, it looks old."

"Can I see it?"

I take the pink box out of my desk and hand it to her. She takes the box out of its plastic bags and takes out the bible. "It's beautiful," she says. She opens it to the front cover then turns the page. "His parents were Samuel and Clarisse. Maybe we should find out what we can about them?" She turns a few pages then holds the book, spine up, over the desk and riffles through the pages. A piece of paper drops out and flutters down onto the desk.

I reach forward.

"Don't touch it," Stammo says. "It might be evidence."

"Do you guys have any nitrile gloves?" Jen asks.

"Yeah, that's another thing we bought when we started the company but I don't think we've ever used them." He wheels over to the stationery cabinet and gets out the box.

Jen dons a pair of the purple gloves and picks up the

paper. She unfolds it once, twice and scans it with her eyes. "It's a letter from Annie to Denis. It's dated Sunday, November twenty-fourth. That's four days before the bombing." Her eyes scan some more then she starts to read out loud, "*My dear Denis, I hope all is well with you and that you are remembering to take your meds every day. I really need you to be on your meds because I need you to do something very important for me. Do you remember I told you that I have been having an affair with my boss, Neil? You told me Daddy wouldn't have approved. Haha. Well, I was at his town house last night and I woke up in the middle of the night with a terrible headache. I got up and crept into his study because he always keeps Extra Strength Tylenol in his desk drawer, only this time the drawer was locked. His desk was a mess, it always is, and as I was rummaging around to see if there were any pills there, my arm must have touched the mouse because his computer screen lit up. He couldn't have had a password set for waking up from sleep mode, he's very careless about that sort of thing. I knew I shouldn't but I couldn't resist looking. There were some documents on the screen that really worried me. I think I need to talk to someone about them. They are illegal, very illegal. I found the folder where they were kept and there were others too. I was really worried. There is something terrible going on. I didn't know what to do so I emailed the documents to myself with a copy to you. I was just about to delete the email after I'd sent it, when I heard Neil coming down the hall calling me. I just managed to close his email program in time and pretend to still be searching his desk for the pills when he walked into the study. I don't think he suspects anything but if he checks his Sent folder he'll know what I've done. Denis, I need you to open that email, encrypt all the files and save them for me while I work out what to do. Please, my darling brother, I need you to do this. Your loving sister, Annie. P.S. If anything should happen to me, I need you to get those files to my friend Sally Hyde at CSIS."*

We sit in stunned silence until Stammo puts it into words. "Ho-ly crap!" he says.

"This Neil guy must have found her emails," I say. "He must have arranged Denis' death. If she hadn't been killed by that terrorist, he might well have silenced Annalise somehow. We need to find out who the hell he is."

"No we don't." Jen's face is white. "There's only one man in the upper management of DND with the name Neil. It's Neil Harris, the Minister, one of the most powerful men in the Federal Government."

"Holy crap squared!" says Stammo. "What are you going to do Jen?"

She shakes her head. "I'm not a hundred percent sure. If the Minister of DND is involved in something criminal who knows who else might be involved? I need to think about this."

I can almost see the wheels turning in her mind. Annie's letter has taken this out of our hands; this, as they say, is way above our pay grade. Jen will have to take it back to her bosses in Ottawa.

"Before I do anything, I need to see those documents. I want to find out what's going on and who's involved." She turns to me. "Cal, do you want to check in with your buddy, see if he's cracked the encryption yet?"

I do.

He hasn't.

"Then we need to find the encryption key. I'm not going to do anything until I see what's in those damn documents."

How the hell do we find what key a schizophrenic, alcoholic, homeless genius would have thought up when our only clue is the word 'garter'?

We all dwell on our own thoughts until Adry says, "This probably isn't relevant but can someone explain to me how you send a letter to a homeless man?"

They all look at me and I shrug. "That's a very good question," Jen says.

9

NICK

Rogan really wanted to come with me to this meeting and, to tell the truth, I'd kinda like him to be here, as backup, if nothing else. I went home and picked up my Glock; it's in the side pouch on my wheelchair, but I still feel a bit uneasy doing this alone. Still, there's no way I want Rogan in this meeting. He might just hear too much. I couldn't stand the shame of him knowing.

As I pull into the handicapped parking spot, my phone rings. I press the button on the steering wheel. "Nick Stammo."

"*Mr. Stammo, Etienne Grey here.*"

Oh crap. "Good afternoon." What the hell am I going to tell him?

"*I was expecting progress reports on your investigation into my wife's activities. We met on Monday, it's now Friday and I've heard nothing.*"

"Yes, I'm sorry about that." Since we started the business, I've never lied to a client, but here I go. "We followed her on Wednesday night but unfortunately we lost her. But, right now, I'm following up a lead, which I think will give us some useful information." The last bit's almost true.

"*And what specifically is that?*" He sounds really ticked off now.

"I'd rather not say at this point, but I will get back to you on Monday. I promise."

"*Please see that you do. If there's no progress...*" He leaves it hanging for a moment. "*I'll talk to you on Monday.*" He hangs up.

I'm starting to regret this plan for getting Susan Grey out of the fix she's in. It sounded easy in the office but now? It's not too late to pull out. I could phone and cancel. I *should* phone and cancel, then just tell her husband the truth, collect our fee and move on. Except that might put them both in danger. *Will* put them both in danger. Who am I kidding, I'm not gonna let that happen.

Decision made, I unlatch my chair from the driving position and activate the lift to get me out onto the sidewalk. It takes a minute for everything to operate and then to stow it back into the truck. I guess a quick getaway is going to be out of the question. The thought makes me grin as I wheel over to the door of the bar. As I get to the door a couple come out; they are holding hands and giggling. The woman holds the door open for me and I wheel in.

This is only my second time in here in five or more years. It's changed a lot. Back then it was a biker bar and if you didn't belong you'd be shown the door. Now it's a lot more of a friendly place but the ownership is still in biker hands. I wheel over to the bar. I feel ridiculous; the bar is at chin level for me.

"Nick Stammo. I'm here to see Tusk. He's expecting me," I tell the barman.

He looks like he's fifteen. He gives me a grin and pours me a beer. "On the house," he says. "I'll tell him you're here."

I reach up and take the glass, drink the first two inches of beer, so that I can put it on my lap without spilling it, and wheel over to a table. I drink some more. It's good. Probably from one of those craft breweries Rogan's so keen on. I run through in my mind the plan that we made when Rogan debriefed us on the details of his conversation with Susan Grey. She told him that the biker gang who own this bar are regular customers of David Fox, the gun dealer she's been forced to work for. They've been buying large quantities of weapons from him, which they are selling on to other biker gangs across the country. I have a history with the top dog in the gang. A history I'm not proud of.

"Well, well, well, Nick Stammo. What can I do for you?" I look up. Roderick Sweet, a.k.a. Tusk, is grinning down at me. He's wearing a suit. Last time I saw him, he was in his biker's colours. It's good to see a thug move up market.

"Hello, Roderick," I say. The grin slips away. He doesn't like to be called by his real name.

"If you're looking for another hand out Stammo, you've come to the wrong place." I was right to come here without Rogan.

"I understand you're a customer of David Fox, Roderick."

"How the fuck did you know that?"

"You'd be surprised what I know."

He mentally chews on that for a moment, then asks, "What'ja want?"

"I have a client. A rich client. A rich, foreign client. He wants some FN F2000s, and he wants a lot of them."

His eyes drill into me. "I thought you were a PI," he says.

"Means to an end, Roderick," I say.

"Stop calling me that," he snaps.

I shrug. "I was hoping you might make an introduction. I'd like to meet with Mr. Fox. There'd be a finders fee in it for you." The last thing I want right now is to meet David Fox and Tusk's greed will make sure I don't have to until it's on my terms.

He sits down across the table from me.

He leans forward and I can smell his aftershave. He has gone up market. He used to smell of sweat. I'll bet the kids at school were too scared of him to call him Sweaty Sweet. He drops his voice. "I can get you F2000s. How many do you need?"

"For the first shipment, I'd need four hundred."

He almost chokes on his surprise. "That's over a million bucks US."

"Well, if it's too big an order for you..."

"No, no." The dynamic between us has changed. "I can handle it Nick, no problem." I can see his slimy little mind doing the math on what his cut will be.

"How do I know I can trust you, Tusk? You've got kind of a rep for short changing people."

"Not on a big deal like this," he tries to assure me.

"So, how much for four hundred and how soon?"

"I'd need to talk to my supplier first. No one carries four hundred F2000s in inventory."

"OK. Fair enough. Just tell Fox that I need 'em quick and I want to see samples. I don't want to get ripped off with some crappy replicas."

Tusk licks his lips. "I'm gonna need a couple of hundred grand deposit, up front."

I chuckle. "With this client that's no problem. But you don't get to see a penny of it until I see those samples."

"Sure, sure. Like I said, no prob."

"OK," I say. "Set it up." I reach into the pouch on the side of my wheelchair and take out a box. This was Adry's idea and it's a good one. It's going to add—what was it she said—'an air of authenticity'. Yeah, authenticity greases the wheels of every good sting. I hand him the box. "There's a burner phone in there with one number in the recent calls list. Call me on that number when you're ready for me to see Fox's samples."

"You got it." He reaches forward and shakes my hand. "How about a glass of champagne to celebrate?"

"No thanks. I've gotta phone my client and let him know we're on and to send the cash." I wheel back from the table. "Don't let me down, Tusk, OK?"

Without waiting for a reply I wheel out of there. I can't wait to make that phone call... and it's not to the imaginary client.

W hen I see her face, I wonder at how the world worked before we had FaceTime. *"Hi Dad."* Her smile is huge. Thank heaven it's also even; no fear of orthodontist's bills in that mouth. *"Ethan said he really liked talking to you. He thought it was neat that you're a private detective. Do you know what, Dad?"*

Mention of her friend's name brings back the unpleasant thought. "No, what?"

"He didn't even know there was such a thing as a detective who wasn't a policeman until I told him there was. Are you solving any cool crimes right now."

"No. Right now I'm talking to you," I say.

"Da-ad! You know what I mean."

"Yes, we are helping a lady who's being forced by a very bad man to do something she doesn't want to do."

"She should just tell him no means no."

If only it were that simple. "Also we're trying to find out who killed a homeless man."

"Who would kill a man because he's homeless? Ethan says homeless people are just like us."

"Ethan's right." I can't delay the unpleasant part of the evening any longer. "Sweetie, would you tell Mommy I need to speak to her. Tell her it's important."

She drops her iPad and I have a view of their living room ceiling while I hear Ellie talking to Sam. There is a pause and she says, *"But he said it's important."*

The iPad is picked up. *"Here she is Dad."*

Sam's face, a face that I once loved more than anything, appears on the screen. *"What is it, Cal?"* I can feel the frost from three thousand, three hundred and fifty kilometres away. This does not bode well.

"Hi Sam." No response. "I want to know if you have any plans to change Ellie's name from Rogan to Cullen?"

"Did she tell you that?" She looks off screen. *"Ellie! I told you I wanted to tell Daddy in my own way, on my own time."*

"She didn't tell me Sam; don't blame her," I say. "It was just that I was speaking to her friend Ethan and he called me Mr. Cullen."

"Oh." She looks uncomfortable. *"Right... Well, yes, I've registered her at school as Cullen and I think it would be appropriate to change her name legally at some time."*

"Have you started the legal process?"

"No," she says, then looks embarrassed and adds, *"Yes."*

"Don't you need my permission?"

"Not really, I have legal custody and guardianship." She got that when I was living on the streets.

"Don't I have any say in the matter?"

"You would need to research that yourself. Anyway Cal, I have to go now. We can talk about it when you come out here for Christmas. Here's Ellie."

Ellie's face appears on the screen before I can object any further. In the background I hear a door close. Her little face doesn't look too happy. She looks off-screen for a moment and then says in a whisper. *"I don't want to change my name Daddy."*

I have to tread a fine line here. "Did you tell Mommy that?"

"Yes but she said I couldn't choose because I'm not twelve yet." Then the clouds disappear and she smiles. *"Anyway she said in Ontario you can't change a name until you've lived here for like a year and we haven't even been here for six months yet. Maybe we can change Mommy's mind when you come here."*

"Good idea, sweetie. We can try."

However, I know Sam. When she latches on to something, even the proverbial wild horses couldn't drag her away.

―――――

"THIRD EVENING IN A ROW, MR. ROGAN." I SMILE LIKE A FOOL and step back to welcome her in. I feel equal parts of happiness to see her and sadness, as her use of my last name reminds me of Sam's intention. Damn. I don't want Sam in my mind right now. She plants a kiss on my cheek and thrusts a bottle of Chianti Classico into my hands. It's one of the more expensive marques.

"Thank you. You look great." And she does. It's the first time I've seen her in a dress and heels. It's red with a gold pattern that brings out the caramel of her skin and a lump to my throat.

"Thank you." She does a pirouette. "I got it in Mumbai." I have an almost overwhelming desire to take her in my arms and kiss her but I'm pretty sure the moment's not right. Yet.

"The Chianti's perfect," I say. "I'm cooking lasagna."

"Yeah, I figured. Guys always cook pasta on a third date."

I hang her coat up and lead her into the living room. She sits on my sofa, slips off her shoes and curls her legs up. I start to pour the wine and she says, "Anything new on the woman we followed, two nights ago?"

I hand her her wine and she pats the sofa beside her. I sit down and breathe in her perfume. Not Chanel. Good, it won't remind me of Sam or Em... yet here they are, unbidden, in my mind. "Just to check," I say, "I assume anything I tell you isn't going to end up in the Daily News Hound."

"Cross my heart and hope to die," she says.

I tell her all about yesterday's events with Susan Grey and Stammo's plan to rescue her from the predations of the arms dealer, David Fox.

"Isn't that dangerous?" she asks.

"Nick may be in a wheelchair but he's a tough old bird who knows how to take care of himself."

She slips her arm through mine.

"You really like him don't you?"

"Yes, I do. I really do. I have no idea how I would get along without him."

"Have you ever told him that?"

"Not in so many words."

"Well you should."

For some reason the thought of telling Stammo how much I rely on him is a bit uncomfortable, so I segue into, "But there was a time when he and I really did *not* get along."

She snuggles closer and I tell her my long and chequered history, how we went from having a bitter, confrontational relationship to being partners and friends.

And I realize how much I have missed just chatting with someone about stuff that matters. I haven't done that since Sam and I were still together.

This is special.

Saturday

Breakfast in the Ovaltine three times in a week, Rocky. We could get used to this couldn't we Tommy?" Ghost's buddy just nods his head as he gums his corned beef hash. An adult life spent mostly on the streets has left him with precious few teeth. "So we done what you said. We handed out copies of that picture you did of the big guy who killed ole Wily. Gave 'em to a whole bunch of folk and told them follow him if they saw him and to let us know where he goes. Told 'em there'd be a hundred bucks in it if they found him. I'll phone you as soon as I hear from anyone."

"Thanks Ghost. If we get anything we'll pay them and you guys'll get a hundred bucks each too."

Tommy smiles and gives us a thumbs up. Ghost says, "Fuckin' A."

Jen jumps in, "I've got another question for you guys."

"Fire away, Miss."

"In that bible of Wily's we found a letter from his sister Annie."

"Yeah, she often wrote to him. They was real close."

"Where did she send them?"

Ghost frowns, "What'ja mean?"

"Wily lived on the streets, he didn't have an address to send letters to."

"Oh... Yeah... I never thought of that. I dunno."

Adry's right, it's probably not relevant but it's bugging me as much as Jen. How the hell did his sister get that letter to him last week?

We get up from the table. Neither Jen nor I ordered breakfast; me, because the withdrawal pains are taking away all my hunger, and her, because she already had breakfast at her hotel. Her breakfast at the Devonshire was definitely more expensive, and certainly more elegantly served, but I'm not sure it tasted any better than a breakfast at the Ovaltine.

Definitely not if Ghost and Tommy are anything to go by.

Tommy swallows his mouthful of hash. "I know," he says.

"Know what?" I ask.

"How he got his letters."

We sit down.

"He was friendly with one of them priests who help out at the shelter. He's a real nice ole guy named Father O'Higgins. Wily told me he knew the Father back in the day, before he was, y'know, on the streets. I think Annie sent her letters to him and he'd pass 'em on to Wily."

"Thanks Tommy, you earned that breakfast for sure." I get up again. "You guys be sure to call me if anyone sees that big guy."

Their mouths are full again so they just nod.

They're good men. If life had dealt them different cards, who knows what they'd be? Again I think of Damien's t-shirt. Is it just luck that they're living on the streets while I have a job I love and Damien owns a multi-million dollar company? It gives me an uncomfortable feeling.

———

THE CHURCH OFFICE IS AUSTERE BUT THE OCCUPANT IS WARM and welcoming. It took me four phone calls to track down Father John O'Higgins, S.J., on a Saturday. He is a very old priest who looks like he might disintegrate and blow away in a strong wind, yet the hand that shakes mine has a firm, if bony, grip.

He smiles at Jen and then me. "How can I help you?" His voice is decades younger than his appearance and still carries the air of Ireland.

"I was wondering if you could help me with some information, Father."

"If I can."

"You knew Denis Lamarche, I believe."

He frowns. "Knew?" he asks.

His question catches me by surprise but then why would he know that Wily was dead? "Yes, I'm afraid he died just over a week ago."

He crosses himself. "That's terrible. It's such a hard life for those poor souls on the streets. How did it happen?"

"He was beaten to death."

He shakes his head. "His poor sister. Do you know how she's taking it? I must call her."

I take a deep breath and Jen says, "We hate to be the

bearers of more bad news Father, but Annalise was killed in the terrorist bombing in Ottawa last week."

"Lord, have mercy on her soul," he whispers, crossing himself again.

He sits with his head down and we give him time.

Finally, he looks up. "They died on the same day. The Lord moves in mysterious ways Mr. Rogan."

"In this case Father, we think it may not have been the Lord." I immediately regret the wording but he doesn't seem offended, so I continue "We believe there's a connection between their deaths and I was wondering if you knew anything about them that might throw some light on it."

"Well I don't know what that might be. What sort of thing are you looking for?"

"I don't really know either. How well did you know them?"

"I knew the family well. I was their parish priest in Sainte-Foy, Québec; I baptized both Annalise and Denis. Did you know they were twins?" He doesn't wait for an answer. "Their mother was a lovely, saintly woman, very devout. The father on the other hand was a—" He stops himself short. "I shouldn't speak ill of the dead but let's just say he was not my favourite person." The Irish in his accent is a little more pronounced now. "He had a knighthood, I'm not quite sure why, but I seem to remember that he might have come to Canada to escape some sort of scandal." There is a look of indecision on his face and he looks hard at me... then decides. "If I know Sir Samuel, there was a woman or women involved."

"What was his last name?" Jen asks.

"Fetherstonhaugh. A typical Englishman of the worst sort, I'm afraid." The Irish accent is really strong now. From his tone, I can feel hints of the decades of oppression to which the English aristocracy subjected the Irish in the nineteenth, and into the twentieth century—long ago but not forgotten. "After their marriage broke down, Clarisse changed her name, and the names of the children, back to her maiden name, Lamarche."

My gut tells me that this kindly old priest may know something that could help in our investigation but I can't for the life of me guess what it might be.

Jen asks. "After their mother's death, they reconnected with their father. Do you know anything about that Father?"

"Not a lot. By that time the Church had moved me out here to Vancouver. I went back to Sainte-Foy to officiate at poor Clarisse's funeral and that was the last time I saw Annalise face-to-face. So I really don't know much about her later relationship with the father. By that time, Denis had also moved out to Vancouver to work at UBC's computer science department. It was about the time his father showed up here that he stopped taking his schizo-phrenia medications. I don't know if the father was the cause but I wouldn't be surprised."

I can't think what to ask him next. I look at Jen to see if she has any ideas but she just shrugs. I hand him one of my cards and ask him to call me if he thinks of anything that might be relevant.

As he rises to show us out, he asks, "Do you know his friends Ghost and Tommy?" When I answer, he asks, "How are they handling his death?"

"With alcohol," I say and the question triggers a thought. "I promised them I would arrange a proper funeral for him. I'm sure he would want to be buried by you, Father, I'd be happy to pay if you could make the arrangements."

The thought of giving Denis a proper resting place

seems to bring some solace to the old priest and we discuss the details before Jen and I leave.

But when we do leave, I still have the nagging feeling we're missing something.

———

"It looks like we've drawn a blank." Jen is not a happy camper.

"Don't worry," says Stammo. "It's like this in every case. Just when you think you're stuck, something shows up. Take the rest of the weekend off and see what Monday brings."

"On Monday morning, I have to be back at my desk in Ottawa. My boss thinks I'm off sick, remember? I was just hoping we could find the connection between Annie and Denis' deaths. But we don't really have anything."

Adry, ever positive, says, "Well at least you found out how to send a letter to a homeless man."

Jen smiles, "Yeah, I guess so." She sighs and the smile slips from her face. "I might as well go back to my hotel and check out. I'm going to see if I can get a flight back this afternoon. It'll give me tomorrow to get over the jet lag and work out how I'm going to tell my bosses that Annalise was having an affair with the Minister of National Defence *and* explain to him how I know that without telling him about my unauthorized trip here. I'll come by and see you guys before I leave."

After she goes, I ask Adry to add our two new pieces of information—the facts that Denis and Annalise were twins and that their father was Sir Samuel Fetherstonhaugh—to our file.

Time to switch gears.

"Nick, we need to go over your plans for getting Susan Grey off the hook that David Fox has her on."

"Don't sweat it Rogan, it's all set. As soon as I get the call from Tusk I'll put it all in motion."

"I know. I just think I should be there with you."

"No. Adding a new face might scare him off. Don't worry, here's how it's going to go down."

As he goes over his plan, I quiz him on the details and I have to admit that he's covered all the bases. It doesn't completely stop me worrying. What if—

"Guys! Come and look at this." Adry's excited yell cuts off my thought.

Stammo wheels towards the reception area and I follow. "Whatcha got?" he asks.

She gives us a big smile. "After you gave me the information about Denis and Annalise's father, I put it in the file and thought I'd do some digging. Guess what I found?"

She laughs at our blank faces and angles her screen so that we can see the Wikipedia page she has open. It is titled *Samuel V. Fetherstonhaugh* and to the right is the picture of an unsmiling face with a severe expression.

"Jeez. I wouldn't want *him* as a father," Stammo grunts.

"What did you find Adry?" I ask.

"Look at the first line. It says, '*Sir Samuel Fetherstonhaugh was a Major in the British army and a member of the Most Noble Order of the Garter.*' That was what Denis meant in the hint file when he said 'garter is the key'. It wasn't about a woman's garter or a garter snake, it was a reference to his father. Maybe his father's name is the key to decrypt the document that was on the memory card."

The stunned silence only lasts for a moment.

"Well done Adry!" I say.

"Atta girl!" yells Stammo.

"Email me the link to that page please," I say. As soon as my phone beeps, I open my email and forward the link to Damien Crotty with an explanation.

"In a minute we may know what was so important about that document that Denis decided to encrypt it," I can't keep the glee out of my voice.

My phone beeps again.

"That was quick," Stammo says.

The email wipes the glee away. It's from Damien, or rather from his email autoresponder. *I have gone hiking for the weekend and will be out of cell range until Sunday night. I will reply to this email on Monday.*

"Damn," says Adry. "I really wanted to know."

"Crap!" Stammo says. "Who the hell goes hiking in the first week of December?"

Then it hits me.

"You know who can probably decrypt it?" I say. "Jen. She's a CSIS intelligence officer. She must have software to decrypt stuff. I'll call her."

As I pull the phone out of my pocket, it rings. I tap 'Accept'. "Hi, Ghost," I say, "I'm in a bit of a rush. Can I call you back."

"Oh, yeah, I suppose. It's just that one of the guys I gave that drawing to has seen him."

"The drawing of the big guy who took Wily out of the Balmoral?" I ask.

"Yeah, him. My buddy Dougie Blake thinks he saw him downtown. You remember Dougie, right Rocky?" He chuckles. *"Him and Roy was always arguing about stuff. Like the time—"*

I cut short what could be a long story. "When did Dougie see him, Ghost?"

"A couple of minutes ago. He jus' called me."

I can feel the adrenaline kick in. "Where was he?"

"I toldja, downtown."

Curbing the urge to scream, I say, as calmly as I can, "Whereabouts downtown did Dougie say he was."

"Oh..." A pause. *"I never asked him, Rock. Sorry."*

"Just give me his number."

He rattles off the number of Dougie's mobile then asks, *"I still get the hundred bucks, eh?"*

"Yes, Tommy too. I'll call you back soon."

I hang up and dial.

"Who's this?"

"Hey, Dougie. It's Rocky Rogan."

"Hello Rocky. Haven't seen you in ages, how's Roy?"

If Dougie doesn't remember that Roy's been dead for some three years, I'm not sanguine about the chances of him having actually seen the person who most likely beat Wily to death. "Listen, Dougie, this is really important." I cut to the chase. "Where are you standing, right now?"

"Right outside where I saw that guy in the picture Ghost gave me."

With all the patience I can muster, I say, "And where exactly is that?"

"Oh, yeah. Right." He chuckles. *"I'm on Hornby. Right outside the Devonshire. It's where the guy went in."*

The electricity shoots up my spine and I can feel the hair on the back of my neck standing to attention.

What's Wily's murderer doing in Jen's hotel?

————

I'M NOT AS FIT AS I USED TO BE. WHEN I GOT NO REPLY FROM Jen's phone, I decided it would be quicker to run the three blocks from our office to the Devonshire than to get my car out of the parkade, thread my way through downtown

Vancouver's lunchtime traffic and then find a place to park near the hotel.

Good theory. Except that it's five blocks not three and I'm standing at the Devonshire's check-in desk trying to catch my breath.

"I urgently need to talk to one of your guests," I pant, "Jennifer Halley."

"I'm sorry sir, you just missed her. She checked out about ten minutes ago."

Damn.

"Was there anyone else looking for her? A big guy, kind of tough looking."

"Oh yes. Only he wasn't looking for her. They checked out together."

My mind revs, trying to process this information.

"He was staying here with her?" I ask.

"I assume so. They came to the desk together."

This doesn't make sense.

"Do you know his name?"

She checks her computer. "The room was booked in her name and there's no mention of another guest."

"Do you know if they checked in together?"

"I have no idea." She checks the computer again. "She was booked in by one of my colleagues early on Thursday morning."

"Would it be possible to speak to your colleague?" I ask. She looks unsure. "It's really important." I can hear the pleading in my voice. So can she.

"Just a minute." She smiles as she picks up her phone and dials. After a moment she says, "Oh hi. This is Melanie at the front desk, I need Jack Novak's phone number." She listens and scribbles down a number, says, "Thanks so much," hangs up and dials.

She frowns. "I'm afraid his phone's not on at the moment. I'm not allowed to give you his number but if you give me your number, I could try again later and get him to call you."

I thank her effusively as I hand her my card.

My mind's in turmoil as I head for the door. I have some big questions buzzing around in my head. I pull out my phone and go to the recent calls list.

He answers on the second ring. *"Who's this?"*

"Hi Dougie, it's Rocky again."

"Hi Rocky, I was just gonna call you."

"That's great Dougie but I need to ask you something. After I spoke to you did you hang around outside the Devonshire?"

"Nah. The doormen there doesn't go for the likes of me hanging around their swanky hotel."

"So you never saw that guy leave there."

"Nah."

Damn.

"But I've seen him again."

"When?"

"Just a minute ago. That's why I was going to call you. After I spoke to you I was walking down Howe and when I got to Hastings, I crossed the road and there he was walking down the street with this good-looking woman."

"Fairly tall? Short, dark hair and blue eyes?"

"Yeah, that's her."

"Did you see where they went?"

"Nah. They just got in a grey car and drove off."

"Did she look like she was being forced into the car?"

"Forced? Nah. She was laughing at something he said."

Nothing makes sense. This isn't good.

"You didn't see what make of car it was did you Dougie?"

"I can't tell one car from another. They all look the same to me, these days."

I sigh. "Ok, man. Thanks. I'll make sure you get a bonus for this."

"Oh, yeah. Ole Ghost said there'd be a hundred in it for me."

"Yes for sure. You've been great."

"So let me ask you something, Rocky," he says and the tone of his voice has changed, and not in a good way. *"How much extra for the license plate of the car they drove off in?"*

My heart misses a beat. "You got the license plate?" He grunts affirmatively. "I'll give you an extra fifty."

"Make it a ton and you have yourself a deal."

"Deal. What was the number."

"How do I know I can trust you? When you were on the streets you did some hinky stuff."

He's not wrong. "Where are you Dougie? I'll come and get you and give you the cash."

"That tiny little park just opposite where Hornby runs into Hastings."

"Stay there, I'm on my way."

I hang up, push through the doors of the Devonshire, take a right turn and start to jog north on Hornby.

If Dougie's right, and it's a big if, then Jen is working with the guy who killed Denis Lamarche.

She's been playing us.

———

I CHECK MY WATCH. SIX MINUTES TO GET TO HORNBY AND Hastings with a stop at the bank to get the cash. The lights are against me and the traffic on Hastings is too heavy for me to run across. I can see the 'park'. It is a strip of land, the width of a building, that runs between the Vancouver Club and the Terminal City Club, two establishments frequented by Vancouver's elite. Shakespeare would have enjoyed the irony of meeting a homeless man between these two bastions of wealth.

The lights change and I sprint across the street.

There's no sign of Dougie in the park.

There are just a few people hurrying through on their ways to or from lunch. I peer through the windows of the upscale Mink coffee shop; Dougie's just ornery enough to go in there. But he didn't. Ahead, I can see the flashing red lights of an ambulance. I stride towards them and as I approach the steps leading down to Cordova, I see him. He's lying, prone and motionless, at the bottom of the steps. He's being attended to by paramedics. Beside him is his shopping cart, on its side, all his worldly possessions strewn down the steps and on the ground.

I run down the steps, taking care not to trip on Dougie's stuff. "Is he OK?" I ask, realizing, too late, that it's a dumb question. The paramedics ignore me. They are trying to attach a collar to immobilize his neck.

"Do you know this man sir?" I turn to the familiar voice. Surprise seeps onto his face. "Hello, Rogan." It's Sarge, a long time member of the VPD. We have history. Latterly, none of it good. "What are you doing here?" he asks.

"I was supposed to meet him here. He had some information for me. What happened to him?"

"Fell down the steps apparently." His eyes drill into mine. "So you knew him." I can't tell if it's a question or an accusation. I nod and give him Dougie's name which he scribbles in his notebook.

The paramedics have affixed the collar and are strapping a board to his back.

"Looks bad. Who saw it happen?" I ask.

Sarge inclines his head. "Lady over there."

He is indicating a tall woman wearing a worried expression and a hijab. "Mind if I talk to her?" He shrugs, so I walk across to her.

After introducing myself, I ask, "Did he just fall?"

"Was he a friend of yours?" she asks, sympathy and concern written on her face.

"Yes, kind of."

"I'm sorry. I think your friend might have been drunk."

"It's after ten in the morning, so he almost certainly was."

She gives a shy smile. "I was heading back to work. As I approached the steps I looked up and saw him glaring down at me. He shouted something about 'terrorists' and took one of his hands, his left hand actually, off the shopping cart and shook his fist at me. It made him lose his balance and he fell, pulling his cart after him."

"Was there anyone near him when he fell?"

She thinks for a moment. "No, I don't think so."

"Thanks," I say. "I'm sorry he shouted at you."

"Since the Ottawa bombing," she smiles ruefully, "he's the third. I'm just sorry that he fell. I hope he's going to be all right."

The unconscious Dougie has been strapped to the board and they are lifting him onto a stretcher. "Thanks again." I smile at her. "You're very kind. Ignore the *slings and arrows of outrageous fortune*. People like Dougie don't know any better."

"Thank you for that," she says.

I just smile and nod and head over to the ambulance. "Which hospital are you taking him to?" I ask the taller paramedic.

"St. Paul's," she says.

"Any idea when he's going to regain consciousness?"

She just shrugs as she slides the stretcher into the ambulance. She climbs in and closes the back door.

I stand and watch as the ambulance pulls away from the curb taking with it our one lead to the murderer of Denis Lamarche. It's firmly locked inside Dougie's head.

12

NICK

It's over twenty-four hours since I talked to Tusk in the biker bar and there's been no contact. Our one hope of getting Susan Grey off the hook does not look as promising as it did when we planned it all out in the office yesterday morning. When I call Etienne Grey on Monday, he is going to be—

Adry's laughter cuts into my thoughts. "Come and see this, Nick," she calls out. I wheel away from my desk and just as I get to the reception area, Rogan backs through the glass doors pulling a Costco cart full of junk. Adry gets up from her desk and holds the door open for him. "Been shopping, Cal?" she asks giggling.

He's not amused.

But I am. "Been blowing your paycheck on luxury items have you, Rogan?" He gets the cart into the reception area and it hits me. "Phew! Did something die in there?"

"I'm keeping it for the one person who might have a clue as to where Annalise and Denis Larmarche's murderer might be."

His words bring me down to earth again. "What happened when you got to the hotel?"

"We've got some stuff we have to work out. Come on, you too, Adry."

He gives us a run down of his trip to the Devonshire hotel and his failed meeting with some character named Dougie.

When he finishes, I look across at Adry and she's sitting there with her mouth open in disbelief. "Jen knows the guy who killed Denis Lamarche?" she says.

Rogan just nods.

"Shit!" I say. "I was sure she was one of the good guys."

"Me too," he says. "But Dougie said she was laughing at what the big guy was saying as they got into his car."

"Why would a CSIS intelligence officer be involved with a murderer?" I ask.

"In the States, the CIA has got involved with some pretty sketchy characters from time to time, maybe we're just catching up."

"Yeah, but this is Canada and I liked Jen," Adry chimes in. "I have a lot of difficulty believing that she's not who she says she is."

"Good point," I say. I swivel my chair and tap my mouse. Fifteen seconds and I've got what I want. I dial the number. It's answered on the second ring. "Can I speak to Jennifer Halley please?" Huh. The answer doesn't help. I hang up.

"What was that?" Rogan asks.

"CSIS. They said 'There's no one of that name on duty at the moment.'"

"Typical government bullshit," he says.

We sit looking at each other and then he says, "You know what doesn't make any sense? If she's in league with the guy why would she sit with Ghost and Tommy to do a picture of him and then have us make copies to hand out to a bunch of guys on the street?" It's a good point. Doesn't make sense to me either.

"What if it was a distraction?" Adry says. She looks at our puzzled faces and says, "She knows that Ghost and Tommy have seen Denis' murderer, so she does a picture with them to seem like she's following up on it. When she told us there hadn't been a match for his face, how do we know she was telling the truth, how do we even know she sent the picture to Ottawa?"

"But why get Ghost and Tommy to send it to all their buddies?" I ask.

"She didn't," says Rogan. "That was my idea. She probably didn't want to say anything against it in case we thought it was suspicious. She probably thought that handing the picture out to a bunch of junkies and drunks wouldn't have any effect."

We slip into an unhappy silence.

"Goddammit!" says Adry banging her hand down on the corner of Rogan's desk, "I really thought she was one of the good guys."

More unhappy silence. Longer this time.

"Wait a minute." It's Adry again. Her face is lit up. "What about this—"

She's interrupted by the ringing of my phone. "Nick Stammo," I say.

"You want to buy four hundred F2000s?" It's not Tusk. This voice is cold and hard. I hold my finger to my lips, signalling Adry and Rogan to stay silent.

"That's right." Better to keep the answers brief.

"How do I know this is a legitimate trade?" He speaks a bit like Rogan. *"You are, after all an ex-cop."*

"Ex- being the main part," I say.

"*But you're a private investigator now. That's not very ex-
is it?*"

"It pays the bills and provides good cover for my other
interests."

He thinks that over for one... two... three... "*Who's your
client? I need to know who wants and can afford four hundred of
these fine weapons.*"

"My client is my business. For the first shipment, I need
four hundred of them and I want the fully automatic version
too—not the semis that they sell to every nut-job in the
States—*and* I need a million rounds to go with them."

"*Nonetheless, I insist on knowing who I am to deliver
these to.*"

My turn now. One... two... three... and four. "I need to
know you can supply what I want and that I don't get fobbed
off with some sub-standard shit. So here's the deal: you
show me some samples of your merchandise and if I'm
satisfied I'll tell you who the end user is."

Another long pause. "*Fair enough. I'll text you an address.
Be there at six this evening.*" The greed for a big deal wins out.
He hangs up.

Six o'clock! We've gotta move fast.

———

SHIT! SHIT! SHIT! WHAT IS IT ROGAN SAYS ABOUT THE BEST
laid plans. We haven't even started yet and I'm hooped. West
end parking on a Saturday night is impossible; I had to park
my truck around the corner and wheel here. And what do I
find? There are twelve steps leading up to the front porch of
the mansion where Susan Grey goes to work for David Fox.

I pull out my phone and reply to the number I was
called on just over three hours ago.

It rings once. Twice. Three times. Four— *"Yes."*

It's the same voice. I decide to land the first punch. "Didn't that idiot Tusk tell you guys I'm in a wheelchair? How the fuck am I supposed to get up to your front door?"

A second's pause then, *"He didn't, I apologize. Please wait a moment."* He hangs up. Still cold but at least polite.

Within seconds, the front door opens and two bouncers come lumbering down the steps. Without a word, each grabs a side of the wheelchair and they carry me up to the porch. They don't even take a deep breath. As I wheel through the front door, I realize there is no way for me to get out of this house without someone's assistance. It's a very uncomfortable feeling. I shake it off and wheel into the house. It's just as Rogan described it; shame he didn't remember the steps up to the porch. The difference is that there are a number of young women in expensive outfits sitting on the couches, chatting and drinking from champagne glasses which are probably filled with ginger ale. Just as well; most of them look way too young to drink alcohol. I'm really starting to dislike David Fox.

"Mr. Stammo. Welcome." He is a stunning looking man. Tall, well built and with a face like Rock Hudson. "I'm David Fox." He extends his hand and I shake it. "If you like what you see, I will be happy to let you take your pick, on the house, after we have concluded our business." He's referring to the girls so I don't think he'd be happy with my choice. Or maybe he would. Maybe he's like Rock Hudson in more than just looks. "Come with me."

I follow him across the 'showroom', through a door marked *Private*, down a hallway to a second door. The bouncers follow behind me. Fox takes out a key, unlocks the door and opens it. He reaches inside and takes out a small, blue, plastic tray. "Please empty your pockets and put everything, and I do mean everything, into the tray." It's OK. We were expecting this. I do as I'm told and he puts the tray on a shelf beside the door. "Come through," he says.

I wheel through the door into a small windowless vestibule. I notice that the door and the doorframe are both heavy steel. We were not expecting that. On the other side of the vestibule is another door, also steel, flanked by the two sides of a metal detector. It's getting worse by the minute. One of the bouncers walks through the metal detector—it doesn't beep for him—and opens the door; he reaches in and switches on a light. I can see from where I'm sitting that it leads to stairs going down to a basement.

"I regret to subject you to this indignity Mr. Stammo." His voice doesn't sound like he regrets anything at all. "Anton here is going to carry you through the metal detectors and down the stairs. Unfortunately, we won't be able to bring your wheelchair down, however, there are comfortable chairs down there."

Time to draw a first line in the sand. "Seriously," I say. "You won't let a man in a wheelchair have some level of dignity." I ramp my voice up a notch. "I'm a goddam customer about to do over a million dollars of business with you and you're going to have your man carry me downstairs into the basement like I'm a baby."

"As I say, I do regret it but it is non-negotiable." He erases my line in the sand. I knew he would. But that's OK.

I stare at him before saying "OK."

Anton comes and lifts me out of the wheel chair like I'm a quarter of my actual weight. He gently maneuvers me through the metal detector that screeches at me. He steps back. Before Fox can speak, I pull up my jacket. "Look," I yell at him. "It's my goddam belt buckle." I show him the lone star state buckle on the belt I'm wearing. "Are you going to make me take this off too? How the hell am I supposed to do business with you if my pants keep falling down." I give him my best glare.

He doesn't speak, just nods to Anton, who walks me through the metal detector and down the staircase into an Aladdin's cave for gun enthusiasts.

Phase one successfully complete.

Except that the metal detector squawked twice when Fox and his other heavy stepped through it.

13

CAL

I just saw the first thing go wrong. How could I have forgotten those steps up to the porch? I recognized one of the two heavies who carried him up; he was here when I checked out the place after I'd followed Susan here. Hopefully everything else will go as planned.

Time to check out that everything's in place. I zip up my new leather jacket and get out of the Healey. I turn away from the house and walk down to the end of the block. I take a right turn and survey the vehicles parked on the street. None of them fit what I'm looking for. I walk to the end of the block and do another right so that I'm looking down the block that runs behind the mansion. Again nothing familiar except Stammo's truck. Now I'm starting to worry. If Stammo gives the signal, and we're—

A blue BMW M3. It could be a coincidence. I walk closer and take a look at the plate. No coincidence. And there's nothing I can do. Stammo has already passed the point of no return, except...

I dash to the end of the block and turn right for the third time. A wave of relief passes through me. Parked on the street are two black Transit vans and a black Dodge. I run to the latter and knock on the passenger window. The passenger's head turns and looks at me. He hesitates for a moment and says something. The back door opens and I jump inside.

14

NICK

The armoury under the house must be close to two thousand square feet. There are shelves like in a library but they are full of guns, not books. To my right are three doors that must lead to other rooms and on my left is a door that must open out onto a garden. I'm sitting in one of those expensive leather wing-back chairs. There are three of them arranged around a teak coffee table. This place is like a freaking luxury-car showroom.

"It's fortuitous that your client wants F2000s. I happen to specialize in them." Now that he's accepted me as a *bona fide* customer, he's all charm and big words but I can smell the snake underneath.

"I want them fully automatic, not the FS and I want them with the grenade launcher module."

He raises his eyebrows seeing the price going up. "We can do that."

"Good," I give him a nod and a smile. "Let's see what you've got."

He gives Anton a nod and the big guy walks down between two of the shelves and comes back with the weapon in one hand and a grenade launcher in the other. He puts them on the table in front of me. It's time. I pick up the gun. "Exc—" I just manage to stop in time. One of the doors on my right has opened and in the doorway is a woman. I recognize her face from the photograph her husband gave us: Susan Grey.

"Who the hell is she?" I ask loudly.

Fox's eyes narrow and the charm is gone from his face. He looks long and hard at me and I get the sinking feeling that he's guessed why I spoke so loudly.

"Why do you care?" He says it quietly.

I scramble for a reply. "I don't like anything unexpected," I say, "like seeing a woman down here." I look back at her.

She looks confused. Luckily she doesn't have a clue who I am. "Sorry," she says. She looks at Fox and he flicks his head at her. She says, "Sorry," again and turns to go back in the room. The room she is going into is directly opposite the door to the outside.

"Wait!" I say. "Look it's me who should be sorry. I kind of overreacted. It's OK if she goes upstairs."

Susan says, "I wasn't going ups—"

"Just wait in the office," Fox interrupts. "I'll talk to you when I've finished with this gentleman."

She nods and does as he asks, closing the door behind her.

Now what the fuck do I do?

15

CAL

Sergeant Steve Waters, my erstwhile partner in the VPD turns around in the front seat of the Dodge. "You were right, she's not only in the house but she's in the basement with Fox and Nick."

I say, "You can't send in the Emergency Response Team if she's there. If Fox and his guys are armed, she might get caught in the crossfire."

Steve turns a questioning face to the man sitting next to me on the back seat. Inspector Wardell's a good cop. He was a sergeant when I was still in the VPD. Before he can comment, Nick's voice comes out of the receiver on the car's dashboard. "Sorry about that. As I say, I overreacted. Let's get back to business. Is the grenade launcher also made by FN?"

Fox replies, "Yes, of course."

"Show me how it attaches?" Stammo's playing for time.

A series of metallic noises come out of the receiver.

Wardell says, "Maybe Stammo can seem to complete the transaction and get them all to go back upstairs. Then we can take them on the main floor."

"Except that Fox offered Stammo the choice of any of the girls," says Steve. "That means there are potentially more people who could become collateral damage."

"Why don't we let Stammo make the call."

Steve and I both nod.

16

NICK

And you can provide me with four hundred of these?" I say. He nods. "OK, let's go back upstairs and discuss the details of price and delivery." He looks at me through slitted eyes. He's trying to intimidate me. He just looks on in silence. He's succeeding. "What?" I say.

"Who's your client?"

"That's one of the details we can discuss upstairs."

"If you ever want to go upstairs again, you tell me who your client is."

Fortunately, I'm prepared for this. "My client is Iranian. The goods are to be shipped to Lebanon for Hamas."

"Really?" he says with a big grin on his face. It's one of those grins that never reaches the eyes. "I'm afraid you're out of your league here Mr. Stammo. You see..." he pauses for long enough to take a Smith and Wesson from a holster in the small of his back. "I just happen to know who arranges armaments for Hamas and it's not a washed-up ex-cop in Vancouver."

Anton's partner follows suit and draws his weapon.

Time to pull the pin.

"Excellent," I say.

17

CAL

I t's the signal. Inspector Wardell says, "Go! Go! Go!" As I get out of the car, the doors of the Transit Vans fly open and the members of the ERT spill out. They break into two groups; one heads up the street to enter via the front door but I follow the second team down the alley that runs behind the house. I ignore Steve's shout for me to stop.

The lead member kicks down the flimsy back fence to the garden and his team follow him to the back door. Two large members swing the red ram at the door, just above the lock. Once. Twice. A split second before the ram hits for the third time, I hear the sound of a gun. The ram connects, sending the door crashing inwards. The guys with the ram step back as their armed comrades run inside shouting "Armed Police!" There is an exchange of gunfire lasting no more than two seconds.

And then silence.

I run towards the door only to get stopped by one of the guys who wielded the ram. He's big and he's solid and there's no way I'm going to get around him. He holds me by the arm. "Just wait a minute sir," he says. "You can go in as soon as they've cleared the place."

I hear a voice shout. "Down on the ground, I said on the ground!"

Then another voice, quieter but even more urgent. "I need paramedics now!"

I struggle to break free. It's no contest. "Please," I plead. It's no use.

Long seconds pass.

Finally a voice yells, "Clear!" and my arms are free.

I dash for the door and go inside.

18

JEN

What a *weird* dream. Aaaaah. Sooooo tired. Time to roll over and go back to sleep. Except I can't. My wrist is stuck. Must still be dreaming. Except I'm not. Where the—? I force open my eyes. Blackness. Must be a dream. I toss my head to wake myself up. As I move, I can feel the roughness of cloth on my face. I try and move my arms and hear a familiar clanking sound. Handcuffs against metal. Each hand is cuffed to something metal. An image of a hospital bed with rails springs into my consciousness.

How?

Think!

OK.

I'm in Vancouver. Good.

What's the last thing I remember? I was about to check out of my hotel. Good. Right. That's when I saw the big guy. The one in the composite sketch. He waved and came over to me. I was a bit freaked out until he showed me his ID with Royal Canadian Mounted Police scrolled under the crest. What was his name?... Harvey. Was it his first name or his last? Why can't I remember? He knew my name though, I remember that. I asked him how he knew who I was and he said that my boss had told him I was in Vancouver and that he needed to speak to me on a secure line. But how did my boss know I was in Vancouver?

I remember checking out and leaving the hotel. Then getting into his car...

Why can't I remember what happened next?

Did we get into an accident?

Am I in hospital maybe?

But why am I handcuffed to the bed?

"Hello?"

Silence.

Not a hospital. Hospitals are never completely silent.

"HELLO!"

Nothing.

OK Jen, you're trained to observe. Is there any sound? I hold my breath for five seconds. Maybe that's the buzz of traffic on the threshold of hearing. Maybe.

My hands are lying on cloth. It's rough. Not quite sacking, but if it's a blanket, it's an old one. I move them. I can feel the other end of the handcuffs with my fingers. They're shackled around something metal. It's not a rail. It's circular and feels rough. The surface is peeling slightly. Rust maybe?

I move my legs. They don't seem to be constrained. I bring my knees up, no problem.

Scritch!

It's faint but distinct: a key in a lock.

The squeak of a hinge that needs oiling.

A closing door.

Silence.

I can feel my heart rate climbing.

More silence.

Then shoes on wooden stairs. They're above me, coming down. I'm in a basement.

Another door opens. This one just feet away.

It closes.

Someone is in the room with me. I know the science. We can tell someone is close to us, not by intuition or sixth sense or psychic power, but by tiny sounds and movements of the air of which we may not be consciously aware.

I know for sure there is someone in the room and he or she is probably standing looking at me.

My heart is playing a tattoo now. The intruder must be able to hear it.

I try to control the urge to speak; to ask who's there. Just to discover if they're only the product of an overheated imagination.

"Good. You're awake."

I know the voice.

"We can get started now."

19

CAL

Relief. Susan is standing in the doorway of a room. She's not hurt. Thank God. I was sure something had happened to her. Then I see the look on her face. It's pure Edvard Munch. As I step towards her, I follow her gaze to the object of her silent scream. One of the ERT members is crouched over a body, his gloved hands pressed on the stomach. Blood is seeping out onto the floor. He yells again, "I need paramedics, right now!"

The body is Stammo's.

I rush and kneel beside him. He's conscious. "Hang in there Nick," is all I can think to say. He reaches up and I grab his hand. "You're gonna be OK Nick."

"Listen, Cal." It's hardly more than a whisper. The effort seems to drain him. He closes his eyes.

"I'm here Nick. Hang in there buddy."

His eyes flicker open. "Tell my daughter, I love her and that..." he fades for a moment and then revives. "Tell her I'm sorry I was never there for her."

I feel a deep pain in my gut. "Just relax. You're going to tell her yourself. You'll see." His eyes close again. "We'll be laughing about this tomorrow." I can hear the desperation in my voice.

He shakes his head and with a struggle, he again opens his eyes.

"And Cal," he takes a couple of quick breaths. "I for..." Another breath, deeper this time, then another. "I forgive you for Matt. OK?"

The pain ramps up and tears run down my face.

His eyes close and his lips are moving but no sound is coming through.

I squeeze his hand, unable to speak.

"Step aside please sir."

It's a paramedic. He's in a bulletproof vest, trained to work with ERT. Nick is in the very best of hands. I get unsteadily to my feet. As I look down, he and his partner start working on Nick. Susan comes and stands beside me. "Your partner?" she asks.

"Yeah," I manage to grunt.

"He's going to be OK, Cal." She puts her arm around me and I collapse into her. We hold each other tight.

I watch as the paramedics work. Nick's eyes are closed now. But I can see he's still breathing, his chest is rising and falling quickly.

In record time they have him patched up, in the stretcher and out the door.

"I'm sure he's going to be OK," she repeats.

Deep down, I know she's wrong.

Because, through the tears, all I can think is, *he never calls me Cal.*

I hear a cough behind me.

It's Inspector Wardell, Steve beside him.

He looks at me. "Nick's a tough old bird, he'll get through this."

It's difficult to look stoic when your face is covered in your own tears. I try, nonetheless.

"Pursuant to your agreement with Nick," I say, hoping that the legal wording will carry some extra weight, "this lady is going to leave now and remain anonymous forever."

Wardell nods. "Thank you for your help," he says to Susan.

I take her elbow and lead her out, through the back garden, to the lane. There is a young uniformed officer standing guard, he is about to say something when he sees Steve beside me.

"Jag," Steve addresses him, "would you mind walking this lady to her car?"

"Yessir," he says.

"Wait," I say. Susan turns to me. "You have to tell him."

She nods. "As soon as I get home. Thank you, Cal, we owe you and your partner everything."

I stand looking after her as she walks down the alley with the officer, treasuring the feeling of her arms around me and just a little bit jealous of the man she's going home to.

"Thanks Cal," Steve says. "This was a big bust. Thanks to you and Nick, we've closed down a big fish in the illegal arms trade and if all his records are here, we may net a few others."

I nod, too full of emotions to speak.

"They've taken Nick to St. Paul's. Why don't you go over there, I'll join you later when we've sorted out this mess."

"Just one thing," I say.

I walk back into the house. For the first time I survey the scene. There are three bodies on the floor. Two are dead and the other is face down and in handcuffs. I walk over to the body wearing the good suit and lying on its side. I look down at him. He's good looking, even in death. I take half a step back, then step into it and with all the rage bursting out of me, I kick him in the face. It hurts like hell. I do it again. I feel something break. But I do it again.

Steve's arms grab my shoulders and pull me away. "Come on Cal," he says gently, "we don't want to make the autopsy too difficult for Dr. Marcus, do we?"

Everything drains out of me.

Without a word, I turn and limp out of there.

St. Paul's is less than a three minute drive from where I'm parked.

Is this the second time I'm going to go there and watch the death of someone I love?

20

JEN

His voice is casual, like we're sitting having coffee. "Let's try this the easy way." I feel his hands beside my head. They are gentle and warm. He removes the blindfold and the world comes flooding in through my eyes. I'm in an unfinished basement, looking up at the rafters above my head. The walls are covered in bare plywood and there seem to be no windows. Looking down, I can see I'm lying on a bed of some sort, with a dirty, old grey blanket over it. I cringe at the thought of the pillow which my head must be resting on. My wrists are handcuffed to rusty iron rings which seem to be attached to the bed frame with multiple cable ties.

I crane my neck to the right to see my jailer. It's Harvey.

"So you're not really a Mountie are you?" I ask. He shrugs. "Impersonating a police officer, unlawful confinement: you're starting to build a list of indictable offences."

He moves closer to the side of the bed. He's not quite close enough for me to use my feet against him, but he's getting there. He may regret omitting to tie down my legs.

He looks down at me. "Before I can let you go, I need some information from you."

"Cut the crap Harvey, or whatever your name is. The moment I saw your face the letting-me-go option was off the table."

He purses his lips and nods his head like a professor considering a student's idea. "True, true. But on a different subject did you know that under torture people always speak. They may hang on for one or two days but they always end up speaking."

"Yes I did know that. But did *you* know that seventy percent of the information elicited from the victims of torture turns out to be false?"

"Correct. So we seem to be at an impasse. I could torture you but there's no guarantee that the information you give me would be true." The bastard's playing cat and mouse with me. "Except for one thing: I actually like inflicting pain. I can torture you until you tell me something. I check it out. If it's false, I come back here and torture you some more. If it's true, I come back and give you the *coûp de grace*."

The sheer matter-of-fact tone to his words sets a worm of fear wriggling in my gut.

"Or maybe we could take a different approach. We could just be friends." His gaze leaves my eyes and wanders slowly down my body. He reaches down, pulls open my jacket and runs a finger in a circle around my left breast. "Friends with benefits."

Even as I cringe at his touch, I know he's shown his first weakness.

"What do you want to know?" I ask.

He looks into my eyes. "Why are you in Vancouver?"

I hold his gaze. "I'll answer your questions if you answer mine in return."

He laughs. "You're not exactly in a position where you can bargain from."

"Perhaps, but if you answer my questions, I'll answer yours truthfully. It'll save a lot of time and unpleasantness."

He chews this over for a second. "Sure, why not?" he says. "I'll go first. Why are you in Vancouver?"

"I was looking for Denis Lamarche." Before he can react, I say, "My turn. I think you lied when you said my boss knows I'm here. How did you know I was here and where to find me?"

"That's two questions," he says slyly. "I'll answer the first one. The RCMP has jurisdiction over the investigation of terrorist attacks. Since the bombing in Ottawa, we've been getting the passenger lists of all flights out. Your name was on one."

So he is RCMP. "Why would you care?" I ask.

"Sorry, my turn." He's enjoying this game. Good. His enjoyment might take the edge off his interrogation skills. "Why were you looking for Denis Lamarche?"

"I knew his sister, Annie. She talked about him. I wanted to tell him about her death."

The back of his hand slashes across my face before I see it coming. My cheek is on fire and there is a ringing in my left ear. My left eye is watering where his knuckle caught it. Without a word, he walks away from the bed. One wall is entirely covered by a pegboard with tools hanging from hooks. The wriggling worm becomes a cold tentacle deep in my bowel as he grabs a pair of pruning shears from among the gardening tools and marches back.

"Listen, bitch," he spits out. "I know a *lot* more about you than you think. So don't try and lie to me again." He holds the pruning shears in front of my face. "You know how in crappy detective books the bad guy threatens to cut off someone's finger?" He snaps them shut just millimetres from my nose. "Well if you lie to me again I'm going to cut off your nose and both of your nipples. Understand?"

I nod.

"Good. Let's start over. Why were you looking for Denis Lamarche?"

Through the fear, I'm wondering what he knows about me and why he cares that I'm here. "I wasn't," I say, knowing that he can hear the quaver in my voice. "I came here because someone tried to contact a colleague of mine."

"Who tried to contact Sally Hyde?" he asks.

My mind goes into overdrive. How did he know it was Sally? I play for time. "My turn to ask a question," I say.

"Fuck you." His urbane cover has gone. "You lost that deal when you tried to lie to me. Who tried to contact her?"

"A private detective named Nick Stammo."

"And why did he want to contact her?"

"He was trying to contact the next-of-kin of Annalise Lamarche, to tell them that her brother, Denis, was dead. He and his partner are investigating the murder."

He goes silent. I can almost hear the gears turning in his head.

Without a word he turns and goes through the door at the bottom of the stairs. I hear him go up and close the door at the top. Then silence.

What the hell is going on? And who is this guy? I'm pretty sure he's an RCMP member and I believe what he said about spotting my name on a passenger list. He's a good interrogator for sure; he spotted my lie immediately. But the RCMP don't kidnap people and threaten to torture or kill them. Why would my name be of interest and why would he care that I took a flight to Vancouver? And he knew it was Sally I was following up on, so he must be plugged into the bombing investigation in some way. But what seemed to be a big surprise to him was that Nick and Cal are investigating Denis' death.

Denis' death! Now I remember what happened to me. After he told me that cockamamie story about my boss wanting to talk to me on a secure line, we walked to his car and when we got in, I was just about to ask him about why he met Denis Lamarche in that pub when he stabbed my thigh with what looked like a hypodermic.

But why?

So many questions.

And I just thought of one more.

How the hell do I get out of this basement?

21

CAL

It seems like we've been sitting here for hours. For what must be the hundredth time I've checked my watch. Adry is sitting beside me; sensing my agitation, she pats me on the arm. "Nick's tough. He's going to be OK Cal," she says. I smile at her and nod.

A man in a white coat enters. I recognize him but can't remember his name. He was Roy's doctor four years ago. He goes to the nurses' station and the nurse points us out.

He extends his hand to Adry. "Hi, I'm Barry Duffus, are you Mr. Stammo's daughter." His British accent is somehow comforting.

She takes his hand and says, "Yes doctor." I'm too shocked to say anything.

"I'm sorry to have to tell you that your father has received a very bad wound. He's in the operating theatre right now and we have an excellent team working on him. I'll be honest with you, his chances of pulling through are only about thirty percent, but if anyone can save him it's the doctor who's leading the team."

"Thank you doctor," she says. "When will we know?"

"Not for some hours yet. I suggest you leave your phone number at the nurses' station and we'll contact you with any news."

"Ok, thanks," she says.

"Oh, by the way," he adds, "your father was in and out of consciousness but he said to tell you he loves you."

Adry looks uncomfortable as she thanks him again.

We sit back down. "I told him I was Nick's daughter because they won't give too much information out to non-family members. Now I feel bad about it." It's my turn to pat *her* arm encouragingly. "Anyway," she adds, "I called his daughter in Ontario, she and his ex-wife are on their way out here."

We sit in silence for a while. I try not to think of what life would be like without Nick. I remember Tina saying that I should tell him how I feel about him and now it may be too late. Tina! I look at my watch again. "Oh my God," I say, "I just remembered I have a date tonight." I feel a wave of guilt that I haven't even thought of Tina today.

I pull out my phone, get up and walk out into the corridor.

She answers on the second ring. *"Hi Cal, I'm so glad you called."* Her voice soothes away some of the worry I'm feeling. *"I had a deadline on a story so I got a bit behind and I'm running about half an hour late."*

I feel a flush of emotions that I haven't felt in a while. For a second, I think about taking Dr. Duffus' advice to leave until they call, and take Tina out for dinner somewhere close by. Instead, I tell her about Stammo. She listens without comment until I've finished, then just says, *"Stay there, I'm on my way over."* Before I can respond, she hangs up.

I go back and sit down next to Adry. "I guess I'm about to have my first date in a hospital."

She smiles. "They do say the food in the coffee shop is divine." Then her face becomes serious. "Cal, I've been thinking about Jen."

In the excitement of the last couple of hours, I had almost forgotten our other case. "Yes. I can't believe we were fooled by her," I say. "But I think I know why. If she's in league with the guy who killed Denis, she was probably trying to put us off track somehow, maybe get us to drop the case."

"Yes, maybe." She sounds unsure. "It's just that I really believed her. I somehow can't accept that she's not who she says she is. What if the big guy somehow fooled her or maybe forced her to go with him."

"I wish I had a hundred bucks for each time I've really believed someone and then been wrong about them. In this business everyone is suspect. Facts are facts. Dougie said she was laughing when—"

Of course!

I get up. "Come on," I say. I stride over to the nurses' station.

The nurse smiles up at me. I ask her, "The paramedics brought in a homeless man early afternoon today. His name's Dougie Blake. Is he still here?"

She checks her computer. "Yes, he's being kept in overnight for observation. He's in neurology on the fifth floor of the Providence building. Just go into the corridor and follow the blue line on the floor to the elevators."

Within minutes we are standing at the foot of Dougie's bed.

"Hello Rocky," he says, "what are you doing here?"

"I got to the park, just after you had your fall. I thought I'd come in and see how you were doing."

"My own stupid fault," he says, "I was being a complete asshole. I'd had a drink or two and was hassling this Arab lady; I don't know why, the booze just brings out the anger in me. I let go of my cart and it ran off the steps. Like a fool, I tried to hold on to it with my other hand but it pulled me down. Now I'm in here and I've lost all my stuff."

"Well, I've got some good news Dougie. I picked up your stuff, put it in your shopping cart and it's safe in our office."

His face lights up. "Thanks Rocky. You turned out all right. Old Roy would've been proud of you. You've made my day."

"Dougie, you remember that big guy in the picture. You saw him get into the car with a tall woman with short dark hair."

"Yeah absolutely. A knock on the head isn't going to affect *my* memory. I remember her perfectly. She was pulling one of those little suitcases on wheels."

"You said you got the plate number."

"Yeah," he says with a rueful chuckle. "If I hadn't've asked you for extra money, I wouldn't've been in the park waiting for you and I wouldn't've had that fall." He chuckles again. "It was *The insatiate greediness of my desires.*"

"Shakespeare Dougie?" I laugh, amazed.

"Yeah. Richard the Third." He laughs back. "I used to be an actor. I was the Duke of Buckingham when Bard on the Beach did it. It was quite a few years back now. *Good time of day unto your royal grace!* That was my first line."

Every day I see homeless people on the streets—and I was one of them a few years back—but I can still forget that so many of them had normal, productive, often successful lives before they were unlucky enough to take that first hit, or to have been unlucky enough to have a genetic pre-disposition to alcoholism or schizophrenia.

He gives a sigh. "That's all in the past now but it's nice to remember it now and then." He sits a little more upright in the bed. "Anyway Rocky that licence plate you wanted, I wouldn't normally have remembered but it was RAJ 1961."

"You're sure Dougie?" I ask.

"Yeah. I remembered it because R A J stands for Romeo and Juliet and nineteen sixty-one was the last upside-down year." He looks at me and then at Adry and smiles at our puzzled looks. "One, nine, six, one: if you turn it upside down it still reads nineteen sixty-one. There's not another upside-down year until six thousand and nine." He breaks into laughter. "I'm looking forward to it."

Adry and I both laugh with him. It feels wonderful. Then I remember Nick down there in the operating room fighting for his life.

"Thanks Dougie, you're a marvel but we've got to go. And remember, you're still going to get that bonus." I hand him my card. "When you get out of here, come by my office. You can pick up your cart and we'll give you the money then."

"Thanks, Rocky. You always were one of the good ones." He looks at Adry, "'Bye Miss, I was very pleased to meet you."

She takes his hand, leans forward and kisses him on the cheek.

"'Bye Dougie. See you soon."

He's grinning like a Jack-o-Lantern now.

"You definitely will; you've made my day," he says.

We can still hear him chuckling when we are halfway down the corridor.

THERE ARE TWO NEW PEOPLE IN THE WAITING ROOM AND I AM delighted to see them both, for quite different reasons. As soon as she sees us, Tina gets up, comes over and gives me a big hug. I hold on for as long as I can without making it feel weird. Which turns out to be quite a long time. It feels good. She takes my hand and looks up at me. "How is he?" she asks.

"I'll go find out," says Adry. She extends her hand. "I'm Adry, by the way." They shake. "They think I'm Nick's daughter," she adds in a whisper, before heading for the nurses' station.

We walk over to where Steve is sitting. Tina is still holding my hand. When the introductions are over, Adry gets back. "Still in surgery, no news," she says.

We lapse into an awkward silence.

I wonder how we're going to manage Stammo Rogan Investigations if there's no Stammo.

Steve speaks first. "I've got some good news. In David Fox's office, there were no paper records, but in a desk drawer there was a sticky note with a user ID and password. We logged onto Fox's system and there was all sorts of stuff. We and the RCMP are going to be arresting people for months to come."

"What was the user ID?" I ask.

"Sooze1977. Why?"

"You can thank our informant for leaving that there for you."

"Thank her for me," he says.

"There's one way *you* can thank her," I say.

"Anything," he says.

"Tell me who owns a grey sedan with registration RAJ 1961."

He looks at me askance. "How will that help her?"

"Come on Steve, cut me some slack here."

He gives me a long look, followed by a half smile, a shake of the head and a deep breath. Then he takes out his phone, does a few taps and asks, "What was that number again?"

I give it to him.

After several long seconds he looks up at me and says, "What's going on here Cal?" There is no smile on his face any longer.

"I'm looking into the murder of a homeless man, I think he might be implicated."

"Are you out of your mind? I know this guy. He's RCMP."

My thoughts go spinning out of control. Ghost and Tommy must have got it all wrong. The big guy wasn't there to kill Wily, aka Denis Lamarche, he was probably there to inform him of his sister's death in the bombing that day. Maybe he and Jen were colleagues. Maybe he was giving her a lift to the airport. Except she said that after she had checked out, she was going to come back to our offices and say goodbye. Then again maybe she was able to book an earlier flight and had to rush off. There are too many maybes but there's one thing I know for sure... and it doesn't fit. "Are you sure?" is all I can think to say.

"Yes I'm sure," he says.

"I'd really like to talk to him. He was the last person to see our victim alive. Can you give us his name and contact information?"

"His name's Harvey Clegg." Steve taps his phone a few times and turns it towards me. I enter the guy's details into my contacts.

"Thanks, Steve."

Before he can reply, my stomach sinks. I see Dr. Duffus walking towards us. His face is set in a way I have seen before. Not a good omen.

He is not the bearer of good news.

22

JEN

At the very edges of my awareness, I can hear a murmur of conversation. No, not conversation. The murmur is too consistent. One voice. Then again maybe it's an hallucination. My arms hurt now. For at least an hour I have been holding the rusty iron rings, to which I am handcuffed, and scraping them against the plastic ties that bind them to the bed frame. The right-hand one is making the most progress. One of the ties has worn through and the others are looking frailer than they were but my muscles are screaming at me, telling me I can't keep it up for much longer.

I stop for a fifteen second break. I hear the murmur more clearly. Then it stops. I continue my efforts for what seems like an age and I feel another tie breaking on the right. Only two more on that side. I work harder on the right-hand side. If I can break my right arm free it will be easier to work on the left.

Stop!

The door at the top of the stairs is opening. Footsteps

down. I look to my left and see the door open. He looks at me and steps into the basement. His demeanour has changed. There is no sign of the taunting humour he originally exhibited.

He picks up the pruning shears. "What exactly, do they know?" he asks.

"Who?"

"Stammo and Rogan."

They say the truth will set you free. I'm guessing not in this case but he is too good for me to risk lying. The thought of those pruning shears disfiguring me is too raw. "Rogan used to be a junkie, living on the streets. One of the street people he knew asked him to look into Denis Lamarche's murder."

"They know his sister died in the bombing?"

"Yes."

"And they know about Sally Hyde?"

"They know she was my friend and that she died in the bombing with Annalise."

"Nothing else?"

What else is there? Maybe there's something I don't know. Or something I *do* know that I don't know the importance of. I look puzzled and shake my head.

"Did they say anything about finding some files?"

"Files? No." I say it fast enough to mask the lie. I think. I hope.

He thinks for a moment. Has he spotted the lie? In my mind I can feel the pruning shears slicing through my flesh. "What do they know about the murder?" he asks. The relief floods in but I try not to show it. No more lies from now on.

Feeling a deep sense of betrayal, I say. "They think you killed Lamarche."

His eyes go wide for a moment then I think he realizes it might be a tell. He relaxes his face. "Why do they think I killed him?"

I tell him about the composite sketch.

"Do they know who I am?"

"No. Just what you look like."

He looks hard at me.

And smiles. "Good. Now I'm going to do you a small favour." The false urbane manner is back. "My orders are to kill you now." He watches the fear which I can't keep from flooding my face. "However, I'm going to break... no... bend would be a better word; I'm going to bend those orders so we can have a little fun first."

He reaches down and grabs my breast in his meaty hand.

"Mmmm," I say. I bend my right knee and place my foot flat on the bed and with every ounce of my strength, I push down with my right leg, arch my back and pull up on the iron ring. The ties part and I smash my hand and the ring towards his head.

He lets go of my breast and his hand darts up to block the blow. He's not fast enough and my hand arrives at the side of his face and drives the ring onto his skull. He staggers back and slams into the door. He's still conscious but dazed. I swing my legs off the bed and push myself upright. I look down at my left wrist. One of the plastic ties has parted. I pull and twist them. Once, twice, three times. Another tie parts and my world explodes in bright white light.

Then darkness.

———

THROBBING IN MY HEAD. IT'S ALL THERE IS. IT'S DARK. JUST the throbbing. I reach up. My hands won't move. And it all comes rushing back in. As consciousness returns the pain ramps up. I take a deep breath but it all comes in through my nose. I try and move my lips. I can't. I can't open my mouth. My legs won't move either.

I breath in again and the smell is familiar. Adhesive. It's the smell of duct tape. I am completely immobilized.

Harvey's not taking any chances this time. Damn it. I moved too soon. If I'd just waited...

Listen.

Nothing but the sound of rain.

Then a sound.

Shoes walking on hardwood floors.

I wait for the sound of the door to the stairway opening.

It doesn't come.

Silence.

Rain.

A door closes.

More silence.

More rain.

A car starts and the sound of a garage door opening is very clear. A pause and then it closes.

Silence.

Rain.

This is my last chance right here. I have to work out how to free myself. My hands are duct taped to my thighs. If I can just free them enough. I wriggle them side to side. They move a little and I realize that my thighs are bare. I move my legs, the tape pulls at my skin. When I squirm my arms about they rub my sides, skin on skin. The bastard stripped me naked. I feel the rush of embarrassment and the violation of being undressed while unconscious.

Oh no! Oh God! Did he also...?

I don't think so. It doesn't feel like it. I can't tell.

Maybe he took off my clothes to make the duct tape more effective.

I have to get free before he comes back.

I try and roll my hands. They move part way but the tape is really tight. I roll them back and forth. Is the tape easing or is it just my imagination? I increase the speed. Nothing. I squirm my body but it's too painful. I want to scream in rage but—

Ding dong dong dong.

The opening notes of Beethoven's Fifth Symphony.

It's the doorbell.

"Mmmmngh." My scream for help is futile. I try it again. "Mmmmmmmmnnnnngh." It's not loud enough to wake a napping mouse.

There *has* to be a way I can attract the attention of the caller.

I try and buck up and down in the bed but the tape is too tight. Maybe I can topple the bed over. I shake my body from side to side, ignoring the pain of the tape tearing at my skin. Still no effect.

Ding dong dong dong.

"Mmmmmmmmnnnnngh." I try again. Maybe if I could bite through the tape. I try to force my mouth open. I can force my teeth apart but my lips are firmly taped. I try to force them apart with my tongue but I don't have enough time.

I listen.

Silence.

Rain.

Time passes.

The caller has left.
Silence.
Rain.
Even my sobs can't be heard.

23

CAL

We all turn towards Dr. Duffus. I feel Tina's grip on my hand tighten. A stab of pain courses through. Heroin would take that away and maybe help me through the next moments. He addresses Adry. "Your father is out of surgery now but I'm afraid the prognosis is not good. He lost so much blood that he had a stroke and we are not yet sure how severely it will affect him. In addition the bullet went through his liver and it must have ricocheted off a rib, because it nicked his transverse colon. We don't know if he'll make it through the night."

"Can we see him?" Adry asks.

"I'm afraid not. He's in the ICU and we can't take any risk of infection. We'll come and tell you if there's any change in his condition." He pats her gently on the arm and leaves.

We just stand in stunned silence for about a minute.

Steve is the first to speak. "I'm going to have to go. Call me if there's anything I can do, anything at all. And Cal, let me know when there's any news." He nods to Adry and Tina and leaves.

"Why don't you guys take a break," Adry says. "I'll stay here and wait for news and I'll call you immediately if they tell me anything, I promise. And Cal, you should try and get some sleep, it's been a long day."

She's right. It seems like an age since this morning when I was sitting in the Ovaltine with Jen asking Ghost and Tommy how Wily got his mail. I yawn and nod. Sleep would be great right now. But there's one more thing I have to do. And I need to go to the office first.

———

"YOU CERTAINLY KNOW HOW TO SHOW A GIRL A GOOD TIME Cal." We are sitting in the Healey, eating McDonald's take-out and watching the small house on east Eighteenth Avenue, just off Main, owned by RCMP Corporal Harvey Clegg. It's dropping a cold December rain and the occasional drip finds its way between the soft-top and the windshield and drops on the console between us.

"I'm usually a better date than this," I grin.

"I don't know. This is the second one sitting in your car on a stakeout." She takes the last, noisy slurp of her chocolate milkshake. "But I do admit it's kind of fun."

I take all the leftover containers, stuff them back in the paper bag they came in and put them on the back seat. I peer through the rain at the house. No change. One light is on, on the main floor.

"How have you been feeling?" Her voice is more serious now, and concerned.

"It's strange. The withdrawal pains have just disappeared. I thought it was all because of all the adrenaline that's been pulsing through me for the last, what?..." I check my watch, "five hours but, except for a twinge at the hospital, right now I'm pain free."

We lapse into a warm silence in a cold car. I check the house and, yet again, there's no change.

I hear Tina move in her seat beside me and, as I turn, she puts her hand behind my neck and places a feather-light kiss on my lips. It sets my spine tingling. The next three kisses are each a little firmer and I respond... the fifth one is passionate and I lose myself in it.

When we finally break apart she sits back in her seat and smiles. "Thank God for that," she says. "I would have been so disappointed if you hadn't been a great kisser."

I start to laugh and find I can't stop. The pent-up emotions of the day flood out of me in laughter. Tina looks at me and realizes what is happening and leans over again, this time to hold me in her arms. I feel as if the laughter is starting to turn into tears. I'm not ready for that. I open my eyes and blink... and see a grey BMW sedan, RAJ 1961, pulling out of the driveway beside the house. The hysterical laughter snaps off.

The car turns away from us and, in the rain, I can't tell if Harvey Clegg is driving and whether or not Jen is with him.

"He's on the move," I say.

Tina slides back into her seat. "Are we going to follow him?" she asks. "I've always wanted to do that."

"Sorry to disappoint you. No."

"You haven't disappointed me yet." A quick grin. "What *are* we going to do?"

"*We*, nothing. Not yet anyway. *I'm* going to go into his house and see what I can find. It may be that he's a regular up-and-up RCMP member but my gut tells me he's not. My gut says that he's got something to do with the murder of a homeless man."

"How are you going to get in?"

I pull out the items that I stopped off at the office to get: my trusty lock picks, taken from a burglar when I was still in uniform. I remember the last time I used them: on the garage door of a townhouse in Kitsilano where an accountant had been brutally murdered. Not a good omen. The second one this evening.

I lean over and kiss her on the cheek. "Can you drive a stick shift?" I ask. She shakes her head. "OK, if that BMW comes back, call me."

I pull a rain jacket from the back seat behind me and climb out of the Healey. I run across the road and up onto the porch of Clegg's house. Before I even think about using the picks, I do the obvious first step.

I press the doorbell.

It teleports me back to ringing the bell at my late best friend's townhouse. Dah, dah, dah, daaaah. The Eighteen-Twelve Overture. A third bad omen.

I listen for movement inside. I can hear nothing but the rain on the porch.

I wait a moment.

I press it again.

I get to fifteen Mississippis before pulling out my picks.

I'm inside in fifteen seconds and there's no alarm. You'd think he'd have better security being a cop.

I find the light switch and turn it on.

The front door leads straight into the living room. It's obsessively tidy. Nothing is out of place. To the left is a staircase leading up, and to the right is a round dining table with four chairs all pushed in. Beyond the dining table is a counter and the kitchen which runs the width of the house. There is what looks like an IKEA storage unit on the right-hand wall. A quick check reveals nothing but children's

games, tablecloths and napkins and books. Everything carefully placed in neat rows. Even the books look like they were
selected by an interior designer to look 'just so'.

No desk, no computer, nothing.

I slip off my shoes. Not because it's the Canadian thing
to do but just to be quiet. Just to be safe, I switch off my
phone's ring. The wall against which the staircase is situated
is shared by the house next door. And just maybe I'm not
alone in the house.

I head silently upstairs to a landing with three doors
leading off it. All closed. I gently turn the handle and open
the first door as silently as possible. A bedroom, also
immaculate, bed made, pillows plumped, everything in
place. It looks like no one has ever slept here. I open the
closets. Five suits, three pairs of pants, seven shirts all neatly
arranged on hangers. Sock drawer, underwear drawer.
Nothing on the shelf above.

I slide back the closet doors, making sure they are fully
closed and return to the landing.

Door two is the bathroom. Everything immaculate. One
bath towel, one hand towel, the cupboard above the sink
with just the bare necessities: one bar of soap, unused, a
toothbrush, a toothpaste tube full, with no dents in it.

Back to the landing. A phrase from my childhood pops
into my mind, from where I don't remember. *What's behind
door number three, Monty?* I reach for the handle and the
answer is... nothing. Literally nothing, except the blinds on
the window.

I pad back downstairs.

Just out of interest I walk through to the kitchen. Same
story: minimalist and anally arranged. The fridge is empty.

Nobody lives here.

So what was Harvey Clegg doing here tonight?

Picking up mail? Meeting someone?

He's RCMP. Maybe this is a safe house. Except it looks like it's never been used.

My suspicion that Harvey Clegg is not just an RCMP member has just quadrupled. Time to blow this pop stand. I head for the front door. Underneath the staircase I see another door, it obviously goes to the basement. Maybe I should check—

I jump. The vibration of my phone feels like an electric shock in the quiet of the moment.

It's Tina.

"Is he back?" I keep my voice a little above a whisper.

"No. I was just feeling a bit worried. Is everything OK?"

"Sure no prob. I'll be right out."

I slip my shoes back on and leave, closing the front door quietly behind me.

Move on. Nothing to see here.

24

CAL

Sunday

I am running, terrified and naked, along the seawall in Stanley Park. At least, I think it's the seawall. Except that the view is different, instead of English Bay and the North Shore mountains all I can see is a vast expanse of stark, brown land. I stop and step off the seawall and onto the soft earth. It smells of coffee. Not just any coffee. Good, freshly roasted coffee. I breath it in and slowly open my eyes... to an unfamiliar bedroom.

"Good morning, sleepy head." Tina's words pull me up from the tatters of the dream. She's standing beside the bed in a patterned, silk dressing gown. The memories of last night, equal parts of passion and tenderness, flood in and I smile. She hands me a coffee. "It's black, no sugar." She sits on the bed. "As I was making it, I wondered if it's OK to sleep with someone when you don't even know how they take their coffee. But I guess it's a bit late for that."

I feel the glow of a deep contentment. I pull myself upright and kiss her cheek before sipping the dark, hot brew. "Perfect," I sigh. As my mind clears, I remember it's Sunday. "What shall we do today?"

"Maybe we should check on your partner." She says it gently, with no judgement in her voice, but I feel guilt stabbing me as I think of Nick fighting for his life. *If thou survive my well-contented day* Shakespeare adds unbidden.

I grab my phone off the bedside table.

I just look at it, dreading to make the call.

Tina slides over and puts her arm around my shoulder.

I let out the breath, which I was unconsciously holding, in a long sigh and say, "Hey, Siri, call Adry."

It takes a while to connect and I almost hang up, wanting to delay the bad news as long as I can. But I don't. I have to know.

One ring.

Two rings.

Adry answers on the third ring. *"Hi Cal,"* she says, *"Good news. The doctor just told us that Nick's going to be OK."*

Thank God. Thank God. Thank God. I collapse into Tina's hug.

"Is he awake, yet?"

As she hears my words, Tina gives an extra little double hug for victory.

"Yes. His real daughter is with him right now. I'm sitting in the waiting room with Brenda, Mrs. Stammo." Nick's ex-wife. I wonder if she will be able to stay sober enough to see him. "They're only allowing one visitor at a time."

"Were you there all night?"

"Mostly. I went and picked up Brenda and Lucy from the airport." Lucy is Nick's daughter; I never knew his wife's name until now. "Their flight arrived at six this morning. I'm going to wait to see if I can see him for a moment and then I'm going home to sleep."

After I hang up, Tina says. "Drink up your coffee we've got a hospital to visit." She grins and kisses me. "And it's still raining hard so we can take my car. It doesn't leak through the roof."

———

As I see them I feel guilt. Twice over. Once for what I did to them six months ago and twice for allowing Nick to risk his life facing down David Fox yesterday. "Pleased to meet you, Mr. Rogan," Nick's daughter takes my proffered hand.

"How is he?" I ask.

"He's still a bit woozy from the anaesthetics, but he knew who I was. The doctors say we can have some more time with him later on."

I turn to Stammo's ex. "I'm really sorry about Nick," I say.

She shakes my hand. "Nick always was one for getting into scrapes." There is no sign of alcohol on her breath or in her demeanour. "He's a tough one. He's going to be just fine."

"Is there anything I can do for you?" I ask automatically.

"No, we're fine. But I do want to thank you for covering the flight out here, that was very kind." I look over at Adry and she smiles sheepishly. I give her a smile back and nod.

"My pleasure, it was the least we could do. You should thank Adry, she did the arranging."

Relieved that I'm OK with the agency paying for their flights, Adry says, "I spoke to Mrs. V., Nick's landlady. She said that Brenda and Lucy can stay there while Nick's in the hospital. It'll be a bit tight, but they're OK with it." Brenda and Lucy nod.

I raise my eyebrows. I've only been to Nick's place once and he has a small bedroom with a single bed.

Before I can say anything, Tina stretches up and whispers in my ear.

"Are you sure," I ask. She nods.

"I've got a two bedroom apartment," I say. "You're welcome to stay there. There's food in the fridge and the supermarket's a block away. You could stay there and I'll stay at Tina's. It will be a lot more comfortable than sleeping in Nick's single bed."

"Are you sure it wouldn't be a problem?" Brenda asks.

"No problem at all."

"Cal's car's a two seater," Tina adds, "we could drive you over there this evening, in my car, after you've visited with Nick some more."

Tears well up in Brenda's eyes. She hugs Tina and then me.

It feels good to do a favour.

———

It feels strange being driven. The last time I remember being driven by someone was years ago by Sam. It wasn't a happy experience. Being a passenger reminds me of being in a police car and I find myself scanning the parked vehicles and the sidewalks as we drive towards my apartment. I need to tidy up and change the sheets before Brenda and Lucy settle in.

It's kind of exciting, the thought of staying at Tina's place. It's waaaaaaay too soon in the relationship but I'm pretty sure it's going to work out just fine. We just had a great breakfast downtown and she told me about her career as a journalist and I told her all about the last major case we had. She said it was perfect for her planned book about unusual killings in Canada.

"Turn right just up ahead," I say. She pulls onto my street. "It's about halfway down the block on the right." We're in luck. There's a parking space right in fr— "Keep driving. Whatever you do, don't stop." She senses the urgency in my voice and turns towards me. I turn towards her so that the back of my head is towards the window. "Just keep driving and take another right at the end of the block."

"What is it, Cal?"

"Just do it." She continues along the block and turns right. "Sorry about that," I say. "If you can find a place to park I'll tell you what's going on."

About three-quarters of the way along she finds, and backs into, a parking space.

"What is it?" she asks and I can sense an eagerness in her voice.

I tell her what I saw and her eyes widen. Not in fear but in excitement. And it doesn't even change when I tell her what I want her to do next.

I give her the detailed instructions I just thought up.

———

I BREATHE A SIGH OF RELIEF AS I SEE HER COMING DOWN THE street. She gets into the car and says breathlessly, "Did it."

"How many were there?"

"Just the one. Just like you described."

"You're sure?"

"Absolutely. I checked the back seat as I walked past."

Good. Hopefully I'll find out why he's alone. "Did you get it?"

"Yes," she chuckles as she opens her purse. "Is it legal?"

"It's a grey area." I take the Glock from her, check the magazine and the safety and put it in the pocket of my rain jacket. "OK, here goes."

"Wait. Why don't I drive you around the block. That way he won't see you coming."

"Definitely not! I don't want him to see your car. He's trained. He would probably get the plate number and that could put you in serious danger."

She leans across the car and kisses me. "Good luck."

I grin and as I get out of her car; I say, "If I'm not back in thirty minutes, call Steve Waters at the number I gave you and tell him everything, then go home. Don't even think of going around the block to see what's happened."

The words bring a look of worry to her face. She just nods.

I close the door, pull my Vancouver Canadians baseball cap out of my pocket and onto my head. And set off down the street. I turn right at the end and when I get to the end of that block, rather than turn right immediately, I cross the road and start down the sidewalk on the other side of the street. If he's checking his mirrors I will be partly shielded by the cars and SUVs parked along the curb.

As I draw level with Harvey's grey BMW I have my two options clearly in mind. I do a quick check: there are no other pedestrians on the block. I take my Glock out of my pocket, walk briskly across the road and pull the rear-passenger, driver-side door handle. It opens. Option one. Thank you BMW for unlocking the doors when he put the car in park. I'm inside the car before he can turn around and see my gun pointing at his face. "Face forward and put your hands on the steering wheel." He does it. I push the gun barrel against his neck. "Reach down with your left hand and lock the car doors." He does it and then returns his hand to the steering wheel. "Now give me the key." He passes it back and again returns his hands to the wheel.

I lower the gun. No point in showing it to a passing pedestrian, out for a Sunday morning stroll. "My gun is pointed through the seat at the back of your spine."

"You're a PI and an ex-cop. I don't think you're going to pull that trigger."

He's right. I think. "I'm sure you checked me out and found that I'm suspected of killing a politician and a drug dealer, right?" He nods. "Well, I put you in the same category as them."

"What do you want?"

"Information."

"How do you know I'll give it to you?"

"Let's try. Where's your partner?"

In the rearview mirror, I see his eyes narrow in momentary puzzlement. Then understanding dawns. His eyes flicker to the right. "She's pursuing other lines of enquiry." It's a lie. So where is Jen? Is she pursuing *this* line of enquiry. Or maybe Adry's right. Maybe he tricked her, maybe she's not his partner. Except how did he know I even existed if Jen didn't tell him?

"Why did you kill Denis Lamarche?"

"Who?"

Then suddenly, I remember Annalise's letter that was hidden in Denis' bible. I know the answer.

"Was it because Denis knew his sister was having an affair with the Minister of National Defence?"

The shock on his face is palpable. He looks at the rearview mirror and sees my eyes drilling into his. My shot in the dark hit the bull's eye.

Before he can speak I ask, "Why are you staking out my apartment?"

He fights to recover his composure... and succeeds. "Really? You live in this dump?" His eyes hold mine and there is a mocking gleam in them.

I don't really care. I'm sure I now know the answer.

I think back to Friday morning when we found Annalise's letter to her brother. Jen scanned it first and then read it to us. If she were in league with Harvey, she would never have read that letter to us; she would have claimed some national security bullshit. And even if she had read it to us, she would have reported the fact to Harvey. But from his reaction, I'm sure he was monumentally surprised that I knew.

It leaves me with just one other question: what to do with Harvey? I can't release him into the wild, he's too dangerous for that. There's no point calling Steve; Harvey's an RCMP member and I have no proof of any sort that he's also a killer. My only option is to kidnap him but how the hell do I do that?

"Look over there Rogan." His voice pulls me out of my thoughts. He's looking out the side window. On the other side of the street are a couple with two young children: the parents are holding hands, one kid's in a stroller being pushed by her mom and the other kid's perched happily on the other mom's shoulders. I hear the click of the car's locks. Before I can react, he has opened the door and got out. He strolls across the street and walks along beside them, throwing a grin back at me.

I concede defeat. No way I'm going to put that family at risk.

But maybe it's only a partial defeat.

I open my door, get out of the car and get in the driver's seat. I slip the key into the ignition and the Bavarian-made engine roars into life. I check the side mirror, no cars are coming, but I can just pick out the look of rage on Harvey's face as I accelerate down the street.

I tell my phone to call Tina.

She needs to be safely at home.

I know what I have to do and I don't want her anywhere near me when I do it.

———

I BACK THE CAR INTO THE DRIVEWAY, REMOVE THE KEY, GET out of the car and lock the doors. It's the polite thing to do. As I run to the front door I throw the key into the bushes. You can take politeness too far. This time I don't bother with the doorbell. My picks have me in the house in seconds. I don't have a lot of time. Harvey is probably on his way here. If he was lucky enough to find a cab he might be here in minutes.

I go to the one door I never opened on my previous visit here: the door down to the basement. I run down, taking two stairs at a time, and push the door at the bottom. Except it's locked. The stairwell is illuminated only by the light coming in through the doorway above but I can just see the key. I turn it and open the door. It's an unfinished basement. In the middle of the floor there's a bed. There's duct tape everywhere, on the bed, on the floor. It looks like someone was kept here. I step inside and my world explodes.

25

JEN

Cal!! Oh my God, what have I done? I drop the gardening spade and crouch down beside him. He's very still. I try to roll him onto his back. He groans. Oh, thank heaven. "CAL." I shake him and he groans again. "Cal wake up." His eyes flicker and open. He looks at me, confused, and closes his eyes. "Cal! Open your eyes." No response. I repeat it and after a few seconds he does; he looks at me again; then he looks down in puzzlement. Does he not recognize me? He looks back at my face and silently mouths my name. Then I get why he's confused. I feel the flush of embarrassment. That bastard Harvey took my clothes. I'm naked.

Cal closes his eyes. "Take... jacket," he croaks.

He keeps his eyes closed while I help him to sit up. Gratefully, I slip off his rain jacket, put it on and zip it up. He's a couple of inches taller than me so it pretty much covers everything.

"I'm OK now," I tell him. "Let's get you up." It's a struggle but I manage to get him to his feet.

He sways. "I... ahhh... gotta sit down." I help him to the bed and he slumps down. I keep him upright.

"No rush, let me look at you." The side of his head which came into contact with the spade is a mess of blood and hair. The blood is still trickling down his face and soaking into his shirt. It's bad but not life threatening. "I am so sorry, Cal," I say. "When you're feeling up to it, we'll take your car and I'll drive you to the hospital and get you checked out."

"Car," he mumbles. "Gotta go now." He tries to get up but I push him gently back down.

"Just wait until you're a bit more steady on your feet," I say soothingly. "Listen, I'm going to go upstairs and see if I can find some bandages for your head, OK?"

"Wait," he says; there's a lot of agitation in his voice. "Gotta go NOW." Then his eyes go wide.

"DON'T MOVE."

I flinch at the feel of the cold metal at the base of my skull.

"I SAID, DON'T MOVE."

The gun barrel pushes harder forcing my head onto my chest.

Rule one: do the opposite of what he says.

I spin to my left, swinging my arm up to face height. I feel it come into contact with his hand and simultaneously hear the detonation in my left ear. I grab the lapels of his leather jacket and pull. I drop my head an inch and I feel my forehead pummel his nose. Over the ringing in my left ear I hear him grunt. With all my strength I snap my knee up into his groin. He grunts louder.

I do one more half turn to the left and grab his wrist. I scythe my right arm between us and over the top of his bicep, then curl it around his elbow. With all my strength I push down on the wrist and up on the back of his elbow. He yelps and I hear the gun clatter to the ground. Now for the finale. Still holding his wrist I move my right arm forward and snap the elbow back into— "Arrrrgggghhh." The pain is excruciating. My kidney's on fire. The waves course through my entire body like electricity. Hands grab me and toss me like a rag doll. I feel my back smash into Cal, forcing him back onto the bed with me on top.

Paralyzed by the pain, I watch Harvey wipe away the tears brought on by my head butt, crouch down with a sharp groan and pick up his gun with his left hand.

"You fucking little bitch," he wheezes. "I am so gonna fuck you up." He stops to pant for a moment, his huge chest heaving.

I feel Cal trying to move underneath me but I can't move off him. It feels like my muscles no longer function. I hear a long groan escape my lips.

"First, I'm going to kill your little buddy there. Then I'm going to chain you down and fuck you and not just once, I've got all the time in the world. Then when I've had enough of your skinny ass, I'm going to go to work on you with the garden shears and keep at it until you're begging me to put you out of your misery."

I can feel Cal's hand on my butt. What the hell is he doing? Is he so out of it he's groping me?

Harvey takes another couple of breaths and steps closer.

Cal's hand lets go of my butt and I feel it groping at my side.

"You! Rogan!" he shouts. "Open your eyes, I want you to see who's killing you."

He levels the gun in Cal's general direction and with every ounce of my strength I aim a kick at him.

But my limbs just twitch.
Then he says, "I said... open... your... eyes!"
Then he smiles. "That's better."
Then he aims carefully.
Then his face explodes.

26

CAL

Still lying on my back, I pull the Glock out of the pocket of my rain jacket and place it on the bed, as far from us as possible. My head is still pounding from the blow that Jen delivered. I want to just lie back and sleep for a week. Not an option. We need to clean up this mess and get out of here. Two shots have been fired within seconds of each other and someone may have decided to call the police.

Jen groans as I move her off me. I push myself up into a sitting position and look at her. Her face is white. I saw the terrible blow that Harvey delivered to her kidney with every ounce of his considerable strength. She may be badly damaged and bleeding internally. "Jen, can you hear me." She nods. "How bad is it?"

"I'll survive," she grunts.

"Can you sit up?"

She tries but ends up shaking her head.

A number of priorities compete for my attention. We need to get out of here before the cops show up, which could be any minute; although it was self defence, Harvey was a RCMP member and we're going to be arrested and held for who knows how long. We need to clean up every bit of evidence that shows we've been here, before we leave; that's going to take at least an hour and even then we'll probably miss something. If Jen is bleeding internally, she needs to get to a hospital fast.

Another groan from Jen.

Decision made.

I dare not call an ambulance. If they come here and find us in the condition we are in they are going to call the cops and all will be discovered. "Jen, I'm going to take you to the hospital. This is going to hurt but I'm going to sit you up." She just nods.

I put my arm around her and pull her into the upright position. She tries to suppress the shriek of pain and only partly succeeds. There is no way she can walk. I'm going to have to carry her. If I can.

Harvey's body is slumped against the door leading up the stairs. As I lean down to take his arm, the pounding in my head would outdo a Gene Krupa-Buddy Rich drum battle. I pull his hundred-and-twenty-kilo body away from the door so that I can open it. It exhausts me. God knows how I'm going to carry Jen upstairs.

I slip one hand under her thighs and the other around her back. I lift her up. She gives another suppressed shriek but not as bad this time. I sway on my feet and get a light-headed feeling. I think I can do this.

I step over Harvey's body and start the ascent.

Every one of the thirteen steps is an application of sheer willpower for me and horrific pain for her.

It takes us five minutes to get to the top.

I start towards the front door. Then it hits me.

I don't have a car. The Healey is parked outside Tina's

house and Harvey's car is locked, in the driveway, with the keys somewhere in the bushes.

Then the second hit.

Sirens.

Police sirens.

All I know is that I don't want the police inside this house. If we can just get outside and close the door, I'll think up some reasonable explanation as to why a man with blood all over his head and a woman—dressed only in a man's rain jacket and suffering from kidney damage—are sitting in the rain on the porch of a house they don't own. Easy peasy.

Moving as fast as I can, I get to the front door, wrestle it open and get us outside. As gently as possible, I sit Jen down on the top step, close the front door behind us and stand and wait.

The sirens are getting louder as I search my mind for that 'reasonable explanation.' Nothing. Not even Shake-speare could have written the plot for us. I look down the street towards Main and can see the reflection of the red and blue lights on the side of a building. Then I hear the Doppler effect as the police car crosses Eighteenth and speeds on its way down Main.

My sigh of relief is audible.

"Jen, I'm going to find the keys to Harvey's car then I'll drive you to the hospital."

She just nods.

As I walk across the lawn towards the bushes, cursing myself for having thrown the car key so cavalierly, I feel the bite of the rain on the cold December wind. Jen must be feeling it much worse; she is naked but for my jacket. I remember approximately where I tossed it and get on my hands and knees so that I can part the leaves of the laurel. In the grey of the afternoon, I take out my phone and tap on the flashlight feature. I search in the bush and on the earth beneath. Nothing. Maybe it was a bit to my left. I shuffle across on my knees and immediately see it on the ground. As I pick it up a voice says, "Are you OK miss?"

I spin around. There's a man, probably in his late sixties, standing in front of Jen.

"Yes, I'm fine," she manages to say.

"Are you sure?" he asks in a French accent.

"Hi," I say walking up to him. He is short, with close-cropped grey hair and a brightly coloured scarf wrapped twice around his neck, but there is something about him that says he is a force to be reckoned with. "I'm just about to take my wife to hospital. She's had a bad fall. As I came down the steps, I stumbled and my car key went flying out of my hand." I hold up the evidence.

"Do you live 'ere?" he asks.

"Yes." I'm hoping it's not a trick question.

He looks at me for a moment. "I live next door." He indicates the house which shares an adjoining wall. "I'm Gilles." He extends his hand and I step forward and shake it. As I move into the light from the porch, he sees the blood on my face. "Did you fall too?" he asks.

"Yes."

His hand snakes out and takes the BMW key from me.

Busted!

I don't want to have to fight this man. Not only because he's twenty or more years older than me but also because he looks like he could whip my ass, given the condition that I'm in.

"I'll drive you to VGH," he says with authority. "Get your wife in the car before she freezes to death and I'll 'ave you there in no time."

I feel an immediate rush of relief. "Thank you so much," I say.

He strides across the lawn to the driveway and I pick Jen up and carry her over. He has the back door open and I slide her onto the back seat then run around the back of the car and get in beside her. While I am still buckling her in, he has the car underway.

He is a fast but expert driver and I feel in good hands.

"Given your wife's attire, I won't ask you what you were doing when you both fell. I'm French, I understand." He chuckles.

"I really appreciate your help, Gilles."

"It is my pleasure, Harvey," he says, raising the hairs on the back of my neck.

"How did you know my name?" I ask.

He looks at me in the rearview mirror. "The post office put a letter for you into my letterbox about six months ago. It 'ad a government envelope so I took it over to you. You weren't in so I just slipped it into your letterbox."

"I appreciate it. Thanks."

"I'm surprised we've never met before." He says it casually but I wonder if there is an undercurrent of suspicion.

Jen groans and looks at me. She feels the same way.

I use the excuse she has given me.

"How are you feeling, honey?" I say. "We'll be there soon."

"Good. It's hurting," she says.

I check out the window. We're on West Twelfth just a block from the hospital. "Soon be there," I say.

With no further questions, he turns right onto Laurel then right again and into the area in front of the emergency department doors.

"You take her in there and I'll park the car and join you," he says.

When I check into the hospital I'll have to use my real name. I don't want him to discover that I am not Harvey Clegg. "You've been very kind," I say. "I don't think I will be up for driving us home. It would be great if you could take the car back and park it in our driveway. Just drop the key through the letterbox."

"If you are sure..." he says.

"It would really help."

Gilles shrugs in a very Gallic style then comes around and opens the door so that I can pick up Jen and carry her into the hospital.

As he drives off, I have a sneaking suspicion I am going to see him again. And not in a good way.

————

HE LOOKS SO OLD. ABOUT TWENTY YEARS OLDER THAN GILLES. His hair is unbrushed and his skinniness makes him look so very frail. He is connected to more tubes than there are on the London Underground.

"Nick," I say softly.

His eyes flutter open and seem to have difficulty focusing. "Rogan?" he says.

"How are you feeling, Nick?" Why do we always ask dumb-assed questions at moments like this?

"Just aces," he says with the shadow of a smile.

"I'm sorry about this."

"Did we get Fox?" he asks.

"Yes. And they found a bunch of records that will lead to a lot of arrests."

"Then it was all worth it." He looks at me as if actually

seeing me for the first time. "What the heck happened to you?"

I look around the ICU, looking for ears which might hear what I say. Seems OK.

"You remember Jen was seen with the big guy who we thought murdered Denis Lamarche?" He nods. "Well he did. I tracked him down and he damn near killed Jen and me." I tell him the details of the last few hours and end with, "Anyway, VGH emergency patched me up and let me go but they're keeping Jen in for observation."

"Jeez, Rogan. I can't leave you alone for five minutes without you getting yourself into trouble." His chuckle comes out more of a rasp. "You've got to go back to that house and clean up any trace of you and Jen having been there."

"I will. I'm going to go over there tomorrow."

"Do it tonight."

"I'm bushed right now. It'll keep. It's some sort of safe house, I think; nobody will ever go there. I need to speak to Ellie and then I'm going over to Tina's."

"Who's Tina?"

I grin. "My girlfriend. I'm staying at her place so that Brenda and Lucy can stay at my place."

"Girlfriend. I didn't know you had a girlfriend. How long have I been in here?"

I check my watch. "Twenty-one hours."

"Jeez Louise. I better get out of here fast, in case I miss the wedding."

My chuckle is subsumed by a jaw-cracking yawn.

27

CAL

Monday

"Mmmmmmm. That was lovely." She stretches and rubs her naked body against mine. "Early morning sex is so much better than breakfast." I hold her tight. I really want to tell her I love her but I'm scared. It's too soon. I really don't want to freak her out.

"Maybe," I say, "we should just stay in bed for a while and see what late morning sex is like."

"You are a very naughty boy. I should have got up hours ago to check the news coming out of Ottawa. I have people to interview and words to write. Know what I mean, Jelly Bean," She giggles, throws off the covers and gets up. Again I am awestricken by her beauty as she stands naked and looks down at me. I reach out and stroke the side of her thigh. "You *are* a naughty boy." She turns around and heads for the bathroom.

Reluctantly, I stretch and get up. And my day floods in. I know what I have to do this morning and it is unpleasant in the extreme. I need to get dressed and get to it. I hear the sound of the shower. I'll need a shower after my toils. I hear her singing in the shower. Maybe the task I have set myself can be delayed a few more minutes. Full of hope, I step into the bathroom.

———

I'M REALLY WORRIED ABOUT THE TASK AHEAD. I NEED TO eradicate all evidence that Jen and I were ever in Harvey's house. This includes retrieving the bullet that killed him, assuming it's not still trapped inside his skull. I have mentally retraced all of my movements in the house and I have a good idea of all the things that I touched and hope I can intuit all the places where I need to remove Jen's fingerprints. I'll have to remove all the duct tape and the covers from the bed she was confined to. Those will be full of her DNA.

And the body. I have to stage that as a suicide. My plan is to sit him up against a wall and take his hand, holding his gun, and fire another bullet along the same trajectory taken by my bullet. Hopefully when Dr. Marcus gets to do the post mortem, she won't discover there are two bullet tracks.

The one problem to which I don't have a solution is Harvey's next-door neighbour, Gilles. When the body is finally found—which hopefully won't be for months—the police will talk to all the neighbours and Gilles' story will strike an inconsistent note with the findings. He got a good look at Jen and me and if shown a photo of Harvey, he will know we were imposters.

Still, I'm thinking too far ahead. I have all the cleaning products, including some bleach, and all the household items I need to do the job. I just have to do it and hope for the best. I pull off Main onto Eighteenth and find a parking spot behind a black Dodge Charger right opposite Harvey's house.

One deep breath to gird up my loins and—

There are three men on the porch. The front door is open. One of the men is Gilles. The others are in suits. They are both tall, well-muscled and have the look. Cops. My mind is racing. Something we said must have alerted Gilles and he called the VPD. I can't for the life of me think what, but in the heat of the moment, it could have been anything. And Gilles knows that Jen is in VGH. I have to get her out of there. Maybe there are other cops already on the way there to question her. Whatever, we are blown.

I pull out of the parking space and drive sedately down the street. At least Gilles didn't look in my direction. I turn left and head down to Sixteenth. If I drive the Healey like it was built to be driven I can be at VGH in five minutes.

———

IT TOOK SEVEN MINUTES, THANKS TO VANCOUVER'S burgeoning transportation issues. One of the hospital greeters points me in the right direction and as I walk onto the ward, I almost bump into Adry. "What are you doing here?" I ask.

"Jen called me and told me they were going to discharge her, so I came over to pick her up."

"Oh, good. But why did she call you?"

"You are *such* a guy. Why do you think?" She laughs at my blank look. "You left her here last night with just your rain jacket. She needed clothes and as we're about the same size, I brought her some over."

"OK. Great. Where is she?"

Adry points. "Behind that curtain getting dressed." She sees the look on my face. "What's up?"

I drop my voice. "We need to get her out of here fast. I'll explain later."

Jen pulls the curtain aside and steps towards us carrying my bloodied rain jacket in her hand. She has folded it so the bullet hole is hidden. She looks a lot better than she did last night but she is obviously still in some pain. "We've got to go," I tell her. I lead her out of the ward and along the corridor to the exit door.

Then I see him. I can't be sure. He may be one of the men from Harvey's porch but if not, he's cut from the same cloth. He's waiting for someone at one of the intake desks to finish his phone call. Maybe I'm being paranoid but sometimes paranoia's good. Any sudden change of direction will give us away. Still holding her elbow, I move slightly in front of her so that I have to turn back around a little bit more to look at her, thus shielding my face and hers. We are just going to have to walk past him.

When we are just two steps away, I hear the receptionist hang up the phone. "How can I help you sir?"

"I'm looking for one of your patients," he says. "Jennifer Halley."

I grip Jen's arm. Then I see Adry's face. She's just about to speak. "Adry, can you take her other arm," I say, just a bit too loudly. She looks at me and I shake my head. She gets it and takes Jen's other arm. As we pass the intake desk I hear the tapping of keys. "She's only just been discharged," he says. "If you go along that corridor and take the first door on your right, she might still be there."

The man grunts his thanks and heads off in the direction we just came from.

Jen winces as I speed up. We need to get out of here

before the cop discovers she has just left.

I push the first set of double doors open and then hold the second one open for Jen and Adry. "Where's your car?" I ask the latter.

She points. "Just over there on Laurel, at a meter."

"Go with Jen and take her to the office."

They walk as quickly as Jen can manage, which is not nearly fast enough for me, and I take up a position behind an ambulance. I have a clear view of Jen and Adry and can see the exit doors through the windows of the ambulance's cab.

If the cop comes out before they are out of sight, I'm going to have to create some sort of distraction, without drawing attention to myself. Sounds like mission impossible to me.

For once in this whole affair, I get lucky. I see them get into Adry's little Mazda and drive off, just as the cop burst through the exit doors. I see his lips perform a four-letter expletive. Twice. Then he pulls out a phone and dials.

He walks off talking to someone. By the look on his face it's a superior officer. Good.

As the rate of adrenalin pumping into my blood eases, I get the feeling I'm missing something.

Something important.

———

"MAYBE WE SHOULD GO TO THE VPD AND HAND OURSELVES in." Jen looks really tired. I can picture the massive blow inflicted by Harvey's fist and I'm surprised she even lived through it.

"Maybe," I say but I'm not convinced.

"How did you know they were cops, Cal? Did you recognize them?" Adry asks.

"No. But VPD has thirteen hundred sworn members and I haven't worked there in three years, not to mention they could have been RCMP. So the chances of me recognizing them would be slim to none."

"So how *do* you know they were cops?"

"I don't know, they just had the look. The neighbour must have suspected something and called them."

We lapse into silence.

Adry is the first to speak. "Where are your own clothes Jen?"

"Harvey took them. He took them off me when I was unconscious."

"That is *so* creepy. You must have felt terrible."

Jen just nods.

"So maybe the cops found them at the house. You must have had your ID in one of your pockets or in your purse."

"Maybe." Jen sounds unsure. "When I managed to free myself from the duct tape, I looked for them but they weren't in the basement. I didn't have time to check the rest of the house because I heard Cal show up and I thought he was Harvey. Sorry about that by the way."

"No prob. And that was good thinking Adry. That house was unnaturally tidy. I would have seen the clothes if they were anywhere on the main floor. If he put them anywhere it would have been upstairs during the time between my two visits there.."

"What about your suitcase, where was that?" Adry asks.

"That's another good question," says Jen. "It's probably still in Harvey's car. That's the last place I put it. But I'm pretty sure there was nothing in it to identify me."

Adry's good at this, she's a natural in fact.

"Oh my God," says Jen. "It's Monday. And it's two o'clock

in Ottawa. I'm supposed to be back at work. I have to talk to my boss."

"What are you going to tell him?" I ask.

"The truth, I guess."

"Yeah, except that implicates me in a murder and you as an accessory."

She thinks about it. "OK, part truth." She goes and sits at Nick's desk and I get a twinge of guilt that I haven't been to see him and update him on what's been happening.

She dials a number. "Hi Tony," she says. A pause. "Actually I'm in Vancouver." A longer pause. She takes a deep breath. "I've been looking into the fact that Annalise's brother was killed in Vancouver at the same time she was killed in Ottawa." Another pause. "Yes, I know but—" A longer pause, a lot longer. "OK... Yes... Straight away."

She hangs up. "I'm not in his good books right now. I have a meeting with him first thing in the morning." Adry is about to say something but Jen holds up a finger. She thinks for a long moment and continues, "Tony sounded weird somehow." She thinks some more. "I'm already up shit creek, so what the hell, if the cops come looking for us we need to have answers, so let's start over again," Jen takes a deep breath. "Let's go through what we know. Annalise is having an affair with her boss Neil Harris, the Minister of National Defence. She tells Sally Hyde, my colleague at CSIS, that she wants to discuss something that effects national security and she sends some documents to her brother. She and Sally are both killed in a terrorist bombing. At the same time, her brother is killed in Vancouver by a rogue RCMP officer, Harvey Clegg. He learns that I'm here and kidnaps me and tries to kill me. Cal rescues me and kills Harvey. Does that about cover it?"

"There's one other thing," I add. "I forgot to tell you

about it. Clegg was staking out my apartment, he knew *we* were involved in this whole thing. That was why he wanted to kill me."

"Well," says Adry. "When you put it all together like that, it sounds like some sort of conspiracy. I'll bet the answers are in those documents."

She's right and it's Monday. Damien's back from his trip. I pull out my phone, dial and press speakerphone. We do the polite stuff then I say, "We know what that 'garter' reference was. The person who encrypted those documents was the son of an Englishman, Sir David Fetherstonhaugh. He was a member of the Order of the Garter."

"Wow. Order of the Garter, that's the most senior type of knighthood in the UK. He must have been a big deal," says Damien. A chuckle comes over the phone. *"I should have thought of that usage of the word garter."*

"We think that his father was the clue to the encryption key. Could you give that a try? And Damien, this is a matter of life and death."

"Hang on a second." I hear a muted clicking of keys and some subvocal muttering for about thirty seconds, then, *"I tried his name and the words 'order of the garter' but nothing. Encryption keys are usually longer than that anyway. I'll get one of my guys to work on it and see if he can get a combination of words in his name and title with and without capitals and spaces and hyphens. See if we can get a key that works. We've got some software here that he can use to help us generate a whole bunch of different options."*

"That's great man, I really appreciate it."

"Sure. I'll call you as soon as we get something."

I hang up. "I wish Nick were here, I'd like to know what he might come up with."

Jen was deep in thought while I was on the call. "Let's

assume your buddy Damien can't crack the encryption key," she says, "and we never get to find out what's in those documents. Where do we go from there?"

"You're in CSIS, why don't you get an appointment to go and see her boyfriend?" I ask.

She looks at me like I've lost my mind. "Lowly intelligence officers like me don't get to interrogate Cabinet Ministers. Neil Harris is like one of the top five people in the federal government."

"Well, without the documents, he's the only person who might know what's in them that could have got Denis murdered."

"OK, so *you* interview him." She laughs as she says it.

I think back to the first thing that Jen said and I follow it through to its logical conclusion. I get up. I know what I must do now.

"I've got to go see Nick."

———

Nick looks a lot better than he did yesterday, though he's still hooked up to all sorts of drips and machines. He has the TV on and he's watching CBC news. I update him on the happenings at Harvey's house and when I was picking Jen up at VGH. He hears me out without comment until I get to the end, "So I was wondering if I should go and turn myself in to Steve? They're going to find my DNA in there soon enough, so I think it's better to get out in front of it. What d'you think?"

He looks at me for a moment, frowns and asks a question I wasn't expecting. "You said there were three members?"

"I suppose there must have been. There were two at the

house and then one at VGH. I drove as fast as I could from the house because I wanted to pick Jen up and get her out of there before the neighbour told them about taking her to the hospital last night. When I got there Jen was already dressing and ready to leave and as we were walking out, he was already at the front desk asking for her. I can't be sure he wasn't one of the cops on the front porch of the house but I don't think so."

"Weird."

"Why?"

"Think it through," he says. "The VPD are there because the neighbour called them, right?"

"Sure, why else would they be?"

He doesn't answer but continues, "Last night, the neighbour thinks you're Harvey Clegg and Jen's your wife. He takes you and Jen and drops you off at VGH. He goes home, parks Harvey's car in the driveway and goes to bed. Next morning for some reason he thinks something's wrong. Maybe he got nosy and looked in through a basement window and sees the late Harvey with his face blown off. Whatever. He calls nine-one-one, uniforms arrive, enter the premises and find the body. It looks like a suicide or a murder. What do they do? They call for a detective team. That's one, maybe two detectives and the crime scene guys." He pauses and looks straight at me. "When do you ever remember three detectives going out on a suspicious death call? Where did the third one pop up from?"

He's right. It never happens.

"And there were no crime scene personnel there," I say.

"The third guy," he asks, "are you sure he was looking for Jen?"

"Absolutely. I heard him ask the person at the front desk, 'I'm looking for one of your patients, Jennifer Halley.'"

His eyes go wide. "What?!" It's almost a shout.

And I get it. That must be what was bothering me after we got Jen out of there this morning.

How did he know her last name? A cop would have been looking for Mrs. Jen Clegg.

"Those guys weren't VPD cops," I breathe.

"You better believe they weren't."

We sit in stunned silence.

"So who the hell were they?" I finally ask.

"And what do we do now?" he adds.

More silence.

This time Nick breaks it. "OK, we'll worry about who they were later. Right now, Rogan, here's what you've got to do. The real VPD are going to find that crime scene and your's and Jen's DNA is going to be all over it. The last place those phony cops are going to look for you is back at that house. You've gotta go back there and clean it up just like you were planning to do this morning. If you can stage it to look like a suicide, so much the better. Oh, and if you can find that neighbour, ask him if he called the cops or if they just showed up there. I've got fifty bucks on them just showing up."

No takers on that bet.

We chat about all the implications of who these guys might be and what it all means for us. Then I ask him a question and he asks me one.

For once we completely agree with each other.

I turn to go.

"Wait," he says. "Look." He's pointing at the TV. The face of a young man peers out at us. He looks nervous in the photograph and his eyes point in slightly different directions. I listen to the voice of the newscaster. "...*released the name of the bomber who killed eleven people last month in Cana-*

da's first-ever, terrorist bombing. He was Hamza Kashif from the Ottawa suburb of Nepean. Neighbours told CBC News reporter John Wilcox, that they were shocked. According to most of them, he was a quiet young man who was always polite and friendly. We go over now to John who's currently in Nepean..."

I'm looking at the face of the man who killed Annalise Lamarche.

———

I MULL OVER ALL THE IMPLICATIONS OF MY CONVERSATION with Stammo as I drive up Main Street. The traffic's heavier than usual. I hear sirens and see flashing lights in my rearview mirror; they remind me of hearing sirens on Main last night. I pull over. This time the sirens are from a fire truck. As soon as it passes, I pull away from the curb and follow it as closely as I can. It's a good way to cut through the traffic. I follow it across Fifteenth, Sixteenth and Seventeenth, flashing past the vehicles which have pulled over to allow the red monster to lumber past.

To my surprise it hangs a left onto Eighteenth.

I see its destination.

It's my destination.

Harvey's house is ablaze and is taking the house next door with it. The fire has really taken hold with tongues of flame licking their way out of the upstairs windows. I know what this means. Vancouver's fire department is organized so that every address in the city is no more than four minutes from a fire hall. This means it's no more than four minutes since someone called in the fire, yet the house is almost consumed already. I foresee the word arson on the investigator's report.

As the firemen unroll their hoses and attach them to

hydrants, I watch the blaze gather strength in the neighbour's house. and hope our good samaritan, Gilles, is out. I scan the crowd but don't see him there. I back the Healey into a parking space and grab my phone, run across the road and turn back towards the faces, all mesmerized by some atavistic fascination with the overwhelming fury of fire. I take several pics of them. Maybe one of the arsonists has returned to examine his handiwork. I text them to Adry with instructions to have them printed on the largest size sheets she can find.

The firemen are now pouring jets of water onto the houses but they are lost. The roof of Harvey's house collapses in a profusion of sparks.

I now no longer need to worry about DNA and fingerprints. They won't survive. But two things will: the shattered bones of Harvey's skull and the remains of the bullet that did the shattering.

———

Adry already has the pictures printed and she and Jen are looking at them.

"Adry, book tickets for Jen and me to Ottawa this evening. Nick okayed the expense."

"On it," she says and returns to her desk.

"Do you recognize anyone in the pictures," I ask Jen. She shakes her head. I pull a magnifying glass from Stammo's desk drawer and scrutinize the first print. Adry has had them magnified and printed so that there are about eight faces on each sheet. I put each face under the lens and search my memory for a match with the men that I saw on the porch from about fifty yards away and the man whom I glimpsed at the hospital some five minutes after.

On the third sheet, I get a possible match. It could be the man from the hospital. I grab a sharpie off my desk and circle it. "I think that's the guy who was looking for you at the hospital. What d'you think?"

She looks at the face and shrugs. "I didn't really see him."

I examine all the other faces but only the one looks familiar.

Gathering all the prints into a folder, I update Jen on my talk with Nick and on the fire.

"Most conspiracy theories are nonsense," she says, "but I'm starting to agree with Adry; there's something going on here and it sure as hell involves the Minister of DND."

Adry walks back into the main office. "Done, I texted you your boarding passes. Air Canada flight three-four-four at five o'clock, it gets in at half past midnight their time."

I check my watch. "We'd better get going."

"You've got four hours," she says.

"I know but I have to stop off at three places before we head out to the airport. Come on Jen, let's go."

"It feels funny," she says, getting to her feet. "Everything I had when I came to Vancouver is gone. All I've got are the clothes Adry lent me and the burner phone she bought for me with your company credit card."

"Adry, can you access the company's computer system from home?"

"Well, duh." She looks at me like I'm crazy so I take it as a yes.

"The guys who burned down Harvey's house know about us. I want you to close down the office, go home and work from there. Make sure all our current clients know that there will be delays in their cases."

"On it," she says. "You guys have a good trip."

She and Jen have a big hug and we head out the door.

As we get to the elevator, Adry calls, "Cal! I forgot to tell you, I did some research about that garter thing, I thought the key might be—" The elevator dings.

"No time," I call. "Text Damien and let him know."

She gives a big thumbs up and again I feel the twinge of worry that the people who burned down Harvey's probably know about the existence of Stammo Rogan Investigations Inc.

———

ALL ERRANDS DONE, I GOT US TO THE AIRPORT IN GOOD TIME. It took us a while to get through security because Jen had no ID. But she did have an image of her Passport and her Ontario Driver's Licence in cloud storage, so they were able to check her identity. I'm enjoying my last BC draft beer before our flight is called and Jen is breaking the law by telling me about the security measures in place for Canadian Cabinet Ministers.

My phone rings. This could be good news. "Damien," I say to Jen. "Hey man," I say to him.

"Cal, you need to come to my office." His voice has an edge to it that I've never heard before.

"I can't. I'm at the airport waiting for my flight to leave."

There is silence on the line for a good five seconds. *"Sorry Cal, you're gonna have to miss that flight."*

It's my turn to pause. "What have you found?" I ask.

He gives me another pause. *"I was in a meeting when your colleague texted me so I only just got to it. You should give her a raise by the way, a big raise. She worked out the encryption key."*

"What was it?"

"Honi soit qui mal y pense."

"What?"

"It's the Latin motto of the Order of the Garter. It means 'shame to him who thinks evil.'"

"So you were able to decrypt the documents?"

"Yes. Well, some of them. You have to miss your flight and get over to my office right now."

"Why can't you just email them to me?"

Again with the silence. Then, *"I do a lot of work for the federal government and I have a top secret security clearance. If I don't turn these documents over to them, that clearance is at risk. I can't afford to lose it. I must be mad but I'm going to let you see them before I turn them in because I'm going to have to tell them I got the documents from you. I can't even take the risk of emailing them to you. Either you come here or..."*

He leaves it hanging. I process what he's saying... for less than a second. "One hour," I say and hang up.

I finish the Trash Panda in three good gulps and stand up. "Damien decrypted the documents," I tell Jen. "It's better if we get a later flight to Ottawa, if we can go there and have the documents with us."

"Why doesn't he just email them?" She asks. I tell her Damien's reason. She thinks for a moment. "Better I meet late with my boss, with some evidence in hand, than meet early with nothing." She stands up. "Let's do it."

We head for the exit.

———

DAMIEN SEEMS SURPRISED, IMPRESSED AND A LITTLE RELIEVED when I introduce Jen as a CSIS intelligence officer. He leads us into a conference room with blinds drawn and a large screen on one wall. He locks the door behind us. "Help yourself to water or coffee." He gestures towards a fancy coffee machine and two baskets containing designer water and healthy-looking snacks. I realize I haven't eaten yet today and take a couple of nutty granola bars and press the buttons to deliver an espresso. Jen just takes water.

As we sit down, Damien opens his laptop and after a couple of clicks his desktop appears on the wall screen. He opens a folder titled 'Cal', inside it there are two more folders, one titled 'EUCs' and the other titled 'Opdocs'. "This is what I found when we decrypted the file," he says. "The 'Opdocs' folder is full of documents, but they are individually encrypted with a different key, or keys, so I don't know what's in them, and I don't know if they were encrypted by the same person but I'm guessing they weren't; why double encrypt them? I've got one of my guys working on decrypting them. However there are twenty-one documents which were not double encrypted."

He opens the 'EUCs' folder which is full of PDF files. He selects them all and opens them. They all pop up on the screen. Although I can only see the ones on top they all look the same. They are all headed with a logo of the Canadian flag and the words 'National Defence, Défense Nationale'. Under that are the words 'END USER CERTIFICATE'.

"Whoa!" Jen says loudly. I look at her and she has a stunned look on her face.

"What's an end user certificate?" I ask.

She gathers her thoughts and answers, "When a company that manufactures guns, or munitions of any sort, sells their weapons to a foreign country, they need an export permit from their own country before they can ship them. To get the export permit, one of the documents you need is an end user certificate from the government of the country that's buying the weapons." She turns to Damien. "Zoom in on one of them, please."

He clicks his mouse and one document fills the screen. The first paragraph reads, 'This is to certify that the following items, for the needs of the Armed Forces of Canada, have been purchased from Unimax Weapons Systems Inc., Bethesda, Maryland, USA to be shipped by USCAN Import Export Corporation, Vancouver, British Columbia, Canada.' Underneath that is a list of weapons and quantities purchased. There are three thousand machine guns, fifteen hundred grenade launchers, tens of millions of rounds of ammunition, granades and a whole bunch of various accessories, most of which I don't understand. Beneath the list is a declaration which reads, 'National Defence Canada hereby certifies that the items listed in this End User Certificate are for the exclusive use of the Armed Forces of Canada for peace keeping purposes and will neither be re-sold, re-exported or transferred to any third party nor used for any purpose other than described herein.'

The document has a seal and a stamp on it and the signature of Neil Harris, Minister, National Defence. It is dated five months ago.

"It looks legitimate," Jen says.

"It is, up to a point," Damien agrees. "I priced out the probable cost of this order, it's around forty million dollars. And it's reasonable that Canada would be buying this quantity of weapons for the army. But look at this one." A different end user certificate appears on the screen. "This is for weapons from the UK. It's for about eighty million dollars and it was signed three months ago. While I was waiting for you to get here, I went through all of them. Each one is for weapons from a different manufacturer and they are from countries all over the world, including places like Serbia, Bulgaria, Finland and others. Each certificate is reasonable on its face but taken together they represent about five billion dollars of purchases. The oldest one is dated eight months ago and the latest one is last week. There is no way that the Canadian armed forces are buying that amount of armaments from seventy different suppliers over a period of less than a year."

Five billion dollars! That makes the man who shot Nick a very small time dealer.

"They're all signed by Neil Harris?" Jen asks. Damien just nods. "I have to get these to my boss. Can you copy those onto a thumb drive for me?" He nods again. She checks her watch. "We need to get booked onto a later flight."

"There's not one. Adry booked the last fight of the evening." A part of me is glad because it means I get to spend another night with Tina before flying off to Ottawa for who knows how long.

"Damn, I really wanted to get these into Tony's hands first thing tomorrow. Any idea when the earliest flight is?"

I pull out my phone to check and get interrupted. "Maybe I can help," Damien says. "Our people have to go all over the world, often at a moment's notice, so a year ago I got a private jet. It can get you to Ottawa tonight. It's at the airport right now; it's yours if you want."

My excitement of taking my first-ever flight in a private jet is balanced by my disappointment at not being able to see Tina tonight.

Then an idea tips the balance.

Not just an idea... but a great idea.

28

NICK

I t's good to be out of the ICU. It was so busy there, sometimes I couldn't hear myself think. It was a bit odd saying goodbye to Brenda; now she knows I'm not going to die she's gone back to Toronto. But Lucy is staying for a few more days. It's nice to have her here and catch up on her life. With Matt gone, she's my only family. I finally got around to telling her I'm gay. She gave me a big hug and said, "I know Dad." I didn't ask her how she knew. She's gone back to Cal's place to spend the night but I can't sleep.

One of my nurses is pretty cute. I've thought about saying something to him but I've been in the closet all of my life and I don't know how to go about it.

Rogan's being a bit melodramatic about these guys who burned down that safe house. Still I'm glad he came by before he went to Ottawa. I grab my phone to check the time. Eleven. It's two in the morning in Ottawa. He'll be there now. I can't believe he's seeing someone, staying at her place too. He's lucky.

Why can't I sleep?

My door is opening. In the semi-darkness I can't see if

it's the cute nurse. He's wearing scrubs but moves more like a soldier than anything else. Or a cop. My senses go on overdrive.

"Mr. Stammo?" he whispers.

"Yes." I roll onto my side, facing away from him.

"One of our alarms is beeping outside and I just want to check you're connected to the monitor OK." He comes around to the right side of the bed to face me. Good. Then he crouches down and before I can react, he is holding a knife to my throat. Not so good. I feel him push something soft and squishy, like cold gelatin, over my mouth. I don't know what it is, but it silences me better than any gag. I slide my right hand under the pillow. "Unfortunately Mr. Stammo, you and your partner know too much. One of my colleagues is dealing with him even as we speak. You, however, will be easier." I move my hand further up and feel it. "I have something for you, something undetectable. You just have to breathe it in and sleep."

He moves his hand off the gelatin-like stuff and it stays firmly in place. The hand reappears in front of my face holding a rubber, bulb-like thing with a short nozzle. I shake my head like mad and it works: he doesn't notice the movement of my hand under the pillow. I get my hand around the grip and release the safety. He's trying to push the nozzle into my face as I jab my gun into his side and pull the trigger. The bulb thing flies out of his hand and he staggers upward and backwards, swaying. I aim at his middle. "Freeze!" Except no sound comes out of my mouth. He drops out of my line of sight beyond the foot of the bed. I hear him scrambling across the floor. I try to sit up but the pain from my surgery cuts through me. I scream against the stuff in my mouth. The door opens... and then closes. For a moment all is silent and I make a promise never to call

Rogan melodramatic again. Bringing me my gun was a stroke of genius.

Then I remember the words. 'One of my colleagues is dealing with him even as we speak.'

But Rogan's in Ottawa.

And Lucy's at his house.

I grab my phone. Then realize I don't know his home number. I always call him on his cell. I don't even know if he has a home number.

Only one thing to do.

I pull the gel thing out of my mouth. it comes away with a sickly, sucking sound. I press my phone's home button.

And around me all hell breaks loose.

29

ADRY

Damn. I was just getting to sleep. It'd better not be one of those damn telemarketers. I grope for my phone and squint at the screen. "Nick, do you realize it's—" The urgency in his voice snaps me fully awake. "Cal doesn't have a landline at his place. Why?" There is a lot of shouting in the background and I can hardly hear what he's saying. "He lives a couple of blocks from me but I don't remember his exact address. Why?" I find myself shouting to match him. I can just make out what he's— "What?!"

"Who is this?" The voice isn't Nick's. Someone's taken his phone from him but I can just make out Nick's shouts in the background. *"Get the cops over there, Adry!"*

The strange voice says, *"I said, who is this?"*

I hang up.

I scroll through my recent calls until I find the one with the four-one-six area code and I tap it.

It rings several times and then I hear her voice. *"Hello."*

"Lucy. Thank God. You have to get out of there right away."

There is a short silence. *"Why?"* she says. There's kind of an echo, like it's on speakerphone.

"Your Dad just called me. Someone tried to attack him. He thinks someone is coming over there to get Cal. You need to get out of there like *immediately*."

Another silence, then, *"OK, I will. Thanks, Kate."* She hangs up.

Kate?!

OMG.

30

LUCY

He throws my phone next to me on the bed. "Who was that?" His voice is calm. It makes him like a hundred times more scary. He's standing beside the bed looking down at me.

"She works for my Dad."

He thinks about it for what seems like a long time then says, "OK. Fine. Let's get back to you. All you have to do is tell me where I can find Cal Rogan and I'll go and never bother you again." He's a lying sack of shit. He is *not* going to leave me around as a witness. I have to play for time.

"I don't believe you. I've seen your face."

"You've been watching too much television." He smiles as he says it. Creepy. "I just need to know where Cal is, then I promise I'll go."

"If I tell you, how can you guarantee not to hurt me?"

Still in the same friendly tone he says, "If you don't tell me, than I guarantee I *will* hurt you. And I'll hurt you a lot."

"Maybe you don't have time," I say.

"What do you mean?" He doesn't sound so smooth now.

"You heard what she said on the phone. She said that

someone *tried* to attack my Dad. My Dad will have sent the police over here. They'll be here any minute."

"If the police were on their way, why did your friend Kate call? Why wasn't it the police?"

He's right. Why did Adry call? Why didn't Dad call the police. Maybe it doesn't matter. She'll know something's wrong because I called her Kate. *She'll* have called the police, *surely*. If he thinks the police are on their way...

"OK," he says. "Enough." He puts his hand behind his back, under his jacket. I can feel a horrible tingling in my gut as he pulls out a knife. It's one of those knives used by fishermen. Sharp on one edge and serrated on the other. "You're very pretty. I can make you very ugly, very quickly." The tingling gives way to something far worse. "Where is Cal Rogan?"

I feel the wetness spreading over my legs. "The police are on their way now. She will have called them."

"I don't think so."

"She'll know something's wrong."

He leans forward and holds the knife right up to my face. "Where's Rogan?"

In desperation, I shriek, "Her name's not Kate."

His eyes go wide. For the first time I see indecision in his face.

Then his eyes go wider as he hears the sirens.

"You bitch!"

His arm jerks back and then slashes forward.

31

ADRY

I hear the sirens as I run down the street towards Cal's building. I only know where he lives because I often jog down here and I once saw him driving out of the building's car park in his cute little English sports car. Note to self: have everyone's home address on file. As I get to the front door of his building, I put my phone back to my ear. "It's two, four, one, seven," I pant to the dispatcher.

"They'll be there in less than sixty seconds," she says. I hear her voice telling the patrol car the full address. I move to the curb so that I can wave at them.

I see the movement out of the corner of my eye. Someone's leaving the building. It's a tall, good-looking guy wearing black. I run to the door and he holds it open for me. "Thanks." I hold the door open and wait for the arriving cops. The tall guy smiles, nods and marches off down the road. Definitely hot.

I only have to wait a few seconds before the cop car pulls up and the officers stride over to me. "Are you the one who called it in?" the older one asks.

"Yes, but I don't know the apartment number."

"It's four-oh-three," he says. How did he know that? "You wait here miss and we'll go and check it out." They head for the elevator. I watch the numbers above the elevator door go up to four and then stop. The number above the other elevator is a G. I can't wait down here, not knowing whether or not Lucy's OK. I run to the elevator and get in. It takes what seems like forever to get to the fourth floor. I follow the arrow pointing left and see that the door to apartment four-oh-three is open. Taking a deep breath, I step inside. I hear the cop's voice talking on his radio. It's coming from down the hallway. I walk towards the sound of his voice and look through the open bedroom door. Lucy is on the bed with the cops standing, looking down at her.

I take out my phone.

I have to be the one to tell Nick.

32

CAL

Tuesday, Ottawa

The great thing about flying by private jet is that there was no airport security to go through so I was able to take my trusty Glock with me. It's safely back at the hotel because it would never get through the security here. Tina's press credentials as a reporter from the Daily News Hound got her in here and my hastily forged credentials get me in here as her photographer—the second advantage of private jets is there's no baggage restriction so I'm decked out with all her camera equipment.

Tina has been busy trying to get quotes and comments on a variety of topics from a variety of politicians who have passed through this corridor on their way to do the nation's business in the Parliament building. I've stood around trying to look useful, but it's all a prelude to the main event. There are a few other members of the fifth estate milling around doing the same thing as Tina. She walks over to one of them. I recognize his face from the CBC News.

"Hey Ian," she says.

"Hi Tina. Nice to see you in the nation's capital again."

She introduces me as Cal, her new 'video guy.'

"I'm hoping to get a comment from Neil Harris," she says.

"What about?"

"A big new scandal." She gives him a mischievous grin.

"What new scandal?" I see all his reporter's antennae twitching.

"Hang around and see," she says.

Before he can ask anything else, she spots the Prime Minister with his coterie of advisors. All the newspeople converge on him and bombard him with questions about whether his minority government will be able to keep control of parliament after his latest, inopportune comments on a video, taken at a NATO Summit, that went viral. As he fields their questions, I see Neil Harris, Minister of National Defence, striding in through the entranceway. He sees the mob of reporters around the PM and looks both angry and disappointed that they are not milling around him. As my hero once wrote, he's *choked with ambition of the meaner sort*. We'll see if he is going to choke over something else.

I tap Tina on the shoulder and indicate our advancing target. She taps her colleague, Ian, on the arm and steps away from the crowd around the PM, onto a trajectory that will intercept Harris. As I follow her, I give a glance backward and see that Ian has got a couple of others to come with him.

Harris' frown gives way to a smile as he sees the small group detach from the crowd and head towards him. Tina hangs back and lets Ian and one of the others get ahead of her. Ian is the first to get to the Minister. He thrusts his microphone forward and his cameraman aims his lens.

"What do you think about the PM's comments at the summit, Minister?" Ian asks.

He slows his pace but continues walking. "I'm sure we have all done things that we regret," Harris says, somehow managing to convey that he doesn't personally have any such regrets, "and I am sure that the PM has moved past those unfortunate comments," he adds, giving every indication that he doubts it. It's the perfect hatchet job. The words are supportive of his boss but the delivery is a condemnation. Maybe Neil Harris has his sights set on the Prime Ministership. I watch as Tina changes direction to place herself right in the Minister's path. He fields one other question then comes to a stop in front of Tina. I pretend to be the cameraman my pass says I am and point Tina's expensive video camera at Harris.

"Minister, I have a national security question," she says. He nods and smiles. "Is it true that a late, um... shall we say, *friend* of yours, stole some documents from your home office?" Her voice drips innuendo.

For a fraction of a second, he looks like he has been slapped in the face, but he recovers almost instantaneously. "I have no idea what you're talking about." He walks around her, increasing his speed.

Tina matches his pace, leans toward him and says quietly, "Certificates?"

His face has taken on a nasty snarl but I can see fear there too.

"No comment," he growls and walks quickly along the corridor.

Tina stops and lets him go.

"What was that about stolen documents?" Ian asks her.

"What did you whisper to him Tina?" another reporter asks.

She just smiles at them. "Check out my column in the Hound, gentlemen," she says and taking my arm she leads me towards the exit door.

Phase one is complete.

Now we just wait.

33

JEN

Tony Hille is a good boss. He listens to everything that I tell him about my trip to Vancouver, without interjecting either questions or comments. If I wasn't used to it, his unflinching stare would be unnerving but I know he's analyzing everything I say and probably spotting things I missed. As I agreed with Cal, I don't leave out anything except for Harvey's death. I just told him that Cal rescued me from the house while Harvey was out.

When I finish, he looks at the ceiling for what seems like a long time.

"This investigator, Rogan, how much do you trust him?"

"With my life," I say. "I checked him and his partner out, before I went to Vancouver. Rogan's a former addict and his partner has some baggage but I trust them completely."

He nods. "Have you got the USB drive with the end user certificates," he asks. I take it out of my purse, hand it over and watch him plug it into his computer. He looks at all the end user certificates, clicking between them. "All from different countries, all bound for Canada." I nod. He clicks some more. "All shipped by different companies, but all of them are registered in Vancouver. That's odd. Vancouver's hardly the shipping capital of the world." He clicks through a few more. "This is evidence of a multi-billion dollar gunrunning operation. Well done Jen." Tony rarely gives praise and even more rarely calls me Jen. It's almost always Jennifer. "I have to take this upstairs to the Director."

"Can you delay that?" I ask.

He raises an eyebrow. "Why?"

Here's where I hope his ambition and mine are aligned. "Neil Harris can't be doing this all by himself. There must be others in the government who are involved. Rogan's girl-friend is a reporter. She's going to put a scare into Harris and see what transpires. Rogan thinks he can find out who the other people involved in this are. If you take this to the Director now, he's going to have to tell his boss because a government Minister is involved. The Director's boss is the Minister of Public Safety and Emergency Preparedness and he's going to tell the Director to hand it over to the RCMP; it'll be out of our hands and they'll get all the kudos. If you can put off telling the Director for a day, two days tops, we might be able to have a lot more to go on."

I watch the wheels spinning in his mind. He has a tell when he's undecided. He kind of grips his teeth together causing his jaw muscles to pulse. He's doing it now. I know he's itching for a promotion. This could swing the scales for him.

The pulsing stops. He pulls the USB drive out of his computer and puts it in his pocket. All he says is, "End of day tomorrow, I take it upstairs."

"You won't regret it Tony."

I hope he won't.

I pray I won't.

34

CAL

December in Ottawa is way colder than the Vancouver version. Although I have several layers on under my leather jacket, we've walked a mere one hundred and fifty metres from our hotel and I'm freezing. Tina's arm is curled through mine as we walk along the Rideau Canal. It feels good. We come to our first destination. The area is still cordoned off but is surrounded by bunches of flowers in memory of the eleven victims of Canada's first terrorist bombing. There is still scaffolding around the Shaw Centre as they fix the damage caused by the blast which killed Annalise Lamarche. I wonder why the bomber chose this particular spot. Just a quick walk across the bridge and he could have detonated it in front of the Parliament Buildings.

We stand in silence for a while just looking and thinking.

Then Tina checks her watch. "It's lunchtime. Are you sure he's going to call?"

"Absolutely. He'll want to know what *you* know. I'll bet

money he's got people asking your buddy Ian who you are and how to get hold of you."

"Let's go have lunch. Seeing as you are giving me what may be the biggest story of my career as a journalist, I'm buying." She points across Colonel Bye Drive to the Westin Hotel. "There." She adds.

It's close and it's warm and it's expensive. How can I refuse.

———

AS SHE PAYS THE BILL, HER PHONE RINGS. "TINA JOHAL," SHE says. She looks at me and nods enthusiastically. "Yes Minister," she says. There is a pause. "Absolutely." Another pause. "I can't meet this evening, unfortunately. How about first thing tomorrow morning?" She listens for a while. "I'm afraid I can't sir." She smiles as she listens. "OK... Got it. Thank you, Minister. I look forward to meeting with you, too."

She hangs up. "Done," she smiles. "He didn't like that I wouldn't meet him later today—and I must say it went against all of my reporter's instincts to ask him to delay until tomorrow—but he agreed. I just hope he doesn't call back to try and rearrange it."

As if on cue, a phone rings, except this time it's mine. I wrestle it out of my pocket and take a look. "Hi Damien," I say.

"Hi Cal, you remember there was a folder called `Opdocs'? Well my guys managed to decrypt one of the documents in it. We used up a lot of computer cycles doing it, but it was worth it."

"What was in it? Can you email it to me?"

"I can't tell you what was in it and no, I can't email it to you.

This document is classified, I'd be breaking the law big time if I sent it to you. I emailed it to intelligence officer Halley via an encrypted email. I'll let her make the decision as to whether she wants to share it with you."

We say our goodbyes and hang up.

Then I call Jen.

———

THE CSIS BUILDING IS MODERN AND PURPOSE BUILT. I HAVE been through multiple layers of security, which have included me leaving my phone and the contents of my pockets with a security officer. Tina wasn't allowed in and is unhappily cooling her heels outside in the rental car. I left my Glock in the hotel; no way I'd get in here with that in my possession. Jen has even had me sign the Official Secrets Act.

Jen and I are in a secure conference room with Tony Hille, her boss. He seems like a good guy but I'm going to reserve judgement. She connects her laptop to a cable protruding from an enclosure in the centre of the table. Two clicks and the wall screen springs into life. There is a document displayed.

"Is this the document that Damien decrypted?"

Jen just nods but Tony adds, "He's a very talented guy. I've asked some of our people to try and decrypt those documents and they estimated it would take at least a week. He seems to have decrypted the first one in about twelve hours. I'm going to contact him and offer him a contract to try and decrypt the other documents; he should do very well out of it."

The document is headed 'SHIPMENT #17'.

It starts off with a list of military equipment. It looks familiar. "Weren't these weapons in one of the End User Certificates that Neil Harris signed?" I ask.

"Yes," Tony says. "The one for the Serbian weapons. The value is about thirty-seven million dollars Canadian."

Jen scrolls down the document, it reads,

SHIPPING AGENT: DKSY SHIPPING INC.

SHIPPING DATE: 2019-11-19

SHIP FROM: DUBROVNIK, CROATIA

SHIP VIA: S.S. ROSE OF BELGRADE

DELIVERY DATE: 2019-11-24

SHIP TO: BEIRUT, LEBANON

LANDED PRICE: $52,300,000 US

PAYMENT 1 RECEIVED: 2019-11-07 (50%)

PAYMENT 2 RECEIVED: 2019-11-27 (50%)

"You realize what this means, Cal," Tony says. "An End User Certificate, signed by the Canadian Minister of National Defence, was used so that someone could buy weapons, ship them to Beirut and make almost thirty million dollars profit."

"We can't be sure that he signed them," says Jen. "They could be forgeries."

Tony shakes his head. "Unlikely. The weapons manufacturer in Serbia would have to have had contact with senior officers in the Armed Forces and likely with the Minister himself. They wouldn't ship that quantity of weapons just based on paperwork."

I say, "When Tina asked Harris about documents stolen from his office, it was like a slap in the face. He knew what she was talking about."

"About that, Cal," Tony says, "I originally told Jennifer that I would give you some time to find out what you could from Neil Harris, but now I've seen this, I have to take it upstairs to the Director. I have an appointment with him in an hour. This is now an official CSIS investigation. I wanted to show you this document so that you would understand what I am about to say. I really appreciate you and your girl-friend's help but you have to back off now. Go back to Vancouver and leave it to us to deal with. I can't order you to do that, but if you do anything more about this issue, you will be putting yourself, and possibly her, in legal jeopardy and I *will* take action against you." He stands up, shakes my hand and leaves.

"Sorry, Cal," Jen says. "I know you wanted to help us but it's out of my hands now."

"No prob, Jen," I lie. "Glad we could help."

"I'll walk you out," she says. We take off along the corri-dor. "You can tell your buddy Damien thanks for the flight in his jet. He can probably expect some lucrative contracts from us if he can decrypt documents that fast."

"I will." When we get to the elevator, I ask her, "Who in Lebanon can afford to buy fifty-two million dollars worth of weapons?"

"Good question. No one. My guess is that the weapons were paid for by Iran but are being shipped to Hezbollah in Lebanon. They'll use them to attack Israel and maybe share them with their Hamas buddies in Palestine."

The words trigger a memory.

I can't wait to get my phone back. I need to make a call to Vancouver, fast.

———

"He told us to what?" Tina says, incredulous. "Clearly he doesn't know me very well, does he? No government dweeb tells Tina Johal to back off. *We*—well actually, *you* —uncovered this story and *we're* going to see it through, right?"

I know why I love this woman: she thinks like I do. Wow, second time I've used the L word. I suddenly have a strong desire to say it out loud. I look at her and smile.

"Right, Cal?" she repeats.

"Right." Now's not the time. Instead, while she drives, I tell her about the meeting and only when I've finished do I realize, with only the slightest twinge of conscience, that I've just broken the Official Secrets Act which I signed less than an hour ago.

I pull out my phone and dial. It's seven-thirty in Vancouver, he'll be awake now for sure. I reach forward to turn down the volume of the radio which is tuned in to CBC News.

"Hi Cal," Steve says. There's the usual wariness in his voice. *"How's Nick?"*

"He's much better, Steve."

"Good, tell him the whole Department's thinking about him."

"I will. Listen, Steve, I'm following up a case and I'm in Ottawa. You remember when Nick was in David Fox's house pretending to do the gun deal with him? It all went to hell in a hand basket when Nick said he was buying guns for Hamas. David Fox called him out on it; he said he knew who bought guns for Hamas and it wasn't Nick."

"Sure.Twenty seconds later we were knocking down his doors."

"You've still got Fox's man in custody eh?"

"Sure do."

First comes the big lie. "The case I'm working on turns out to have some national security aspects and I'm working with CSIS on it." Now comes the big ask. "Could you do something for me? Could you find out if Fox's guy knows anything about anyone involved in buying weapons for Hamas. I'd really appreciate anything he knows. Tell him that anything he tells you will help lessen his sentence; anything to get him to talk."

He's silent.

"It's really important, man," I add.

"You're a lucky bastard, Cal Rogan. I've got some questions for him. I'm going in to see him this morning. I'll be with him in about an hour. I'll see what I can find out."

"You're a star, Steve. Thanks."

"Sure, sure. I'll call you later, OK."

He hangs up.

Tony Hille's decision to talk to his boss in an hour has forced a change of plan.

Time for me to drive while Tina makes a call.

———

"WHO THE HELL IS THIS?" NEIL HARRIS INCLINES HIS HEAD IN my direction.

"He's my driver and my video guy. Just pretend he's not here," says Tina.

He digests that for a moment. "Ok. Please sit down."

She does as he asks. I don't. Instead, I stand by the door surveying his office. It's not as plush as I would have imagined the office of a federal cabinet minister to be.

"Ms. Johal, I agreed to see you to clear up a misunderstanding you seem to have that—"

She interrupts. "Minister, let's cut to the chase shall we? You were having an affair with one of your employees." His eyes go wide. He ain't seen nothing yet. "She saw some documents on your computer, documents she copied and sent to her brother in Vancouver; documents so important that he was killed in an effort to retrieve them." He takes a breath and is about to say something but Tina holds up her finger and his mouth snaps closed. "Among other things, there were a large number of End User Certificates signed by you. I'm giving you a chance to get in front of this before I go to press and publish what I know."

To give him credit, he recovers from the initial shock very fast.

"I have to congratulate you," he says. "Your investigative skills are excellent. However your conclusions are wide of the mark. I did indeed sign a number of End User Certificates but in a very good cause. I can't yet share it with you for a number of reasons, national security being one of them. However, I can certainly promise you a scoop if you can hold off publishing for a couple of days."

"A couple of days is a long time in the news business, Minister. My competitors can move fast. When I talked to you this morning, CBC and the Globe and Mail were hovering around. I'll need more than the promise of a scoop."

This is it. Either we'll get what we want or we might as well go back to Vancouver.

"Seems like we're in a Mexican stand-off," he says.

"Yes," Tina agrees. "Maybe if you could give me a little more information, I could maybe hold off going to press."

He smiles. "Perhaps we could talk somewhere else, somewhere private but away from the office." He purses his lips for a moment... then makes his decision. He takes a Post-It note from his desk and scribbles on it then hands it to her. "Come to my townhouse, both of you, at six this evening. We can talk this over and come to an accommodation beneficial to both sides."

Bingo!

"Thank you Minister and maybe we can also talk about another very incriminating document. One about a specific shipment. Number seventeen, I think."

This time he has a real struggle to keep it together.

35

NICK

When I see her face, tears start to well up. I've got to get a hold of myself. There's a small Band Aid on her face, smaller than I expected. That's good. Then she's right beside the bed and putting her arms around me. I just hug her even though it makes the pains in my gut go through the roof. "Thank God you're alright, Luce," I whisper in her ear as I feel the tears running down my cheeks. So much for getting hold of myself, still, who cares? Over Lucy's shoulder I see Adry smiling. She's going to remind me of these tears sometime and I'm betting she's going to do it in front of Rogan. I just hug Lucy until the pain gets too bad. Lucy pulls back and kisses me on the cheek.

Adry pulls over a couple of chairs.

"I don't know how I can ever thank you," I tell her.

"I just did what you told me. I just wish I could have got there with the cops a little earlier, before he slashed at Lucy."

"It's no prob," Lucy chimes in. "When he pulled back his hand holding the knife, I knew he was going to slash at my throat, so I just rolled over fast and his knife only made a tiny nick on my cheek. I rolled right off the bed and then slid myself under it. The sirens from the cops' car were getting loud and I knew he wouldn't try and get to me under the bed, he couldn't waste the time. He just ran off. Next thing I knew, the cops were in Cal's apartment and I was safe. All thanks to Adry." She reaches over and gives Adry's arm a squeeze.

"I didn't know it at the time," Adry says, "But when you described him to the cops, I realized it was the hot guy I saw leaving the building just before the cops arrived.

"Yes, the cops got us both doing pictures of him using their computers, then we compared them and finally came up with a pretty good likeness."

"How bad's the scar on your cheek?" I ask. Lucy gets her good looks from Brenda. I don't want to see her lovely face ruined.

"It's nothing. The cops made a big fuss and took me to VGH but the doctor didn't even need to give me stitches and he said he didn't think there would be much of a scar at all."

"Did the police have any idea who he might be?" I ask.

"No, they said they were going to get their computers to try and identify the guy using facial recognition."

"They won't find a match. The guy's not a criminal. His mugshot's not going to be in the system."

"You're probably right. I think he was a soldier," Lucy says.

"I think so too," says Adry. "When he came out of Cal's apartment building, there was something in the way he walked that made me think that."

Adry's got good instincts, cop instincts, she's probably right.

"What made you think he was a soldier, Luce?" I ask.

"I was in the apartment and I'd just got into bed when suddenly the bedroom door opened and he was there. He told me to keep completely quiet or he'd kill me."

"There's your first mistake," I say. "When someone like that tells you to do something, *always* do the opposite. If he says be quiet, you scream; if he tells you stay where you are, you run."

"I'll remember that next time I see him," she says with a grin. "Anyway, he wanted to know where Cal was. I told him Cal was staying with his girlfriend and that I didn't know where that was. He thought about that for a bit then he called someone on his cell and he asked to speak to 'the General'. Then when the guy came on the line he called him 'sir'. That's what made me think he was a soldier."

"What did he say to this general?" Adry asks.

"He said Cal wasn't there and what should he do now. Then my phone rang and it was you Adry."

She tells me about the phone call with Adry and how she told her there was a problem by calling her Kate. That's my girl, smart as a whip. It's nice to have her around. I wonder if I can persuade her to move out here. Mrs. V has another bedroom in the house, maybe Lucy could—

Adry breaks into my thoughts. "If he *is* a soldier, his picture will be in a government database somewhere. I batted my eyes at the cop who did the composite sketch thing and asked him to print me off a copy. I'm going to do a high-resolution scan of it and send it to Jen; maybe she can feed it into her computer and find out who he is." Jeez, I'm in a room with *two* women who are as smart as whips.

If Jen can put a name to the soldier who tried to kill my little girl, we may have another clue as to what the hell is going on. My gut tells me this general may be another piece of the puzzle. I wonder who the hell he is.

36

CAL

We have some time to kill until our meeting with Neil Harris. We've already killed a very pleasant hour back at the Chateau Laurier, our hotel. Now for another, but different, pleasant time. As I wait for the connection, I run through in my head my plans for tonight's meeting; the Minister of National Defence is going to be in for a big surprise!

FaceTime connects. *"Hey, Dad. You're early. Well actually, you're late. You were supposed to call me on Sunday, so you're two days late."*

That means today's Tuesday. The last few days have been a blur. "I'm sorry about that sweetie, on Sunday I was..." I have to think it through. "I was saving a friend from a killer and yesterday, I flew in a private jet."

"A private jet. That is so sick!" I grimace at her use of the word 'sick' to mean cool. But I guess language evolves, even if I don't like it. Her face is lit up. *"And you saved your friend too. Who was the killer? Did you put him in jail?"*

"He used to be a policeman, he killed someone I knew." I

avoid answering the second question. I am *not* going to tell her about the demise of Harvey Clegg.

"I'm sorry about your friend Daddy, the one he killed, was he — Wait a minute. Where did you go in the private jet?"

"Ottawa."

"Ottawa?!" She screams. *"That's in Ontario. We're in the same province. Why don't you drive over here?"*

"Ottawa's four hundred and fifty kilometres from Toronto, sweetie, it takes over four hours to drive. But when I've finished my work here, I'll ask Mommy if it's OK for me to start our Christmas visit a few days early."

Sick!" she grins. Then a new idea sprouts from her fertile mind. *"Ottawa's where they had the bombing. While you're there, maybe you could find the bad man who did it."*

That's way above my pay grade. Through my chuckle, I say, "I don't think that's going to happen. The man who did it was blown up in the explosion."

"Oh... Why?"

I take refuge in a parental favourite. "It's complicated, sweetie." Time to change the subject. "How's your boyfriend Ethan?"

"He's NOT my boyfriend. He's a boy who's a friend, OK? But you'll never guess what he did today."

Her happy prattle soothes me and I just bask in it. I look over at Tina and she has a broad ginger-cat smile. She and Ellie are going to love each other.

And I am abruptly aware of how important that is to me.

———

OTTAWA IS STRANGE IN SOME WAYS: ON A DRIVE THROUGH THE city, the view often changes several times from beautiful to ugly and back again to beautiful. Right now we are in a beautiful part. Neil Harris' Ottawa abode is three floors high and wider than your average townhouse. In Vancouver it would cost a couple of million.

"Are you sure you want to go through with this?" I say.

"Absolutely."

"We end up in jail if things go wrong," I remind her.

"Bring it on!"

I lean over and kiss her before we get out of the car. I pull the canvas bag from the back seat and we cross the street.

The front doors of the townhouses are all painted in different, bright colours. Harris' door is lime green. It harks back to a memory of Roy; he used to sing a song from his youth called *Behind the Green Door*. One of the lines of the song was: *Green door, what's that secret you're keepin'*. Hopefully I'm going to find out.

We go through the gate, take the four steps up and Tina stretches out her hand towards the bell.

I grab it just in time and pull it back.

She frowns and is about to speak when she sees the look on my face. I put my index finger to my lips and nod my head towards the door. She follows my line of sight and sees it.

The door is ajar.

I gently push it open.

The entryway is in darkness.

I step inside.

It's eerily quiet.

I run my hand along the wall until I find the light switch. When I press it nothing happens. I slide my hand further. There are three switches on the switch plate; I press the other two.

Nothing.

Signalling Tina to stay where she is, I take two steps further. "Minister," I call.

More nothing.

As my eyes become accustomed to the dark, I see that there are three doors leading off the entranceway. One is open. I put the bag on the floor, step through and inch forward, rubbing my hand along the wall as I feel for a light switch. I don't feel one. I feel some more.

Stop!

Some primitive sense clicks in and I leap backwards.

Inches from my nose, I see a blur and feel the rush of air. There is a clunk at floor level and I feel the vibration through my feet. Whoever attacked is behind the door. With every ounce of muscle I can muster, I explode my whole body into the door and am rewarded with an "Ooof!" from the other side.

I pivot and slam the door closed. He's silhouetted in the light from a side window. I see what looks like a baseball bat on it's upswing. I step in close, grab his lapels, arch my back then propel my head forward into his face.

His groan is followed by the clatter of the bat on the hardwood floor. Still holding on to him, my leg jerks upward and I get an exhalation of breath in my face as my knee connects, right on target.

I step back and bring an elbow down hard on the crown of his descending head.

His body hits the floor with a satisfying thump and I suppress a yell at the pain in my elbow.

Two and a half seconds of action and I am gulping air into my lungs. Time to start using that gym membership, Rogan.

Then the thought hits: maybe he has a partner.

Tina!

I turn and open the door. I find myself looking into the barrel of a gun.

I freeze.

37

DAMIEN

There are three of them. That in itself is strange. Two of them look like veteran officers and the third guy looks more like he works for me. I make a point of checking the credentials of all three. I've seen enough of them to know that if these are not genuine, they're excellent forgeries. Normally, I would welcome the appearance of members of the Royal Canadian Mounted Police. I would love to have them as a client. However, clients don't show up without an appointment. I have an uncomfortable feeling that I know why they are here.

I address the oldest one. His credentials identified him as a Superintendent. That's a very high rank to just drop in for a visit. He's the number one guy here. "How can I help the RCMP?" I ask him.

He looks at his number two and nods.

Number two says, "I believe that you have in your possession some documents that are the property of the federal government." His voice sounds like the voice of a life-long smoker.

"Of course we do. We do a lot of government business."

"These particular documents were not given to you by someone from the federal government. They were given to you by a private detective named Cal Rogan."

I was right. "That's correct."

"Those documents are classified sir. Your possession of them is a possible violation of the Official Secrets Act."

"I have them on the authority of Jennifer Halley an intelligence officer with CSIS." For a second I get a horrible feeling. I only have her's and Cal's word that she is actually a CSIS intelligence officer. If she's a fraud, I've just put my entire business in jeopardy.

"Intelligence officer Halley overstepped her authority. We have been ordered to retrieve all copies of the documents and ensure that you delete all copies from your systems and from any backups you've made. Will you now comply with that request?"

It's couched as a request, but it's not a request.

"Yes, of course."

Number two nods at number three.

Number three points to a laptop at the end of the conference table. "Can you access your servers from here?" His voice is a high-pitched counterpoint to his colleague's rasp.

I nod.

We sit at the end of the conference table and I log on. He makes a big point of looking away when I enter my password. He hands me a USB drive. "Please copy the files onto here." I do as he requests. "There's a script on the drive, I want you to use it to delete the documents." I look at the script. Smart. We both know deletion doesn't actually delete the files. This script will scrub the files and any copies from the server. Again I do as he asks. "Now let's access the backups and do the same there." This takes a little longer.

When I have finished he takes the USB drive, stands up and nods to number two.

Number two takes a sheet of paper from his briefcase and slides it across the table. It is a document confirming that, under pain of prosecution, I swear I have no other copies of the documents. I read it, sign it and slide it back. It's returned to number two's briefcase.

Number two looks to number one.

Number one speaks. "Thank you Mr. Crotty. Your co-operation has been noted." He shakes my hand. He's a bone crusher. I try not to wince.

I see them out and go back to my office.

As I sit down, my screen pops into life. There is a message box. *No more valid files.* The program that was attempting to decrypt the files has finished running. Deleting the files will do that. I click the *OK* button. Another box appears. *Thirty-three files attempted, two files decrypted.* Two files! During the time I stepped out of my office and the time I destroyed the files, the program decrypted a second file.

I am transported back to my time at Harvard. I remember taking a moral philosophy class; Professor Sandel frequently asked us to evaluate a moral dilemma. Now I have a real live one of my own.

Look at the decrypted file or delete it?

And if I look at it, what then?

38

CAL

The barrel of the gun is unwavering. It is not in the hands of an amateur. "Point the gun at the ground, Tina," I say quietly. She does so and as she releases the trigger, I hear the click as the safeties reengage. My exhalation is distinctly audible.

She removes the magazine, ejects the chambered round, puts it back in the magazine and returns magazine and Glock to the canvas bag.

"Where did you learn to do that?"

She grins. "I did my Masters in Chicago, which is *not* the safest city in the world. I decided to make use of my second amendment rights and bought a handgun. But I made sure that I had a ton of hours of training and time on the range before I bought it."

I gather my thoughts. "Do you know what a circuit-breaker box looks like?"

"That's a bit of a sexist remark, Mr. Rogan. But yes."

I take the flashlight out of the bag and hand it to her. "Find it and turn the lights back on."

I take the duct tape out. We were going to use it to

immobilize Neil Harris. I take it into the darkened room. My erstwhile assailant is still on the floor. For the first time I notice he's wearing a Fed-Ex uniform; it makes sense, everyone opens the door for a Fed-ex delivery. By the time I have him trussed like the Christmas turkey, the lights come on.

The room is a study.

It has one wall full of bookshelves, another wall full of trophy photos of Neil Harris in various prestige-boosting situations, a messy but expensive-looking antique desk, a computer with three screens... and a dead body on the floor.

I crouch beside the body. He has been beaten to death, probably with the baseball bat that is now lying by the door. Echoes of Denis Lamarche, a.k.a. Wily. But this time the face is recognizable as Neil Harris, Minister of National Defence.

"Is that who I think it is?" Tina says from behind me.

I nod.

"The best laid plans..." she says.

"Indeed. Neil Harris is the only person we know who was involved in this major-league, gun-running scheme."

"Now what do we do?"

"Call the police, I guess."

"Maybe we should call Jen," she says.

"Yes, you're probably right."

I call her and tell her to get over here right away. She is not a happy camper.

I stand up from my crouching position beside the body and look at the desk. In my mind's eye, I see Annalise Lamarche creeping in here, looking for something to relieve her headache, but disturbing the mouse and seeing the documents that got her brother killed. I remember something she said in her letter to Denis. Something about how

Harris was lax about passwords. Maybe all is not lost with Harris' death.

I sit down behind the desk and jiggle the mouse. The screen springs into life. Harris clearly didn't learn his lesson. Even the operating system is an outdated version of Windows. There are two apps open. One is the file system. I click around but he has hundreds of folders and documents; it would take an age to go through them all. I silently curse myself. I should have brought a USB drive to copy his files. Maybe he has one. I pull open the desk drawers; they are full of the usual detritus of an office desk, including the Tylenol Annalise was looking for. There's lots of stuff but no USB drive.

I look back at the screen. Maybe I should open WORD and see if he has any recent documents that might be of interest. The other app already open is a conference call program. I click on it then click 'File'. As I move the cursor down to the 'Close', it passes over 'Recent'. I click it; one of the options is 'The Ruling Group'. That is one mother of a conference group name. I click on it. Three windows open, accompanied by an irritating pinging. All three are blank. The pinging continues and suddenly the middle window goes grey for a second, then shows the face of a man. "Is it do—" For an instant there's fear in his face. "Who the *hell* are you?" he snarls. He stares into my eyes. Then there's what looks like the dawning of a bad dream. The window goes blank.

If I can just put a name to the face I saw for three seconds, we may have another piece of the puzzle.

———

I OPEN THE DOOR. JEN PUSHES PAST ME INTO THE entranceway and looks around furtively. "What the hell do you think you're doing in the house of a government minister?" she says in a loud whisper. "Tony told you to leave this alone and go back to Vancouver. Are you crazy? You could be in serious trouble here."

"No need to whisper," I say. "But you do need to see this." I walk into the study and she follows. I point to the body.

"What the f—" Her expletive is deleted as she sees the assailant. He's awake now and silenced with tape across his mouth.

"Victim, murderer and murder weapon." I can't keep the smugness out of my voice.

"The perfect trifecta," Tina adds.

Jen is silent for a long time. Finally, "What exactly happened here?"

I tell her in detail up to the part about the man on the conference call screen. I have a raw, pulling sensation in my gut. It's my 'keep quiet' feeling. Something is telling me not to share this with Jen. So, for better or for worse, I don't. "That's about it." I look across at Tina. The question is in her face but she gets it and says nothing.

Silence again from Jen. Then, "Tony took this up to the Director, Markus Heath. Markus told him that the RCMP already has an investigation going into Neil Harris and that we were to back off. Somehow, I'm going to have to explain what I'm doing here. Anyway, I need you two to leave, I don't need to complicate matters by having to explain your presence. And *please*... go back to Vancouver."

———

"WHY DIDN'T YOU TELL JEN ABOUT THE GUY ON THE conference call?" Tina asks, as soon as we are back in the rental car. There's excitement in her voice.

"Dunno. Something in my gut."

"Who d'you think he was?" she says, as she starts the car.

"I have no idea. He looked like... a... well... like a take-charge kind of guy."

"OK, good, that cuts down the field to like about a million Canadians," she chuckles.

"I don't even know if he was Canadian."

"Great, one in ten million. So where do we go from here?"

"I don't have a clue. Harris was our only real lead. With him gone we are just about nowhere. Maybe we should do as we're told and go back home."

"Or maybe we should go back to the hotel and commiserate with each other. Nudge, nudge."

Despite my frustration I can't help laughing.

I lean across to kiss her cheek and my phone rings.

"Hey Steve."

"Hi Cal. I talked to David Fox's guy. Turns out the guys who are supplying arms to Hamas were big-time rivals of Fox and his gang. Fox's guy was only too willing to give up a name. The only person whose name he knew was an Iranian living in Ottawa, his name's Majid Zarin." He spells the name for me. *"I'm sure your CSIS friends will have a file on him."*

"Thanks so much Steve, you're a star."

We're Canadian, so we do the polite stuff and I hang up.

If David Fox's guy is telling the truth and this Majid Zarin is the one buying arms for Hamas, using the End User Certificates signed by Neil Harris, I should really hand it over to Jen for her to pass on to her RCMP buddies. But it still rankles that both she and her boss told us, in no uncertain terms, that we're off the case and should go back to Vancouver.

I turn to Tina.

"We're back in business."

She takes one hand off the wheel and fist bumps me. "So... celebrate rather than commiserate," she says with a big grin.

"I love you." It's out before I can stop it.

She hits the brakes and pulls the car over to the side of the road.

Her eyes are fixed on the road ahead, her hands gripped tight on the wheel. One Mississippi, two Mississippi, three Missi— She turns and drowns me in her huge, brown eyes.

"I love you too."

Wednesday

Email. The curse of the working classes. I have fifty-five new ones since Cal called me out of the office at six yesterday evening. I kind of miss having his brain on the team but Tony was adamant: orders from above. I scan through the email subject lines. I deal with all the urgent ones and then spot one from Adry. I must have missed it yesterday. That reminds me I've got to dry clean the clothes she lent me and send them back to her with a nice thank-you present. I open it.

Hi Jen, we had some excitement after you left. Someone tried to kill Nick. Nick shot him but he got away. Nick is indestructible. :) Also someone went to Cal's apartment looking for him. We think he might be a soldier. I have attached one of those computer images of his face, could you use your fancy-shmancy face recognition software to find out who he is? Hope to see you soon, Adry.

Hmm. Sorry Adry, no can do. All my searches are logged and I've been told to lay off this whole Neil Harris investigation and anything to do with it. The Director told Tony that it was all being handled by the RCMP. When I called the Mounties to Neil Harris' townhouse last night they sent Inspector Saunders, I'll forward the email to him. He's a good guy, I've worked with him before; he can do the searches and I'll ask him to let me know the result.

I double-click on the image file and a face appears on my screen. The shock sends a bolt of electricity down my spine. It's a face I know. It's the guy who killed Neil Harris. I check the RCMP directory and dial. It's seven in the morning but I'm sure he'll be on duty. He answers on the first ring, *"Saunders."*

"Hi Clive, it's Jen Halley over at CSIS. The man you took into custody at Neil Harris' house, do you know who he is yet?"

"Hi Jen. He's keeping his mouth tight shut. He won't say a word to anyone. But we did get him to open his mouth long enough to put in a swab. DNA says he's former Staff Sergeant Anton Wills of the Special Operations Regiment. He served in Afghanistan and Iraq and was honourably discharged in two thousand seventeen. Why?"

"He was in Vancouver yesterday, we think trying to assassinate Cal Rogan."

"Who?"

"The private investigator who discovered the End User Certificates that Harris signed."

"What End User Certificates?"

WHAT?!

"Aren't you part of the team investigating Harris' possible involvement with an illegal arms sales scheme?" I ask.

"No. I'm just investigating his murder."

Unbe-friggin'-lievable!

"Listen Clive, you guys have got a serious case of one

hand not knowing what the other hand's doing. You need to talk to your bosses so you can co-ordinate with the team on the arms sales investigation."

"Thanks Jen. I'll check it out. I owe you one..." His voice is the voice of a confused man. *"I think."*

Jeez. And I thought *we* were the secretive department.

So Adry was right; he is, or rather was, a soldier. I reread her email. He tried to kill Nick, got shot, then went after Cal. I need to talk to Adry. It's just after four in the morning in Vancouver but can't be helped.

She answers on the fifth ring. *"Hi, Jen. Don't they teach you about timezones in CSIS?"*

"Sorry about that, but this is important. I just saw your email. You were right. He was a soldier. Did you say that he tried to kill Nick, got shot, then went after Cal?"

"No. It must have been two guys. One guy tried to kill Nick at around eleven at night, Nick shot him but he got away. So Nick called me immediately and I went over to Cal's house and I saw the other guy just leaving."

"I think you need to tell me the whole story."

When she's given me all the details, one question stands out in bold print. Who the hell is this general that the would-be assassin, former Staff Sergeant Anton Wills, spoke to?

I have some research to do.

40

CAL

I watch mesmerized, still revelling in the warm glow of new love. One lock of curly, black hair caresses her forehead as her fingers fly over the keyboard. "OK, this is him," she says, swivelling the laptop towards me. A handsome, slightly overweight man in an immaculate, blue, pin-stripe suit smiles out of the screen at me. "Majid Zarin, commercial attaché at the Iranian embassy. I thought the name rang a bell."

So, according to David Fox's thug, this is the man who supplies weapons to Hamas. And according to Jen, the arms shipment to Lebanon, detailed in that *Shipment #17* document, was almost certainly bound for Hezbollah and probably Hamas too.

With Harris dead, Majid Zarin is our only lead to uncovering the reason that Denis Lamarche was beaten to death and to find out who's trying to illegally sell arms to terrorists.

"How did the name ring a bell?" I ask.

"I wrote an article about a Canadian company which

was trying to circumvent the Iranian trade embargo. Zarin's name came up when I was researching it," she says

"We need to interrogate him," I say.

Tina laughs. "You're joking," she says. "He's the trade representative of a sovereign state, he's covered by diplomatic immunity."

"Yes, but we're not police or RCMP. We're not constrained by legalities."

"So how do you plan to interrogate him? Kidnap him off the street and tie him up in our hotel room?"

"No. He has to come to us."

"But how?"

Good question.

And I might just have the answer.

———

The Iranian embassy is an unattractive red-brick building on Metcalfe Street a few blocks from City Hall. We are sitting in our rental car just around the corner. I'm in the driver's seat and she is in the back. We have rehearsed this over and over again and Tina is ready for the live performance. She takes a deep breath and dials her phone.

I'm holding my breath.

"Good morning," she says in her brightest voice. "This is Tina Johal from Daily News Hound dot com. I'd like to speak with Commercial Attaché Zarin, please."

A brief wait then, "May I speak with him please." She listens intently for a while. "Yes. Please tell him it's about the shipment from Dubrovnik to Beirut... Yes... Certainly, I'll wait." She gives me a big, excited thumbs up. We wait... and wait. I reach behind my seat and hold her hand. She squeezes tightly. Then, "Mr. Zarin, thanks for taking my call." She listens for a moment and then interrupts. "No, you listen to me. Here's what you need to do. I am sitting in a maroon Chevrolet on Somerset, one block from the embassy. If you are not sitting in the back seat of this car in two minutes from now, I am going to press 'Send' on my computer and the story of how you conspired, with Neil Harris and others in the Canadian government, to ship weapons to Hezbollah and Hamas, will be all over the Internet. Do you understand?... Good. One hundred and twenty seconds, starting now. One... two... three..." She hangs up.

I watch the rearview mirror intently and put the car in Drive. If more than one person comes running around that corner and heads for the car, we are out of here. A woman pushing a stroller with a baby in a bright blue winter jacket... A teenager, with hair dyed orange, on a skateboard... A man with flowing dark hair and an expensive Burberry: Zarin. And he's alone.

I put it in Park, get out and, like a good chauffeur, walk around the back of the car and open the back door for him. When he's inside I walk back and, as I get into the driver's seat, I catch the tail end of his sentence. "... all about?"

I pull away from the curb.

"As I told you on the phone," Tina replies, "I have docum—"

"Ms. Johal," he snaps. "I came to speak to you as a courtesy." His accent is high-class British, probably acquired at Oxford or Cambridge. "If you say you have documents linking me to these arms shipments you speak of, I would like to see them." He seems very confident. Yet here he is, sitting in our car. Why? I check the rearview mirror. There is a black Mercedes behind us. I turn left, it follows.

Tina says, "I'm not prepared to show them just yet but I will tell you what I have. One: an End User Certificate signed by Neil Harris the Minister of National Defence for armaments from a Serbian manufacturer. Two: a shipping document that details a shipment of those same armaments sailing from Dubrovnik, Croatia to Beruit, Lebanon, with your name as the payer of the fifty-two million, three hundred thousand US dollars price." She smoothly slips in the lie about his name being on the document together with the truth of the precise dollar amount. I check the rearview. He's wearing his best poker face but he's weighing options. I take a right turn and the Mercedes follows.

"Ms. Johal," he continues in his refined English accent, "as I'm sure you know, my first name, Majid, is a very common first name in my country and the middle east in general. The same can be said of my last name. I am willing to bet that there are, quite literally, hundreds of Majid Zarins in the middle east. If you even think of publishing anything so inflammatory, you will find yourself and your publication in court," he pauses and fixes his stare on her, "*or worse... and very quickly.*" His emphasis is a not-so-veiled threat. "Driver, stop the car now." I continue down the block and turn right. The Mercedes follows. "I said... Stop. The. Car."

I look at Tina in the mirror. She nods. I hit the brakes and stop in the middle of the road. The Mercedes almost smashes into the back of us. Zarin, sits in his seat, waiting. In the side mirror, I see the driver get out of the Mercedes. His face is vaguely familiar. He walks forward and slips between the cars.

I open my door as he opens Zarin's.

Zarin and I exit the car in unison.

I look across the roof of the car at Zarin's driver.

He glances at me.

I'm looking at a dead man.

41

JEN

There are over a hundred generals in the Canadian Armed forces. Who knew? On top of that, there are hundreds of retired generals, any one of whom could be the one I'm looking for. However, Harris' killer Staff Sergeant Anton Wills was in the Special Operations Regiment and there are only a handful of generals who have had any association with Spec Ops, so I guess that's a place to start. I print off their pictures. As I scroll through the other files, I get a depressing feeling that this is a lost cause. Also it's a cause I have specifically been told not to pursue.

Saved by the bell! I pick up my phone; it's Clive. *"Hi Jen. You said there was an RCMP team looking into Neil Harris and some End User Certificates?"*

"Yes. The Director told my boss to back off our investigation because you guys were handling it."

"I think you must have got it wrong. No one here knows anything about it."

"Are you sure?"

"Absolutely." He chuckles. *"Maybe it's not our left hand not knowing what the right one is doing."*

My head feels like it's spinning out of control. I was sure Tony told me to back off because the Mounties were on the case. Feeling like a complete idiot, I mumble, "Sorry, I guess I must have got it wrong. I'll go ask my boss again."

I put down the phone.

What the *hell* is going on?

I look at the faces of the Generals, current and retired, all of whom had Special Operations responsibilities. There are seven of them. I lay out their pictures on my desk. I pick up the picture of the ex-SO guy who killed Neil Harris. "Which one of these generals do you work for soldier?" I ask him in a whisper. He just stares up at me. "Who sent you and your buddy to try to kill Cal and Nick, then called you back to Ottawa to kill Neil Harris? And Nick shot your buddy didn't he, probably wounded him badly. I wonder how—"

I log into the airline systems and do a search. Air Canada... No. WestJet... No. No record of Anton Wills flying from Vancouver to Ottawa. So how did he get here? I don't suppose he had a friend with a corporate jet... but maybe...

I grab my phone and dial my liaison at the RCAF. After the polite stuff, I ask him, "I need to know details of all military flights that departed Vancouver for Ottawa between midnight on Monday and midday on Tuesday. Can you give those to me?"

I wait. I can hear him tapping away at a keyboard.

"There was only one in that timeframe. A Challenger flew from Uplands to Abbotsford which is just outside of Vancouver. It arrived at oh four-twenty Vancouver time, then left at oh five-thirty and returned to Uplands at thirteen thirty-five EST."

One thirty-five. That would have given him enough time. "Do you have a passenger manifest?"

More keyboard taps then. *"Hmm. Interesting. It's classified. If you want it, I'd need an official request."*

"Do you know who authorized the flight?"

"No. You'd need to contact Four-twelve Transport Squadron for that."

"Thanks. You're the best!" I tell him.

"The Royal Canadian Air Force is ever at your service." I can almost see the grin on his face. I imagine his face. He's cute.

Within minutes, I am on the phone to a Captain at Four-twelve. He is a lot less helpful. The words 'I can't tell you that on grounds of national security' come up three times during the ninety seconds of the call.

I need to escalate this.

———

MY PHONE RINGS JUST AS I'M ABOUT TO WALK INTO TONY'S office. It's Cal. Clearly he's not in a plane back to Vancouver. My irritation fights with my curiosity. Curiosity wins. "Hi... Listen, you were told not to follow this up; you were told, or asked anyway, to go back to Vancouver... Who?... What do you mean you can't tell me?...You'll only tell me in person?... OK, OK, I'll meet you there at, around eleven-thirty." OMG he won't leave it alone.

If Tony thinks Cal's still involved he'll have a cow.

I knock and enter.

"Hi Jennifer, grab a seat," he says.

"Something's come up and I need your help," I say. He nods. "I know you told me to lay off the Neil Harris thing." He nods again but this time there is a look on his face that doesn't bode well for me. "Well, a couple of things have come to light that I need to talk to you about."

"They'd better be earth shattering or..." He leaves the sentence hanging, like a condemned man.

However, he listens with neither comment nor expression, while I tell him about Adry's email and the details of my conversations with her, the RCMP and the RCAF.

When I finish, he rubs his chin like he's stroking a beard. Seconds pass and I know better than to interrupt his train of thought. I watch him as he thinks through all the ramifications. I can see why he got promoted to his current position; in addition to the fact that he has a razor-sharp mind, he exudes an air of confidence and authority. Finally he nods, slowly at first, then faster.

"OK, that's earth shattering enough." he says and I breathe a silent sigh of relief. "I need to talk to the Director again and I might need you to join us. Don't leave the building."

So much for going to see Cal.

———

IT TOOK THE BEST PART OF AN HOUR BUT I GOT THE summons. The Director's office is on the corner of the floor and has a bleak view of the mantle of early-winter snow dusting the Pineview Golf Course. It's so much prettier in summer.

"Firstly, Jen," the Director says. "I want to thank you for bringing this to our attention. Your work on this has been excellent, especially your discovery that there is a Canadian Forces general implicated in this armaments affair. However, you have touched upon an issue that is of the highest security. For that reason, Tony and I have agreed that you will drop all your other work and report directly to me on this case."

Wow. Working with the Director will give a huge boost to my career. "Thank you sir," I say.

"If we are going to work closely together, I think you'd better call me Markus," he smiles.

"OK, I'll leave you to it," says Tony rising. "Well done Jennifer." He pats me awkwardly on the shoulder and leaves.

As soon as the door closes behind him, Markus speaks. "What I'm going to tell you is highly confidential and is not to be talked about outside of this room; not even Tony has been briefed on this. We have known for some time that Neil Harris was involved in some illicit arms deals. But we knew he wasn't the only one. There is a cabal of senior government officials involved and we need to find out who they are. We knew someone in the Army must have been in on it and it looks like this general that you've discovered is the one. We are fairly sure that there is also a senior member of the RCMP involved, so the Minister has given me the responsibility for the investigation. I'm afraid your conversation with Inspector Saunders and his subsequent inquiries may have alerted the cabal."

"I am so sorry, sir, uh, Markus. I should never have contacted him."

"Don't sweat it. It was partially my fault, I told Tony to take you off the case and told him that it was in RCMP hands. Anyway, maybe it's good that you made that call. Maybe it will shake up the cabal and they may do something rash and expose themselves. I have my own mole in the RCMP attempting to unearth who is the bad apple over there and I want you to find out who the hell this general is. If we have these two key members identified we can take action."

"So far, I have a short list of seven generals who might fit the bill. If I can find which one of them authorized a certain military flight from Vancouver to Ottawa on Monday night we may have our man. Unfortunately, the guy at Four-twelve Squadron is refusing to tell me on grounds of 'national security'." I make the air quotes as I say it.

"I can cut through that BS for you. Leave it with me." I realize what a big advantage it is reporting directly to the Director of CSIS.

His phone rings.

He looks at the caller ID with a frown. "Sorry, I have to take this."

"Do you want me to leave?" I ask. He shakes his head.

"Yes," he says into the phone. "Who... OK... When was this?... What did you say?... Uh-ha... OK, I'll follow it up." He hangs up and puts the phone back in his pocket. "That was my mole in the RCMP. He's getting closer to knowing who our target is." He smiles. "Better hurry up and track down that general."

I get up to go.

"One other thing," he adds. "Tony tells me that you have been working with a private detective from Vancouver."

"Yes. Cal is a really bright guy and he's given me lots of help. In fact it was someone in his firm who told me about the existence of the general."

"Yes, Tony told me that. However, I ran a check on them. Rogan is a former drug addict and his partner has some fairly sketchy skeletons in his closet. Due to the highly sensitive nature of our investigation, I think you should sever all contact with them. And Jen, that's an order."

"If you say so." Cal and Nick have been really useful and I enjoyed working with them but if dropping them is the price of working directly with the Director, so be it.

I AM ON SUCH A HIGH. ONE CALL FROM MARKUS TO AN AIR Force General has cleared the way for this call. I try to dial back my glee as I dial the number.

"Hello again, Captain. This is Jennifer Halley from CSIS."

"Yes ma'am." I can tell from his tone that the word has trickled down from four ranks above him. "Can you *now* tell me who authorized that flight from Vancouver to Ottawa on Monday night?"

"Yes ma'am, I can."

I wait. Silence on the line. He resents being told to give up the information.

"So who was it, Captain?"

There's a longer pause than necessary. Finally, *"It was... Major-General Art McNeil, ma'am."* Gotcha! He's one of my seven suspects with Special Ops experience.

"Thank you Captain," I say.

"Yes ma'am." There's a tone in his voice. I get the feeling he doesn't like dealing with women. I hang up on his ass.

Major-General Art McNeil was the least likely of my seven suspects but he's had several postings that were Special Ops related and he could certainly have known Neil Harris' killer, Staff-Sergeant Anton Wills. Now comes the big job. Finding enough evidence to go forward.

My cell rings.

Cal.

I was supposed to meet with him twenty minutes ago. How am I going to let him down lightly?

"Hi Cal."

"How far away are you Jen?"

"Sorry Cal. I won't be coming."

"What?! Why the hell not?"

His tone irks me. "Because, what I'm working on is highly classified and I have been told not to share any information with you."

That draws a long silence. Then, *"If I were to tell you that I know the name of the person Neil Harris was selling arms to, would that change your mind?"*

"Are you serious?"

"Yes. But that's not the biggest piece of information I have for you."

"What are you talking about Cal?"

"Be here in thirty minutes." he hangs up.

If he knows the name of the person who has been buying the arms this could be a big break. I call Markus to get his permission but all I get is his secretary. When I ask to speak to him she says, *"He's meeting the Minister for lunch and then he's going to a meeting at twenty-four Sussex."* Twenty-four Sussex? That's the Prime Minister's residence. Ho-ly! There's no way I can get through to him to get his permission to meet with Cal.

Damn!

42

CAL

Wilfrid's is a bit up market for my taste but I guess I'm trying to impress Tina just a little bit. Stammo won't be impressed with the bill though. Which reminds me I must give him a call and see how he's doing. I feel a twinge of guilt being here. We have a business to run and with Nick in hospital, it must be putting a big load on Adry; she's keeping me up-to-date with emails but I really should be there.

I also feel guilty that Nick's daughter was at my apartment when that soldier showed up, probably to kill me on the orders of some general. Maybe Jen will have had some luck in tracking him down.

We have just finished our lunch when Jen arrives. She walks over and stands at our table. She looks from me to Tina and back to me, indecision written clearly on her face. I sense the change in attitude towards us which I noticed on our phone call. She looks around. Checking to see if we will be overheard by any other diners, I guess. Finally she sits. "You know who Harris' cabal was selling weapons to?" No, 'hi', no preamble just straight to it.

"What cabal?" I ask.

She looks flustered. "Well he wasn't doing it alone was he?" She just answered a question with a question.

"What cabal?" I repeat.

"I'm sorry, I can't share that with you."

Seems like she wants to follow through on that order to cut us out. We'll see.

"There is a Commercial Attaché at the Iranian Embassy, name of Majid Zarin. He is the buyer of that shipment number seventeen."

"How do you know?"

I tell her about our takedown of the Vancouver arms dealer David Fox and how Steve got his surviving gang member to give us Zarin's name.

"How do you know it's the same guy? Majid Zarin is a fairly common name." Her previous suspicion is somewhat smoothed over with enthusiasm.

"That's what *he* said," I say.

"You talked to him?"

"Tina interviewed him. He denied everything but he threatened us, so I figure he's our man."

She furrows her brow. "It makes sense that he would be the buyer. Iran is a big Hezbollah supporter." She mulls it over for a moment. "Cal, Tina, I really appreciate your help with this, I'll be in touch." She stands up. It's time for her to give us the brush off.

"Sit down Jen," I say.

I take out the photograph we printed off the Internet, put it on the table and smooth it out.

"So?" she says.

"I just saw him. He's Majid Zarin's driver."

"But he's dead."

"Yet I just saw him, face-to-face, not two metres apart."

"That's ridiculous. When he detonated the bomb, Hamza Kashif was blown into a thousand pieces along with eleven innocent victims. We have the DNA evidence."

"I know," Tina says. "I covered the bombing for the Daily News Hound. When his name was released, I did a deep dive into Hamza Kashif 's background and I discovered that he had a brother, a twin brother named Rachad. They were born in Palestine, moved to Lebanon as teenagers and then disappeared off the map."

Jen sits down.

"And he's Majid Zarin's driver?"

She looks at me and I nod.

"Are you sure?"

I nod again. "He looks exactly the same as this picture. Same eyes looking in different directions, same shaped nose. Identical."

"But how can that be?" she says.

"Think about it Jen," Tina says. "Neil Harris, and this cabal you mentioned, are making millions selling arms to terrorist organizations and God knows who else. His girl-friend, Annalise Lamarche, steals some incriminating docu-ments and sends them to her brother. They need to get rid of her and Denis. Denis is no problem, he's a drunk living on the streets in Vancouver; they just send their rogue RCMP guy to kill him. But Annalise is more difficult. So they ask a favour of a customer, Majid Zarin, they ask him to get one of his terrorist friends to blow her up."

"But why would they murder eleven other people just to silence her?" Jen looks aghast.

"Yes," I say. "It is extreme. But there would be no murder investigation that could lead back to Harris. Someone might have known about their affair and could have told the police. It's the perfect murder."

"But eleven innocent people as collateral damage? These people would have to be monsters."

Even I have difficulty accepting Tina's theory. Who would do such a thing?

Jen stands up.

"I need to talk to my boss before he goes in to see the PM. Don't leave the hotel. He may want to talk to you guys."

She picks up her briefcase and turns to leave.

"Jen wait!" Tina says. Jen turns back, impatience written all over her face. "After you've made your call, come back. There's something else you need to know."

Jen nods, then strides out of *Wilfrid's* thumbing the screen of her phone.

"What do you want to tell her?" I ask.

"Nothing. It's what *you* have to tell her," she says.

I know what she's talking about. "About the face I saw on the conference call screen?"

"Yes. This whole thing is too big. Jen's boss is meeting with the Prime Minister about this. You really need to tell her. Also it's probably the only way for us to stay on the inside."

I smile at her. "This is going to be a huge scoop for you isn't it?"

She grins back. "Yes. Bernstein and Woodward huge."

I am swept by a desire to kiss her but Jen has reappeared at our table. She sits down. "I couldn't get hold of him," she says. "His cell is switched off." She turns to Tina. "You said I need to know something?"

"Cal has something." Tina smiles at me.

"Adry emailed you a picture of the guy who killed Harris and told you he works for some general. I might be able to identify who that general is." I tell her about the face on the conference-call screen.

"Why the hell didn't you tell me this before?" Her voice is almost a shout. She looks about guiltily and lowers the volume but not the intensity. "That conference software may be able to lead to others who are involved in this."

"Yeah, I'm sorry about that. However, if you keep us in the loop, I can help identify him."

"No need," Jen says. "I already know. He's Major-General Art McNeil." Damn. Our one point of leverage is gone. I look at Tina and can read the disappointment. Jen opens her briefcase and pulls out a photo. "This is him right?" she says.

A good-looking face in uniform smiles at me.

"No," I say.

"Are you sure?"

I nod.

She thinks for a bit. "Yet again," she sighs, "I'm going to tell you something I shouldn't. We know Neil Harris had two associates in these arms deals. One is General McNeil and the other is a very senior RCMP officer. I suspect it's his face you saw." She screws up her face. "So, once again, I'm going to have to break a direct order. You guys better come with me."

———

THIS TIME I REFUSED POINT BLANK TO GO INTO THE CSIS offices unless Tina came with me. After going through all the security procedures, we are in a little conference room with no windows.

When we are settled into our seats, Jen explains, "I'm going to log into a secure system which will give access to pictures of all RCMP officers." She opens the laptop on the conference room table and logs on. The system asks her for a security code. She checks her purse and frowns. Then scrabbles in her briefcase. Cursing under her breath she pulls out several file folders and documents which she places in a neat pile on the conference-room table. On top of the pile is the picture of a distinguished looking man in uniform. On the bottom of the photo is a legend saying 'General McNeil'. Finally she finds what she was rummaging for. It's a small metallic oval with a screen on it. She enters the numbers on the screen into the system's security code. "The guy we are looking for is senior so I'm going to filter the list to just show commissioned officers. There are over six hundred of them so it could take up to an hour to go through them all." She clicks and keyboards around for a while and then slides the mouse over to me. "Go through the list on the side. When you click on a name it will bring up the photo."

I click through the list, looking for a match. Some are clearly not the guy but others I need to look at longer. One Chief Superintendent looks a bit like the face on the conference call; I don't think it's him but I make a note of the name. When I'm about halfway through, Jen interrupts. "I have to go to the bathroom. I'll be back in a second. I'm going to have to lock you in this room; it's a secure area and visitors are not allowed to wander about." She leaves and I hear the door lock behind her.

I'm distracted from clicking through the list of RCMP members by the rustle of paper. Tina is looking at the pile of files and papers which Jen pulled out of her briefcase.

"I don't think you should be doing that," I say.

"Reporter's curiosity," she grins back at me. "I can't not do it. Look, she has a whole bunch of photos of other generals."

"How do you know they're generals?" I ask.

"My father was in the army. I know stuff," she says. "These guys all have little gold maple leaves on their epaulettes, from one for a brigadier to four for a full general, see?" She shows me the photos and one face jumps out at me. Without thinking, I grab the picture from her, fold it over twice and put it in my jacket pocket. "Cal! What the hell are—" There is a buzz and a click as the door lock disengages. Tina quickly puts the other pictures back on the pile and I swivel back to the laptop. As I hear Jen enter, I hope we're not looking too guilty.

———

"Cal Rogan, what were you thinking?" I can't tell if she's amused, angry or afraid. "You just stole a document from a CSIS intelligence officer."

"He's the guy from the conference call."

"Well, duh! I guessed that but you can't just take it like that."

"I know, it was probably stupid."

"Probably?! I think you should turn around right now, give it back and tell Jen who he is. We're dealing with a huge government conspiracy here. It may even involve this guy being complicit in staging a false-flag terrorist bombing. You cannot go it alone."

I think over her words and a feeling rises from deep in my gut. "I don't really trust Jen anymore. I don't really know why."

"You think she's involved in the conspiracy?"

"No. No. Not directly." The feeling gets stronger. "It's just that she seems very keen to get us off the case; to get us to go back to Vancouver." I can feel a raw anger shooting skyward. "If some government cabal, as she called it, is doing arms deals with Iranians and staging terrorist attacks on Canadian soil for God's sake, *and* having innocent, homeless people beaten to death, I'm not just going to stand by and do nothing." I can feel tears of anger in my eyes. "I'm Canadian damn it! No one fucks with innocent lives on my watch. I'm going to get to the bottom of this if it kills me."

"But how?"

"Like a cop, not like a CSIS intelligence officer."

————

LIEUTENANT-GENERAL RICHARD MATHERSON, LIVES IN AN elegant house in the Hunt Club Woods area of Ottawa. Tina's research skills have produced a wealth of information about the man whose face I saw for an instant on Neil Harris' computer. He's a hawkish, decorated officer, known for his outspoken views, and is one of the most senior officers in the Canadian Armed Forces. A widower, he lives alone and seems to have no social life at all; I was hoping this would equate to arriving home early but Tina and I have been camped out in our rental Chevy across the street from his house for the last three hours and it's now seven-thirty. As soon as we start to freeze to death, we crank up the engine for a while to warm us up. And we do what cops always do on stakeouts: we chat.

I have learned all about her childhood growing up as the oldest child of immigrant parents in Belleville, Ontario and she has learned about my dysfunctional childhood moving from district to district in Vancouver. We have had the former spouse/lover chat. She was never married but lived with someone for five years. I have waxed eloquent on the subject of Ellie and she has reciprocated with stories of her baby brother who was born on the same date as Ellie but five years before.

I can feel my feet starting to freeze again. I reach for the ignition key but Tina grabs my hand and signals with her head. A black Jaguar is pulling into the driveway of the house opposite. The garage door glides up and swallows the car. In the harsh, neon light of the garage's interior, I see Matherson get out of the car before the door slides fully down.

"Game on!" I say.

We get out of the car together and walk across the snowy street in step.

I rap the ornate, lion-head knocker on the front door and it is opened almost immediately.

The elderly woman who opens the door peers myopically at us. "Can I help you?" she asks.

Without missing a beat, Tina says, "Yes, we have an appointment with General Matherson."

"Well you're lucky dear, he just arrived home. Won't you come in?"

She holds the door open for us to enter. This is easier than I expected. Too easy in fact. We find ourselves in a spacious entranceway with a curving staircase leading up to a minstrel gallery. The house is larger than it looks from the street. But I don't have time to admire the architecture as the sound of shoes on hardwood announces the arrival of the master of the house.

He is shorter than I was expecting but looks squat and strong. Potentially a formidable opponent. He shows less surprise than on our previous, electronic encounter. "Thank you Martha," he says and without a word she gives an odd smile in our direction and disappears into the rear of the house.

He looks at Tina. "And you are...?"

"Tina Johal of the Daily News Hound dot com," she says, smiling and offering her hand, which he ignores.

"You had better come in," he says.

He strides across the hallway and opens a door, indicating that we should enter. Tina starts through the doorway but I grab her arm. "A study," I say, "with the possibility, even the likelihood, of a concealed weapon *and* with a lockable door. I don't think so, General. The living room would be a preferable meeting place."

He sighs. "As you will, Mr. Rogan." He turns and leads us across the entranceway into a stereotypically masculine-style living room: all wood panelling, oak furniture, vanity photos and the faintest trace of pipe smoke. "Sit," he says indicating the couch.

Tina looks at me. I nod. We sit. He doesn't. I smile at his power ploy.

Tina takes out her notepad and pen and starts scribbling: a ploy of our own.

"Sit down General," I say. "I don't think you're in a position to control the conversation, just by standing up." There's enough of a hint of mockery in my tone to make his gambit feel foolish.

He sits down opposite us.

I go for the jugular. "General, you were conspiring with Neil Harris to sell armaments to our country's enemies." I detect the slightest of flinches.

"That's ridiculous," he says. "Apart from the fact that you have no idea who our country's enemies are, why would I conspire to sell anything to them?"

He looks nervously at Tina as she writes down what he says.

"The very fact that you were in a conference group

named 'The Ruling Group' with Harris and General McNeil would indicate otherwise."

A puzzled look traverses his face before he responds. "I have responsibilities in DND which require that I frequently communicate with the Minister. Why wouldn't I be in a group with him?"

"In a group called 'The Ruling Group'?"

He shrugs. "Harris had a penchant for fanciful names."

I smile. "Talking of names, how do you know my name, General?"

"What?"

"You used my name a moment ago. How did you know who I was?"

There is a soupçon of panic in his eyes as he searches for an answer. I supply it for him. "Someone told you I was the annoying private detective from Vancouver who discovered that Denis Lamarche was killed on the same day as his sister, who unearthed the End User Certificates that Neil Harris signed, who discovered the details of shipment number seventeen to Lebanon, who tracked down Majid Zarin and Hamza Kashif's brother."

He can't keep the shock out of his face; he didn't know this last bit of information. His agitation is doubled by the scratching of Tina's pen.

"I don't know what you're talking about." It's almost a shout.

Now for the well prepared lie. "There's no use denying it, we have been monitoring your communications. We know every call you make, every text, every email, every conference call."

His face has gone white. "I think you had better leave, both of you."

I get up and Tina follows suit. We have achieved our

objectives of chaos and fear. As we walk to the front door, I have just one question. My voice is casual as I ask, "Who *did* tell you my name General?"

"Get out!" he snaps.

And in a flash, I know the answer.

———

WE HAVE DRIVEN AWAY FROM THE GENERAL'S HOUSE AND completed a circuit around the block. We are parked in a different spot but still with a view of the house.

"Do you think it worked?" Tina asks.

"We'll see. I'm pretty sure that we shook him up; great work with the note taking by the way. That really rattled him. If he believes that we are monitoring his communications, he's going to leave the house and hopefully he'll lead us to the next member of this cabal."

"Well, that *was* the plan." She reaches over and squeezes my hand.

And we wait.

The temperature has dropped. Big flakes of snow are drifting lazily downward. I leave the engine running.

Our eyes are drilled in on the house. He has to make a move soon. Come on General. As if on cue, the front door opens. It's the housekeeper. She closes the door behind her and walks down the garden path, crosses the street and gets into a car that was old when I was young. It starts after a couple of tries, pulls away from the curb and meanders down the street. The only possible witness to him leaving the house again tonight is gone. Any minute that garage door will open and his Jaguar is going to—

I hear a metallic click and, too late, I see the movement in the side mirror. Tina screams at the twin bangs as our side windows explode. I feel the gun against my head. "Get out of the car!" The man's voice is used to giving orders. But I'm not used to taking them. I slam the car into drive and floor the gas pedal. The car leaps forward, the side pillar pushing his gun arm out of line with my head. "Get down!" I tell Tina. I doubt that they're going to fire their weapons in the street but you can't be too careful.

A glimpse in the mirror shows two men running to a car. As they get in, we reach the end of the road and I hang a left as fast as I dare on the slippery road surface. We don't get a lot of the white stuff in Vancouver, so confidence in my snow-driving skills is not high. We need to get to a major road with a lot of traffic. I check the mirror. No one seems to be following us. Odd. I ease back the speed. More by luck than judgement, we hit Highway 19, which will take us back to downtown and our hotel. There is still no sign of pursuit. "It's OK to sit up now." I tell Tina.

With adrenaline levels dropping, I become aware of the cold air streaming through the shattered windows as I accelerate up the ramp onto the highway.

"Who the hell was that?" Tina asks. She turns and looks through the back window. "Are they following us?"

"I don't know," I say, firing up the heating to it's highest setting.

"If they're not following us, why not?" She asks.

It's a good question. "They know who we are; maybe they know where we're staying," I say.

"Maybe we should check into a different hotel," she says.

"Good idea. Except these guys are pros. They know there's the possibility we'd do that."

"Maybe they just wanted to scare us off."

"No, they told us to get out of the car."

I run through the sequence of events in my mind. One thing stands out.

"Grab your phone and find us the nearest gas station," I say. She hears the urgency in my voice. After a few taps, she says, "There's a Shell station just off the highway about a kilometre or so ahead."

"Good, it should be busy."

"Are we low on gas?" she adds.

"No. I need to check something."

She gives me directions and I pull into the gas station and up to a pump. There are three other vehicles filling up. Good. "Just put some gas in, please," I ask her.

I turn off the engine, take out the key, pull the lever to open the gas cap and get out of the car.

I check the roof first. Clear. I step back and scan the side of the car. Also clear. Then I see it. On the trunk, snug up against the back window. I pull it off and scan the other vehicles, ahhh: a big, black Ford pickup, perfect. I walk over to the driver; he's an older guy with long grey hair cascading out from underneath his stetson. He's just finished filling up and is putting the pump nozzle back. "Excuse me," I say, "do you know if there's a hotel or motel around here?"

"Sorry, can't help you, I'm from Alberta."

"You're a long way from home," I say.

"Yep, the wife and I are doing the whole cross country thing. We're heading off to Montreal now."

I can't suppress a huge grin. "Well, you have a great trip," I say as he gets back into the cab. I take my hand off the side of his truck as he pulls away, and walk back to the Chevy. Tina has finished topping up the tank.

"You look like the Cheshire cat," she smiles at me. "What was that all about?"

We get in the car and I pull away from the pump.

"Those guys were pros," I say. "A second before they smashed the windows, I heard a metallic click. They knew there was a chance we might make a run for it, so they put a homing device on the car. They didn't have time to conceal it so they just slapped it down on the trunk." I start to laugh, "In about fifteen minutes, they'll be wondering why the heck we're heading down Highway 417 bound for Montreal."

Tina's laugh joins mine as I pull back onto the highway.

———

I THINK THE UBER DRIVER AND TINA ARE LAUGHING AT ME BUT have no way of knowing. They immediately hit it off when she discovered that he is from the same state in India as her parents. They have been chatting away, in what I assume is Hindi, for the last fifteen minutes. Yet another grey car pulls into the parking lot. In the dark it is next to impossible to see the driver. I wait until it has parked. The driver gets out. She stands beside the car, as ordered. "Alright," I grunt.

"This is soooo exciting," the driver says. "I've never been in a stakeout before." He drives over to where she's parked.

I slide down the window. "Get in please, Jen." I ask her.

She does as asked. I hope she is as cooperative for the next stage.

"What's going on Cal?" she asks.

"All will be explained later," I say.

"But—"

"Later." My tone brooks no protest.

We sit in silence for the ten minutes it takes to get to the Travelodge. "Go with Tina," I say.

"You have to tell me what's going on," she objects.

"Later. Just do what I say."

She shrugs and gets out of the car. She and Tina disappear inside the hotel.

"Where are they going?" the driver asks.

"I can't tell you on grounds of national security," I say to him. I've always wanted to say that.

We sit in silence for ten minutes. I don't know what he's thinking but I know I'm worrying about all the things that could go wrong.

They come out. Jen is wearing some of Tina's clothes. Tina is a bit taller than Jen but the latter looks OK.

When they get into the car, Jen glares at me but doesn't speak.

"Next stop," I tell the driver.

He drops us at the Riverside Pub fifteen minutes later. Fifteen minutes during which I have done everything I can to see if we are being tailed and even now I can't be a hundred percent sure. I hand him the second two-hundred-and fifty-dollar envelope and he and Tina say fond farewells. At least I guess that's what they're saying.

He was right; the Riverside is perfect. It's loud enough that we won't be overheard but not so loud that we can't hear ourselves speak.

We choose a booth and order food and drink; I only just realized that I'm starving. After the waitress leaves, Jen leans forward. "What is going *on*, Cal?" she asks.

"We needed to be sure that you weren't carrying any form of recorder or homing device. We'll give you the key to the hotel room and pay for another Uber to take you back there so you can retrieve your clothes and your stuff."

"Yes but why?"

"When we were in your conference room," I say. "I kind of stole the picture of the general I saw on Neil Harris' conference call."

"You took General McNeil's picture?" she asks.

"No it was General Matherson."

"Matherson? He's one of the most senior generals in the Forces. Maybe he was just calling Harris to—"

I cut her off. "We just went to see him." I tell her about the meeting with Matherson at his house.

"Did he admit to anything?" she asks.

"He didn't have to. Right after the meeting, he had a couple of guys show up and try to arrest us." I tell her of our escape from the general's men and the episode with the homing device. I finish with, "Would an innocent man order that?"

She thinks it over for a few seconds. "But why did you put me through changing my clothes and leaving all my stuff in that hotel room?"

"I told you. In case you were wearing any sort of surveillance electronics."

"Why would I do that," Jen asks.

"Because General Matherson knew my name. How did he know it? The only government people who know my name are you, your boss and maybe his boss."

"You think *I'm* involved in this conspiracy?" she asks.

"I don't know, are you?"

"Of course not." Her denial seems genuine but she has been trained in both sides of interrogation. "What about Harvey, the RCMP guy back in Vancouver? He knew who you were didn't he? He made me tell him your's and Nick's names. As I told you, there's a senior RCMP guy involved. Harvey would have told him and he would have told the general."

She's right. My suspicion of her and her bosses is unwarranted. For nothing I've put her through the humiliation of removing her clothes and possessions and leaving them at a strange hotel. I hear Nick's voice in my head; it's his best sarcastic voice: *Well done, Rogan.*

"I am so sorry Jen," I say.

"No prob. You were just being cautious." She is a whole lot more forgiving than I would have been.

The waitress brings our order. My liver, bacon and onions, with mashed potatoes and gravy, smells wonderful. I take a long swallow of my IPA and ask, "Why do you think General McNeil is involved?"

She tells us about her discovery that the Special Ops guys took a military flight from Vancouver, authorized by McNeil.

"So we have two generals involved."

Jen picks up a french fry and nibbles the end of it. "I guess."

"You sound unsure."

"The Captain I spoke to at Four-twelve Squadron, sounded, I don't know, odd, when he told me McNeil's name."

"Maybe he didn't like being forced to tell you," Tina says.

I finish my mouthful of mashed potato and gravy. "OK, so we've got Neil Harris, the late Minister of National Defence, Lieutenant-General Matherson, a high-ranking general, Major-General McNeil, *and* a Senior RCMP guy, as yet unknown. They are in this cabal to make millions of dollars selling weapons illegally." I pause and Jen and Tina both nod. "It's a crime of opportunity. They work in important jobs but get government salaries. They see an opportunity to work together and make hundreds of millions, with little chance of being found out. I get that." I pause again and this time for effect. They both nod again. "Then Annalise Lamarche steals some incriminating documents. Why don't they say 'OK, the game's up', take their millions and go live on a tropical island or in a big city under the finest false identities that money can buy?"

"Maybe they're just greedy," Tina suggests. "They figure if they kill Annalise and her brother, they can just carry on making more money."

Jen nods, "When it comes to money, some people just can't have enough. Maybe they want billions, not just hundreds of millions."

I wave at the waitress to indicate another round of drinks. "I don't buy that," I say. "There are businessmen that are wired that way, all these high-tech billionaires for example..." I pause, the thought of high-tech billionaires reminds me that I must call Damien. "...but these guys have spent a life in public service; they're *not* wired that way." Jen and Tina don't look convinced. "And another thing: I understand them killing Denis by having him beaten to death but why get their big buyer, Zarin, to get one of his people to kill Annalise in a terrorist bombing? Tina, I know you said that it was a way to kill her without there being a murder investigation, but there's got to be more to it than that. There's more to this whole conspiracy than we know about."

We slip into silent eating.

As I savour the good pub food, a new thought hits. "We don't know how big this conspiracy is. We discovered Neil Harris and when we got close to him, they killed him. You have to be pretty callous to kill your own people just so they won't talk. So now that we know about General Matherson, is he dispensable too? Is he next on the list?"

"Or are we?" Tina adds.

Jen says, "I doubt that Matherson is next. He's the one who controls the Special Ops guys who are doing the actual killings." She thinks for a second. "In fact *they* were probably the ones who told him your name," she adds pointedly.

Tina adds, "Plus he's a Lieutenant-General. That's a senior rank, the second most senior rank in the military; there are only about a dozen of them. He may well be the top man in this whole conspiracy."

"We need to find out who the senior RCMP officer is," I say.

"I've already told you more than I should," Jen says, "so I might as well tell you that my boss has a mole in the RCMP who's trying to find out. First thing in the morning, I'll talk to Markus and get an update and I'll tell him about General Matherson."

"Make that second thing in the morning," I say. "There's something we need to check on first."

I take the last slice of the liver, with bacon, onions and gravy, and pop it in my mouth." Man, that Uber driver was worth the five hundred dollars we paid him. This place is great.

43

CAL

Thursday

For better or for worse, we have decided to trust Jen and so far we haven't been arrested but it's still early in the morning. We'll see how the day unfolds. Uplands CFB is not a high security military base and Jen's CSIS credentials get us in with no problems. Captain Vince McCaffery is skinny with a slight stoop, even though he can't be more than thirty-five. He's sitting behind a desk that has definitely done more years of military service than he has. Behind him is a photograph of aircraft flying in close formation. He looks uncomfortable.

"Did you fly with the Snowbirds, Captain?" I ask.

He brightens. "Yes sir, I did."

That makes him one hell of a pilot. Only the cream of the crop get to fly in Canada's famed aerobatic squadron. "Impressive," I say. He smiles.

When Jen speaks, the smile disappears. "You told me on the phone that the flight from Vancouver to Ottawa had two passengers and was authorized by Major-General McNeil. Is that correct, Captain?"

"Yes ma'am." His discomfort level visibly goes up.

I weigh in with, "It's correct that you told her or it's correct that it was authorized by General McNeil?"

He looks down at his hands clasped together on the surface of his desk. His left thumb rubs his right. "I can't say sir."

"Can't or won't?" I say.

He doesn't answer.

"Captain, this is a very serious matter," Jen says gently. "I need you to tell me the truth."

"Yes ma'am," he says again.

We wait. I look around the tiny office with its posters of various military jets and one of a black aircraft on a runway. It resembles Damien's corporate jet that brought us to Ottawa. The word Canada is painted on the side and the number 616 is on it's nose.

"Is that the plane that was used for the flight?" I ask.

He swivels in his chair to look at it. "Yes, sir. It's a Challenger."

I look him in the eye. "The flight was authorized by General Matherson wasn't it?" I say.

He takes a deep breath. "Yes sir. Well, not the General himself, but it was a Lieutenant-Colonel on General Matherson's staff. It was him who called me yesterday morning and told me to say it was authorized by General McNeil. I'm sorry I lied to you ma'am. The fact I was ordered to is no excuse. I don't think it's right to order a soldier to lie to anyone. I hope you can accept my apology."

"No apology is necessary, Captain. You were just following orders. I appreciate your honesty now."

"With respect ma'am, I am a student of military history

and the phrase 'just following orders' has, more than once, led humanity down some very dark paths."

On that cheery note, we get up and say our goodbyes.

———

JEN DROPS ME OFF AT A HOLIDAY INN JUST EAST OF downtown, before heading to her office. I thought a second change of hotel would be wise. I'd like to be a fly on the wall and hear what her boss has to say when he hears that General Matherson is in this cabal and not General McNeil. Especially when she tells him that some private eye from Vancouver found it out.

Tina gives me a big hug as I walk in. "How did it go?" she asks.

When I've told her, she gives me another hug and says, "I want to talk to you about something."

Those are never words you want to hear from a lover.

She reads my expression perfectly. "No, silly. I have a plan. But I want to run it by you."

Phew! My smile returns. "Great! I just need to make a call first. I've kept putting if off or forgetting it, I just need to do it now while it's on my mind. You should sit in on it."

I pull my phone from my pocket, dial and press the speaker button. It rings four times, then, *"Hey Cal, you do know it's six AM here, right?"*

"Sorry man, I just wanted to ask you if you'd managed to decrypt any more of those documents."

Damien is silent for a second. Then, *"A team from the RCMP came to my office and made me hand over copies of the documents and then delete them all from our servers."*

"The RCMP?!" I can feel the hackles rising on the back of my neck.

"*Yes. They sent a Superintendent, an Inspector and a tech.*"

"This is really important Damien. Did they say on whose authority they were there?"

He thinks for a bit. "*No, the Inspector just said that they had been ordered to get the documents back.*"

"Damn!" I say. "We've learned that a Senior RCMP officer is involved in this illegal gunrunning operation; he probably sent them to your office. I was hoping..." I clutch at a final straw. "Do you remember the name of the Superintendent?"

"*Yes... is was Bruce... No, not Bruce, it was Brian, Brian O'Mahoney.*"

Maybe Jen, or her boss' mole, can find out who in the RCMP ordered Superintendent O'Mahoney to retrieve those documents.

"That sucks, they got them before you could decrypt any more of them."

There is a pause. "*Uh-huh.*"

My neck is prickling again. "Was that uh-huh, yes, or uh-huh, no?"

The pause is long this time. "*No. Between the time I left my office to go see them and the time that I deleted the documents, one more document was decrypted.*"

I look at Tina; her eyes are shining. "What was in it?" I ask.

Silence.

"Come on Damien. Was it just another shipping document or was it something more incriminating?"

He gives a grim chuckle. "*Both,*" he says.

"What do you mean, 'both'?"

"*Schrödinger's cat.*"

I let it sink in. Tina looks at me with a questioning frown.

"You haven't looked at the document, have you?" I say.

"No, I haven't. I didn't open the file. I just re-encrypted it with a key of my own and kept it."

"Why?"

"The RCMP guys made me sign a legal document. If I'd looked at the file, I would have been open to prosecution."

"So why didn't you just delete it?"

"Dunno. I just thought that maybe, one day, I would be asked to hand it over to someone who had the legal right to demand it."

"Can you send it to Jen Halley?" I ask.

"Happily, but only if she has a court order compelling me to do so."

"OK. I'll get on that. Thanks, Damien. You're a star."

I hang up and call Jen's cell. No reply. She'll be meeting with her boss. "It's Cal. Call me a.s.a.p.," I tell her voicemail.

I take a deep breath and give another big, but this time, long and out loud, "Phew!"

"What was that about the cat?" Tina asks.

"Never mind. It's too long to explain right now. You said you had a plan."

She laughs. "Yes, I have a plan so cunning you could brush your teeth with it."

"What?" It's my turn to frown in perplexity.

In a deep growl, she says, "Never mind. It's too long to explain right now." I have to admit it's a pretty good imitation of my voice and tone. When I laugh, she relents. "It's from a British TV show called 'Black Adder'. My parents and I lived in England before we moved here. They made us watch a bunch of old TV comedies when we were kids."

I hug her. For a long time. We kiss. And hug some more.

Finally, I release her from my arms. "I'll tell you about Schrödinger's cat over lunch. Right now what's this cunning plan of yours?"

Her face becomes serious. "I've been thinking about this whole thing. Twice since we've been in Ottawa, the General's special Ops guys have tried to take us down. Last night, after you went to sleep, I spent some time worrying about it. The third time they might just get lucky."

"I wouldn't worry about that. Jen's the only person in the world who knows we're at this hotel."

"Yes, but we can't stay cooped up here forever. So I thought this whole conspiracy has gone on in the shadows for far too long. I thought, what if I publish an article in the Hound that brings the whole thing into the light, talks about the End User Certificates and the shipments, names Harris and Matherson and mentions you too. Then they wouldn't dare attack us. It would incriminate them further."

"You can't do that. You'd be breaking the Official Secrets Act."

"I've never signed the Official Secrets Act. Everything in the article is stuff we found out for ourselves."

"But you're bound by the Act, even if you've never actually signed it." I say.

"I am?"

"Yes."

"Then that's a problem," she says, picking up her computer from the desk. She opens it. There, on the screen, is the banner of the Daily News Hound dot com. I read the words in big letters: CANADIAN GOVERNMENT OFFICIALS MAKE MILLIONS FROM ILLEGAL ARMS SALES.

She gives me a lopsided grin.

"Because I kind of... already posted it."

44

JEN

The look on the Director's face is amazement. "You're telling me that it's not McNeil but it's Matherson?" He asks. I just nod. "How did you find this out?" It's the question I knew he would ask and the question I don't want to have to answer.

I take a deep breath. "Cal Rogan contacted me." His eyebrows raise a fraction. "He discovered that it was Matherson who was the General involved in the conspiracy. He went to interrogate the General at his house." The brows go higher. I rush on, "And right after, he was attacked by who he thinks were Special Ops soldiers, but he got away. I have to believe that implicates General Matherson. Then I went to see the Captain at Four-twelve Squadron and he told me that the flight from Vancouver was arranged by an aide to General Matherson, and that the same aide told him to tell anyone who asked that it was arranged by General McNeil."

I take a big breath in.

Markus purses his lips in thought. "Well, I'm not delighted about Rogan being involved but it was a good result. Well done."

I let out the big breath in relief and in silence.

"There's another thing, sir, uh, Markus. I couldn't get hold of you yesterday to tell you this because you were with the PM." I tell him about Cal's meeting with Majid Zarin and then seeing Rachad Kashif and his theory that the bombing was caused by the conspirators.

When I finish, he doesn't say anything, he just leans back in his chair and stares at the ceiling tiles.

I wait on tenterhooks.

Finally he speaks. "It's improbable but not impossible. Here's what I want you to do," he says. "Like it or not, Rogan is involved in this and I have to admit he's been much more of an asset than I thought. You've found the General, so I think it would be good if you and Rogan could work together to find out who the hell is the senior RCMP member in this cabal. I want you both to meet with the mole I have in the RCMP. Let me set it up and I'll text you the details."

"Right," I say. "Who is the mole, by the way?"

His phone rings. He gives a frown of annoyance and looks at the caller ID. The frown changes to one of puzzlement. He picks up the phone. "Yes Minister," he says. "No, I haven't... Which...?" He opens the lid of his laptop and taps some keys. His eyes go wide. "Let me read it. I'll call you right back."

He turns back to me. "I have to deal with this. I'll text you the details." He turns back to his screen and I leave his office.

Listening in on a communication with a Cabinet Minister is probably over my security clearance.

————

"WHY THE CHANGE OF HEART?" CAL ASKS AS WE WALK ACROSS the carpark of his hotel.

"The Director was so impressed that you were able to track down and confirm General Matherson's involvement in the conspiracy, he wanted you to help with finding the RCMP member in this cabal."

He just grunts at this.

When we are in my car, he asks, "So where is it we're going?"

"We're meeting him in the Victoria Building."

"Isn't that near where the bombing was?"

"A couple of hundred metres. It's an old heritage building just across the street from Parliament Hill."

He's silent for a while. Then, "What do you know about this mole in the RCMP?" he asks.

"Nothing. I asked the Director who he was, but before he could tell me, he got a call from a Cabinet Minister. His text didn't say. He just texted me to pick you up from your hotel and go to suite three-oh-seven in the Victoria Building to meet with the mole."

He's silent for the next ten minutes. I get the intuition that there's something on his mind but he doesn't know whether to share it.

I score on the parking and get a spot just a block away.

As we walk up the block, Cal asks, "Did you check the news today?"

"No, why?"

"Did you tell anyone where Tina and I are staying?"

"No. No one asked me."

"You're sure."

"Yes, absolutely. What's it got to do with today's news?"

"Nothing."

"Come on Cal, what's going on?" I wonder if he's often as exasperating as this.

"When your boss reads the news he's going to freak."

Uh-oh. "Why?"

He doesn't answer but pulls out his phone and taps away with his fingers. He spends the time it takes to walk the entire block tapping away and ignoring me.

"Why Cal?" I repeat as we go through the sliding doors of the building. He just stares at his phone. As we enter the elevator, he puts it back in his pocket, sighs and looks up at the floor numbers changing.

"Cal, will you please tell me what's going on?"

We get off at the third floor. "Wait until we get inside. The mole will want to know about this too."

Our heels click as we walk along the corridor's old flooring. The door of suite three-oh-seven has no marking other than the numbers. I knock and enter.

The office is minimalist, probably just being used temporarily. There is a reception desk with a privacy wall behind it. Beside the desk are about fifty, shrink-wrapped boxes of copier paper; they are stacked in two rows. That's a lot of paper. At five thousand sheets a box, it's a quarter of a million pages. Against the far wall are six folding chairs in a drab olive colour; they are clearly government issue. Over all, there is a slight chemical odour. I think I can smell ammonia; it's as if the office has been cleaned with cleaning products left over from the nineteen-twenties, when the building was constructed.

The door clicks closed behind us.

Silence.

"Hello! Anyone here?"

Silence.

The door clicks a second time. I turn around. Cal looks at me and tries the door. It doesn't open.

"Excuse the security," a voice says.

We both spin around.

This is Markus' RCMP mole? She's short and kind of frail looking. Her clothing is... well, the kindest word would be old-fashioned. Her grey hair is tied back in a bun and her lipstick is bright red. But by far, her most striking feature is the silenced Smith and Wesson held unwaveringly in her left hand.

45

NICK

Ping. It's a text. I grab my phone. "Mr. Stammo?" it's the cute nurse. I smile. "We're going to move you out of acute care into a regular ward," he says. "My colleague here is going to take you." He indicates an orderly who looks like he plays fullback for the BC Lions. He grabs my bag of clothes and puts them onto the foot of the bed. I take the book I've been trying to read and put it in my lap with the phone..

He cranks me up into a sitting position, moves behind the bed and pushes me out of acute care. We're joined by the uniformed cop who has been assigned as protection after I shot the guy who was trying to kill me. I knew Carl Smith when I was on the job. He's a good, solid cop but without a lot of imagination. "Hey, Carl, how's it going?"

"Good. They're moving you then?" Good observation Carl.

"I guess so."

We proceed down the corridor in silence and take a right at the end. The next corridor is empty except for a patient at the far end, walking towards us. He's in a dressing gown and is pulling one of those things on wheels with all sorts of plastic bags of medications and drips hanging from them. Poor guy's hobbling along with his head hanging down onto his chest. As he shuffles along, I see that one of his pant legs is up and the other one's down. It makes him look odd; all part of the indignity of hospitals. When they let me get out of bed, I'll probably be wandering along the corridors looking like that. Maybe I should ask Adry to pop over to Mrs. V's and get me some pyjamas.

Pyjamas!

"Carl," I say. He looks at me, his face questioning my tone of voice. "I need you to trust me on this. Get out your weapon, *right now* and *fast*." Carl may not be the sharpest knife in the drawer but he knows how to take orders. He has his gun out in double-quick time. I point at the patient. "YOU!" I yell. "FREEZE."

The head snaps up. In one fluid motion he pushes the drip thing away and, as if from nowhere, an Uzi appears in his hand. A movement beside me catches my eye. Carl is pointing his Beretta and steadying his firing hand. He fires twice and the patient flies backwards, the Uzi falling from his hand and clattering on the floor.

Carl runs forward and stands over the would be killer. I thank the heavens that the VPD sent Carl to protect me. When I was a cop, he was the only man on the force who could outshoot me on the range.

"Let me see your hands!" Carl shouts.

Good, he's alive. Maybe we'll get some answers when he's questioned.

My smile dies as thick fingers grab my throat from behind. The orderly! His thumbs are pushed into the back of my neck and his fingers are crushing my windpipe. I try to shout for Carl but nothing comes out. I look at him but he's still covering the fallen man and is calling in for back up. My fingers try and pry the hands off my throat and I get a sharp pain in the back of my hand. It's the shunt they've put in to connect to my saline drip. Stars are starting to appear in front of my eyes. I grab the shunt and pull. With a tearing pain it comes out. I can no longer see Carl as the darkness starts to creep in. With all my strength I jab the shunt into my attacker's right hand. I feel it sink into the flesh and I rotate it hard to maximize the damage. I hear him grunt out as he yanks the hand away. His left hand is still a vice on my throat. But the shunt is still in my hand. I jab it into his left hand but he doesn't let go. Everything is darkness now. I pull the shunt back and try again for his hand but feel a sharp pain as I miss and spear my shoulder.

The blackness gets deeper. I don't even see stars.

Just a white glow getting brighter and brighter.

46

CAL

My surprise at seeing the woman whom I thought was General Matherson's maid is eclipsed by the shock of seeing the gun in her hand. For an instant, I think of doing the unexpected and rushing her, but everything about her says she knows how to use that weapon. Then any thought of physical resistance is dissipated by the two men who appear from the office behind her.

One face I recognize. I saw it for the briefest instant at the nurses' station at VGH, as Adry and I helped Jen to the exit, then afterwards as he made a phone call to report the failure of his mission. The other I'm not sure about; he could have been one of the men on the porch of Harvey Clegg's house.

They work quickly and efficiently. In minutes Jen and I are bound into two of the folding chairs. They are professionals; we are not going to escape from this. Gags have been applied and our captors are seated across from us.

The Smith and Wesson is cradled in the maid's lap. Ready for instant use.

We wait.

I feel a short buzz against my thigh. It's my phone.

I fervently hope it's Tina and that at least she has seen my text and quit the Holiday Inn for a different hotel.

————

SOMEONE'S PHONE BEEPS. ONE OF THE SPECIAL OPS GUYS pulls it out of his pocket. He gives a couple of taps then gets up and goes to the door. There's a quiet knock. He opens it and a woman enters. She is in sharp contrast to Matherson's maid. She is young and athletic-looking and wearing a nurse's uniform. My heart accelerates wildly when I see she is helping a patient into the room. Tina.

She staggers slightly and her eyes are glassy from the drugs that she has obviously had administered.

I struggle in my chair. It's a futile thing to do but I can't stop myself.

The nurse puts Tina in a chair. The Special Ops guys bind her in, as securely as Jen and I are bound, and they gag her. Her breath snorts through her nose and I want to shout at them to remove the gag until she's fully conscious, but it just comes out of me as a muffled moan.

The nurse opens her purse and takes out a syringe and gauze. She swabs Tina's neck and I get the sharp tang of alcohol in my nose. She slaps the skin and injects the needle. Tina snaps upright and her eyes are like saucers. She looks around; confusion is wreathed about her face. Finally her eyes settle on me and a recognition dawns. She's breathing heavily but without the snorting from her drugged state. She looks at me again and I imagine that she is trying to smile.

The nurse leaves and the guards sit down again.

We wait in silence.

I scan the room. There's no clock on the wall. I need to know how long we've been in here. I'm guessing around twenty minutes. Nowhere near long enough. Hopefully the wait will be longer this time.

But it's not.

The same routine. The guard's phone rings, he stands by the door. But this time, the routine is different. The 'maid' and the other guard also stand. I know who's coming now. As before, a soft tap on the door. He walks in but it's not who I think. He's tall with grey, wavy hair and glasses. I've never seen him before.

I can see from how his minions are standing to attention, even General Matherson's maid, that he is someone high in the conspiracy.

His face is set in a rigid glare. He strides over and with a mighty swing, he back-hands Tina across the face, almost knocking her and her chair to the ground.

I moan and struggle against my bonds as my blood rises to boiling point.

Tina's head is sagging onto her chest. I think he must have knocked her unconscious. I *will* make him pay for that.

He turns to the maid. "Hold your gun to her head," he snaps. The order is obeyed in double time. He grabs a chair and swings it in front of me, sitting down in one smooth movement. "Make any noise and she dies. Do you under-stand?" I nod. He reaches forward and yanks the duct tape from my mouth then pulls out the cloth gag.

I struggle to hold back all the things I want to yell at him.

"Under pain of death, *her* death," he jerks his head at

Tina, "you need to answer my questions honestly. Do you understand?"

I nod.

He fixes me with a stare. I sense he has done this before. Lying is not a good policy with this guy. He's likely well schooled in the interrogation arts.

"Do you know who I am?"

I shake my head. "No."

He jerks his head towards Tina again. "Apart from the article she wrote in that online rag she works for, has she posted anything else?"

"I don't know. I don't think so."

He looks over at Tina and I follow his gaze. Her head is upright and she is looking at him.

He takes the gun from the maid and touches the end of the silencer to my forehead. I feel myself tense, waiting for the click of the trigger, the last sound I'll ever hear.

"Have you posted anything else?" he says. She shakes her head. He keeps staring at her. She shakes her head again desperately. He stares. One Mississippi, two Mississippis, three— He hands the gun back and it is again trained on Tina.

He turns back to me.

"What else do you know that wasn't in her article."

"That you or your people engineered the bombing to kill Annalise Lamarche." And a bunch of innocent bystanders, I think.

He just nods.

"Who else knows anything about this whole business?"

"My partner."

"Anyone else?"

"No."

He smiles. "Good. Your partner doesn't count. He's already dead."

Before I can worry about his words he snaps, "Who knows you're here?"

"No one."

He looks long and hard.

"It's a shame," he says.

"What is?"

"...that I didn't meet up with you years ago. You're resourceful, smart and tough. You would have been a good addition to the team. Too late now of course."

He's given me an opening. I need time.

"Why kill all those innocent people?" I ask.

"Collateral damage." He looks at me as if trying to make a decision. "Canada has become weak," he says. "Our current PM is the most feeble in a line of increasing feeble predecessors. Look around the world Rogan. Democracy is a failure. The politicians in the United States are so caught up in bickering with each other that they can't get anything done and the populace is so confused with identity politics that they'll vote for anyone with a pulse and a good line of talk. The UK, the seat of modern democracy, is no better. They're still spending all their efforts squabbling about Brexit and will continue to do so even after the deal is done—if it ever is." He leans forward. "We are *not* going to let Canada go in the same direction." He stands up. "Here's how it's going to unfold. After a series of terrorist bombings the military will have to take charge. A state of emergency will be declared. Several politicians will be shown to be involved, starting with the late Neil Harris. Parliament will be dissolved and the country will be run by sensible people with vision."

"You being one of them," I say.

He looks down at me.

"Yes, Rogan. Me being one of them."

"What about General Matherson? You can't use him now. Tina's article has blown his cover."

"You're naïve, Rogan. We'll just attribute that to fake news from the gutter press and move on; we'll say that the End User Certificates were part of a sting operation. After an unfortunate accident to his boss, General Matherson will be put in charge of the Armed Forces. The only thing her article has done is to accelerate our schedule." He gives a big creepy smile. "Do you know what this building is used for Mr. Rogan?"

It's a question out of left field. "No. Why would I?"

"It's right across the street from Parliament Hill. Many members of parliament and cabinet ministers have their offices in this building. During lunch hour it's full of them." He looks at his watch. "At twelve-thirty, the second terrorist bombing is going to turn this elderly building into a pile of rubble, sadly, taking with it a great many of the key players in Canada's Parliament. Not to mention you three. You'll be vaporized in the explosion."

He walks to the door. "Carry on," he says.

One of the Special Ops guys steps over and stuffs the cloth gag back into my mouth and reapplies the duct tape. The tape doesn't seem to stick as tightly as before. I might just be able to—

"Goodbye Mr. Rogan." He smiles and leaves.

His minions kick into full gear.

The men start taking the boxes of paper from the piles beside the reception desk and cutting off the shrink wrap. The 'maid' disappears into a back office. As they remove the lids from the boxes, I can smell the fumes. There's what smells like gasoline but there's another smell too. I can't identify it, but it is nothing good. From a seminar long in the past, the word ANFO springs into my mind; Ammonium Nitrate Fuel Oil. It's the explosive favoured by terrorists because it's easy to get the ingredients. They could have used more sophisticated explosives but this one spells terrorist not government cabal.

While they open the boxes and place them in a square on the floor, the old woman struggles out carrying a heavy box. She starts to pull out cylinders with wires attached. I know what they are. She sticks one deep into one of the boxes.

While our three guards are working, I flex the muscles of my jaws and am rewarded with a prickling, as the duct tape starts to peel away from my skin. It only feels like a tiny amount but if I can keep this going...

The team's working fast; already half the boxes are open and half of them have the detonators placed inside them. Every time I'm sure they're engrossed in their work, I flex my cheeks and jaw muscles. The duct tape is so loose now that I have to stop. I don't want it to fall off my face just yet. I sit still and watch the team at work. When they're gone, I'm going to scream this place down until someone comes.

I hear a thump. One of the Special Ops guys has brought a heavy box out of the room. Now all three of them are attaching the wires from the detonators to terminals of the box. It's the trigger device. When they finish, they survey their handiwork. Then one of them moves something on the side of the box facing away from me. Controls for the trigger, I'm guessing.

He stands up and nods to his companions. They all check their watches, then pick their way around the boxes and make for the door. I'll give them three minutes to get out of earshot, then this duct tape is off! I'll spit out the gag and be screaming the place down. The men leave and Matherson's maid stops in the doorway, turns and gives one last sweep of the room with her ancient eyes. She focuses on us, calculating something. But what? She checks her watch again and nods to herself. She steps into the hallway.

But the door doesn't close behind her.

I hear the murmur of voices.

In seconds, she walks back into the room followed by the men.

"Check them," she says.

The men make their way around the boxes. They check that Jen and Tina are both firmly attached to their chairs. When they get to me, they are doubly careful. They turn and look at her.

She looks at us and nods, then her eyes lock onto mine. She picks her way past the boxes to the reception desk. I see her objective and my stomach sinks. It's a new reel of duct tape. She takes it and returns. In seconds, she has wrapped the tape across my mouth and behind my head three times. She does the same for Tina and for Jen.

"On their backs," she orders.

One of the men takes the back of Tina's chair and pulls it back and down until he drops it on the floor with a small thump. Then Jen. Then me. I'm tied in a chair, on my back looking at the ceiling.

I hear them move away. Then the door closes and the lock clicks.

I feel my phone buzz. Please be Stammo. Let him still be alive. Please let him survive the latest attempt on his life. If I die and he lives, he'll get to the bottom of this somehow. King Lear comes unbidden to my mind. *No rescue? What, a prisoner? I am even, The natural fool of fortune.* As always the Bard hits the nail on the head but it is of no comfort to me.

I wonder if there is a digital readout on the side of the box that will trigger the explosion. In the movies, you always see it counting down towards zero. I don't know what's better: to see or not to see; to know or not to know.

Ay, there's the rub!

47

NICK

The sound of the shot and the release of my neck are simultaneous. The pain of the air rushing down my throat is excruciating.

Nothing ever felt so good.

As the mists clear, I see Carl looking at me through a long, dark tunnel. And I hear his words. "Thank God."

"Amen," I say but no noise comes out.

———

I'M WAITING FOR THE X-RAY RESULTS. I'VE BEEN GIVEN STRICT instructions not to try and talk, which is really bugging me. I want to thank Carl for saving my life. No one else could have made those shots. Best of all, both perps are alive and in custody. Maybe we'll get some information from them. As if reading my mind, Carl walks into the room. I give him the big thumbs up and point to my throat. He nods and smiles. "How did you know the guy walking towards us was going to try and kill you?" he asks.

I look down. Through it all, my phone is still in my lap. I

grab it and open the Notes app. I type, *He had one pant leg down. He was wearing pants, not pyjamas. And he was wearing leather shoes.* I turn the screen towards him.

"Good eye. You always were a sharp one, Nick."

I start typing again. *Do we know anything about them yet?*

"I dunno. They're both being treated for the gunshot wounds I gave 'em. I guess no one's been able to interrogate them yet. Anyways, I came to say goodbye. I've gotta go and start all the paperwork that goes with the discharge of a weapon." He shrugs. "Paperwork, eh?"

I type, *Thanks again Carl. I owe you my life.*

He grins, pats me on the shoulder and trudges off.

As I relax back onto my pillow, I remember that just before the orderly came to take me to a new ward, I got a text. I open the Messages app and read it.

I look at the time of the message and the time on my phone.

Holy—

A real uneasy feeling sweeps over me. I don't care what the doctor said about not talking. I dial the once-familiar number and pray that he'll be there.

48

CAL

Again I do the math. Jen picked me up at the Holiday Inn at around ten. It took us about fifteen minutes to get here. Ten minutes for the Special Ops guys to tie us up. We waited about fifteen minutes for the nurse to show up with Tina and the guy with the grey, wavy hair showed up about fifteen minutes after that. He was here for ten minutes then it took them about an hour to set up the bomb. That means they left here at about five past twelve.

The bomb is set for twelve-thirty.

How much of the twenty-five minutes are gone?

At first, I thought it was too melodramatic that he left us here to die in the bomb blast. Why not just put three silenced rounds into our heads? Then, I remembered Harvey Clegg. Bullets survive a fire and so they would probably survive a bomb blast too. They might raise too many questions; they might even be traceable. This close to the bomb, there will be no trace of us, the ropes, the duct tape, not even the chairs. The man with the grey, wavy hair has got to be a certifiable psychopath, he's probably savouring the torment he's putting us through.

I suppose I should, I don't know... compose myself for death. My final case did not turn out so well did it? I think of Ellie. I wonder if her plans to be a cop will change as she gets older. In a way I would like—

Beep-beep-beep. It came from the box that is set to trigger the explosion. Maybe an alarm. A five minute warning?

I roll my head to the right. Tina is looking straight at me. Tina, I am *so* sorry. I try to say it with my eyes.

BANG-BANG-BANG. "Police! Open up!"

"Mmmmmmmmgh!" We all three try to shout behind our gags. I hear a noise to my left. Jen is writhing up and down and feebly banging her chair on the ground, I follow suit and I hear Tina do the same.

"Open up right now!"

We bang and moan in unison.

Five long seconds and the door comes crashing off its hinges. Two armed officers in ERT gear step inside and sweeps the room with their weapons. They take in the scene. "Clear," one shouts. A third officer enters. He has the air of command. He takes one look at the boxes. "Dyson!" he shouts to someone outside. "Call the bomb squad. Fast."

The first two officers make their way past the boxes and enter the office behind us. I hear shouts of, "Clear!"

The senior member calls in some more men. "Untie those people," he says. "Gags first." They come over and the first one pulls my chair upright. He picks at the edge of the duct tape then pulls it off. The last layer pulls out a whole bunch of hair at the back of my head. He pulls the cloth gag out of my mouth. The senior officer is picking his way through the boxes to the trigger device.

"It's set to go off at twelve-thirty," I shout.

He looks down at the side of the box that I can't see. Then he crouches down. "Four minutes, seven seconds," he says.

Four minutes! There's no way we can clear the building in four minutes. But we can't just run and leave everyone to be blown up. "Untie my colleagues so at least *they* can get out!" I say to him. He ignores me, just reaches forward. I hear a click.

He looks at me and smiles grimly. "Unlike on TV," he says. "they always have an on-off switch."

———

We are in the street outside the Victoria Building, waiting for the bomb squad to show up. People are streaming out, many of them visibly and audibly annoyed at being evacuated during their lunch hour. Tina and I each have an arm around the other, listening to Jen talking with the Inspector.

"What I don't understand," he says, "is why you called the Ottawa Police Service and not the Mounties."

"I didn't. When you guys showed up, I was as surprised as I was relieved."

"That was me," I say, "indirectly, anyway."

They turn towards me.

"When you told me, Jen, that your boss wanted—"

"Cal! Don't say any more." She turns to the Inspector. "I'm sorry about that, but this is a national-security issue." He nods. "Just report it up your chain of command." He nods again. "I have to go to discuss it with my superiors."

"OK. Will do." He nods at Tina and me and heads towards his police cruiser.

"Let's go," Jen says and we head down the street to her

car. "Sorry to have to cut you off there Cal, I'll tell you why in a minute. But I've got to know why the police showed up."

"When we were in your car coming here, I kept chewing over in my mind that your boss told you to get me involved in helping you. It made no sense. No police department asks for civilian help in operations and I couldn't believe that CSIS would either. I just couldn't leave it alone. I thought you were leading me into a trap. So when we were walking from your car, I texted Tina and told her to get out of the hotel a.s.a.p. and then I texted Stammo. I told him that if I didn't text back in twenty minutes he had to get our former colleague in the VPD to contact the Ottawa police and get them to have an Emergency Response Team storm the place. It all took a little longer than I was expecting. When that box started beeping, I worried that maybe Stammo thought I was being melodramatic and had ignored the text."

We get to her car and climb inside. "Why the Ottawa police?" Jen asks.

"Well your boss had said that there was a senior RCMP officer in this cabal, so I didn't want Stammo to get the Mounties in on it, in case he did something to delay the ERT."

She pulls away from the curb. "The man who interrogated you Cal," she says.

I finish her sentence. "...was your boss at CSIS."

"How did you know that?" Tina asks.

"At first, I suspected Jen was leading me into a trap, but when they tied her up with us, that kind of exonerated her. So I knew when she told me that she hadn't revealed our hotel to anyone, she was telling the truth. When that nurse brought you in, I worked out that Jen's boss must have had her followed, discovered the hotel and sent someone to take you. Therefore, he was the one in the cabal."

"You're right on all counts," Jen says.

"So what do we do now?" I ask.

"Markus told me that a senior RCMP officer was part of the cabal. If that were true, he would never have told me. I have to assume that no one in the Mounties is involved and it's safe to take this to the Commissioner of the RCMP. If he'll see me."

It's a good plan. "I can probably get you an appointment with the RCMP Commissioner," I say. I can hear the sound of sirens. More emergency response teams going to the scene, I guess.

"How the hell are you going to do that?" Jen asks.

"Larry Corliss is the Minister of Border Security and Organized Crime Reduction. I know him well; I've known him since he was Mayor of Vancouver. I helped with some problem he had in his election campaign. He must work with the RCMP on a daily basis and he probably feels he owes me one. He could get us an appointment with the Commissioner."

I pull out my phone. I have Larry's personal cell number. I press dial.

I check my watch. "It's nearly one. Time's running out. Markus and the rest of the cabal will know the bombing didn't happen. We have to move fast." Larry's phone is ringing.

The sirens are behind us and Jen pulls over to the curb to let the police cruisers pass. Except that they don't. They screech to a halt beside us and in seconds, RCMP members, with firearms drawn, are surrounding us.

"Keep your hands in full view," I say, putting mine against the window so that the armed officers can see them.

Still training their weapons on us, three officers step forward and open the doors. Keeping our hands in view we get out of Jen's car. The sergeant who opened my door, takes the phone from my hand.

As they start to cuff us, Jen asks, "What the hell's going on here. I'm a CSIS intelligence officer. On whose authority are you arresting us?"

"Your boss, the Director of CSIS."

Time just ran out.

———

I HAVE BEEN ALONE IN A WINDOWLESS ROOM FOR NINETY minutes. I know the routine: separate the suspects, let them sweat for a while, and then interrogate. They'll probably go with Jen first but who knows. I hope Tina's OK. She's probably never been arrested before.

Why did Marcus have the RCMP pick us up? Why isn't he worried that we'll tell all? Is he so arrogant that he thinks we won't be believed? Our stories will be identical; surely they must carry some weight. Is it a delaying tactic? Hold us long enough until he, General Matherson and any others can get out of the country. No. He's an egomaniac; there's no way he's going to run for it. It just doesn't make sense. Maybe it's—

The door opens. Two RCMP members enter. The one in uniform has an unmistakeable air of authority. Reflexively, I stand. Old habits die hard. I look at his epaulettes: crossed swords and a crown. He's a deputy commissioner. He reports to the Commissioner; there are only six deputies in the force; why is one of them here to see *me*?

"Please sit down," he says. It sounds like a polite request not an order.

304 ROBERT P. FRENCH

We all three sit.

"On instructions from the Director of CSIS, we have been told that, as a matter of national security, we are *not* to interrogate you." His voice tells me that he is not happy with these orders. "He has asked that we hold you in complete isolation until such time as you are transferred to a different facility." The word facility conjures up images of a 'black site'. I can feel an unpleasant reaction in my gut. "Accordingly, you are not to discuss with anyone here anything about what you may believe to be the reasons for your arrest."

I see a tiny sliver of light. "Might I ask why you're here then sir?" I ask.

"When you were arrested, one of our sergeants confiscated your phone." The sliver of light becomes a thin beam. "As is normal procedure, we ascertained that it was connected. The sergeant saw that the party being called was Minister Corliss. He spoke with the Minister and subsequently the Minister contacted the Commissioner. Although we are unable to speak with you about anything relating to your arrest, the Minister insisted that he talk with you."

His colleague hands me a phone.

"You can make just one call with this phone. My colleague here will be watching you on camera, although he won't be able to hear what you're saying. When the call is over, he'll come in and retrieve the phone."

They stand and leave. I tap the phone. No password. It is open in the 'Contacts' app. There is just one name on the list.

I tap it.

———

THE PLAIN-CLOTHES OFFICER ENTERS, TAKES THE PHONE AND puts it in his pocket. "Come with me please sir," he says. This is not a request. I follow him down a corridor into a larger, equally-windowless room. Jen and Tina are both handcuffed. I look at Tina and smile. She doesn't look in the least worried, just defiant, but Jen looks less than happy. The Deputy Commissioner is also there and he is not happy one bit.

One of the five military policemen in the room, a Sergeant, approaches me with handcuffs. I hold out my wrists. "Behind the back please." I do as he says. I feel the cuffs click closed. This is too quick. Larry Corliss won't have time to do anything for us. Even if he believes everything I told him, it will still take him time to react and set any wheels in motion.

The MP Captain, Laurent according to his name badge, salutes the Deputy. "Thank you, sir." His voice carries a slight *québécois* accent. The salute is returned in silence.

We are walked out into another corridor then into an elevator which takes us to a carpark. There are two Suburbans, in camo colours, engines idling. We are bundled into the backseat of one of them, with me in the middle. I smile reassuringly at Tina. She smiles back but now I can see worry in her face.

We leave the RCMP building and already the cuffs behind my back are cutting into my wrists. In minutes we're on a highway. One that I used last night. This is the way to General Matherson's house. Good. If all goes well, we will be at his house when they come to arrest him. *If* they come to arrest him.

But within fifteen minutes, we are driving through the gates, not of the General's house, but of CFB Uplands and we're heading towards a sleek, black Challenger jet sitting on the runway, engines whining idly; the number 616 is painted in white on it's nose. It's the one in the poster on Captain McCaffery's wall. Beside it is a sleek, black Jaguar, Lieutenant-General Matherson's. He is standing beside it in uniform. We are going to be taken somewhere. We are the pawns that the cabal needs to take off the board. If we get into that jet we're dead meat.

We pull up beside the Jag and the MP Captain jumps out and snaps a smart salute at the General. The General talks to him for a moment. He turns and signals his colleague, who gets out of the front seat and opens the rear passenger door on Tina's side. "Please get out of the vehicle," he says.

Tina starts to wriggle around in the seat. "No!" I say. "Stay where you are, Tina. Don't do anything they tell you." She wriggles back.

"Get out of the vehicle," the Sergeant repeats.

"No," Tina and I say in unison.

The sergeant turns to his captain, who waves to his men in the other Suburban.

They get out. "Take those people out and load them on the plane," he tells them.

"Just resist," I say to Tina and Jen.

"Resistance is futile," says Jen.

"No way. Every minute of freedom is worth it," I say. "They're not the Borg, for God's sake."

The sergeant and a corporal grab Tina but she brings her knees up and pushes her feet against the back of the seat in front of her, jamming herself in place. "Good idea," I say. I lift up my legs and push them between the front seats. I look at Jen; she too has followed Tina's lead. It takes two minutes of swearing and struggle but they manage to get Jen and Tina out. One MP holds their arms and three come to get me.

Despite the pain it causes to my wrists, I slide my bottom forward until I'm on my back, with my feet on the front console. I make my body as stiff as a board. It takes them a long time, and a crippling punch to my solar plexus, before they get me out of the vehicle. I'm praying that resistance isn't futile. I struggle furiously, hoping to keep my captors busy, and yell, "Tina, Jen, RUN."

They both pull away from the corporal who is holding them and Tina breaks free. Despite having her hands handcuffed behind her, she is running like the wind towards the gates through which we entered. One of the men holding me lets go and runs after her. It's no competition; he reaches her and with a push sends her sprawling. None too gently, he pulls her to her feet and drags her back.

Now for the next step.

"Captain!" I say, putting as much authority into my voice as I can muster. "It's Lieutenant-General Matherson whom you need to arrest. He is a traitor who has profited from illegal arms sales—"

"SILENCE HIM," Matherson roars.

"—and he's responsible for the terr— Oooof." The second punch to my solar plexus doubles me over and makes me fight for breath. Through the pain raging in my gut, I hear Tina's voice.

"General Matherson and Markus Heath, the Director of CSIS are also responsible for the terrorist bombing two weeks ago."

"This is preposterous," Matherson laughs. "I don't think I've ever heard such a ridiculous conspiracy theory." I realize how ludicrous our accusations must sound to the MPs holding us captive. "It's these three who are the traitors. I'm here to see that they are transported to CFB..." His voice trails off and over the sound of my laboured breathing, I hear sirens.

I force my body upright and look toward the sound. At the gate, another MP vehicle and an RCMP cruiser, with lights flashing, are pulling up to the barrier.

"Captain," Matherson shouts. "Take the prisoners and bring them on board this plane, right now."

"Captain," Jen says calmly. "I'm a CSIS intelligence officer. I think you know that. Wait until those vehicles get here."

"CAPTAIN! This is a direct order. Take your prisoners on board NOW!"

The MPs start to push us towards the steps leading up to the Challenger's cabin.

The captain looks from Jen to Matherson and back, indecision writ large on his face.

"I think you know the right thing to do here, Captain Laurent," Jen says.

He looks at her and gives an almost imperceptible nod. "Stand down," he orders his men.

"I'll have you court marshalled for this," Matherson spits out. He turns and marches up the steps into the waiting jet.

I look back towards the gate. Both vehicles are speeding along the tarmac towards us but before they can get here, the Challenger's steps fold up and the door closes. The engine whine grows to an unbearable scream, drowning out the noise of the sirens. The aircraft inches forward then rapidly gains speed, when it is a hundred metres from us the cruiser and the MP Suburban flash past us. They just pull up level with the jet and I see gold-beribboned, uniformed arms appear out of the windows and wave at the pilot, but the pilot ignores them and the aircraft outstrips them.

The vehicles slow, u-turn and move toward us. By the time they get to us the Challenger is airborne and climbing steeply.

A general in fatigues gets out of the MP vehicle and the Deputy Commissioner gets out of the RCMP cruiser.

The MP captain and his men all snap to attention and Laurent delivers a smart salute. The general's gaze sweeps over us and comes to rest on Laurent. "Very well done, Captain. You can un-cuff your former prisoners now."

The Deputy comes over to me. "You're lucky to have friends in high places Mr. Rogan. I hope I did the right thing here, if not, I'll be saying goodbye to a career I love."

The volume of the Challenger's engines increases and we all look up. It has done a u-turn and is flying back over us, heading south. We all stare up at it, silhouetted against the cold blue of the afternoon sky. In moments, it will be out of Canadian airspace. General Matherson will live to fight another day, unless someone can get an airforce general to recall the plane and if that happens, will the pilot comply? Maybe he too is part of this cabal we've been chasing after.

As we look at the departing jet, each of us thinking our own thoughts, it bursts into an orange cloud of flame. For a surreal fraction of a second, I still hear the engines, then the percussive boom of the explosion hits my eardrums and I watch, mesmerized, as a shower of aircraft parts rains down onto the end of the airfield and onto the adjacent land.

The Deputy Commissioner was right. Silently, I thank Larry Corliss, my friend in high places.

———

SHE LOOKS AFFRONTED BY THE FACT THAT FIVE PEOPLE HAVE walked into her office unannounced and without even knocking. "I'm afraid you can't see the Director right now; he's on the phone to the Minister."

Jen's boss, Tony, leans over and whispers something to the Deputy Commissioner. The latter thinks for a second and nods. Tony smiles at the Director's PA. "Alice," he says gently, "I'm going to have to ask you to leave the office."

"But I—"

"Sorry Alice. National security," he says. They seem to use that as an excuse for everything but in this case I approve. "Please just wait outside."

Not in the least mollified, she humphs, picks up her purse and leaves.

As the door closes behind her, Tony presses buttons on her phone and the Director's voice comes over the speakerphone, loud and clear.

"Yes, Minister, I feel sure that the PM will agree that these bombings, plus the attempted bombing of the Victoria Building, will warrant using the Emergency Act. After all, his father used the War Measures Act to do the same thing in nineteen seventy."

"But Markus, I doubt that it will pass Parliamentary review." I recognize the well-known voice of the Minister of Public Safety.

"Yes, but while Parliament dithers around, there might easily be another attack, which armed military on the streets might be able to thwart." There is silence from the Minister. Markus Heath presses his point. "The sabotage of a military aircraft requires an armed response. And, but for the bravery of a Canadian citizen who tragically died in the explosion with General Matherson, we would never have known about the bomb in the Victoria Building. Military patrols in the Capital's buildings would certainly deter these terrorists."

"OK, Markus. I'll talk to the PM about it."

"I would be happy to brief him with you, Minister."

"That might be a good idea. I'll get back to you."

They hang up.

Tony looks at the Deputy Commissioner and they both nod. The DC opens the door to the Director's office and walks in, followed by Tony, Jen, myself and Inspector Saunders.

When he sees Jen and me, the annoyance on his face morphs into disbelief.

The DC gets straight to it. "Markus Heath, you are under arrest for treason, conspiracy to commit murder and corruption."

"Don't be ridiculous," he snaps. "You're arresting me on the word of those two." He inclines his head in Jen's and my direction.

"We have far more than that," the Deputy says.

"Like what?" Heath sneers.

"Well for a start..." the Deputy stops in mid-sentence. "No, why don't you tell him Mr. Rogan?"

"Apart from the fact that we are going to find your fingerprints on the door handle of suite three-oh-seven of the Victoria Building, together with the fingerprints of your colleagues. And apart from the fact that you were the only person, other than Jen Halley, who knew at which hotel Tina Johal was staying, so you could kidnap her. And apart from the fact that you admitted to three witnesses what you were plotting. And apart from the fact that several of your men have been arrested and one of them is bound to talk. Apart from all that, there is documentary evidence." I stop and smile.

"What documentary evidence?" The sneer is still in his voice.

"The Deputy Commissioner here made a couple of phone calls and discovered that it was you who requested that the RCMP send a team to the offices of Chaos Star Security in Vancouver to delete all copies of the documents that Annalise Lamarche sent to her brother Denis. The only problem for you was that one document was decrypted just before it was deleted. The CEO of Chaos Star sent it to the DC this afternoon. It was a Microsoft Project document showing the detailed plans of your little cabal. It mentions names, dates and places. Based on that, the RCMP and the Military Police are in the process of making arrests right now." I remember one other detail. "Oh, and the other documents have been sent back to Chaos Star for them to decrypt."

"You fools," he sighs. "Our 'cabal', as you call it, was the only hope for Canada. Democracy is the deadest concept in the modern world. We can only survive as a nation if we have a strong hand on the wheel." His voice grows more forceful. "You people could be in the vanguard of a new chapter in our glorious history. Just think what—"

The Deputy Commissioner cuts him off. "You can contemplate all that during the years you'll be spending in jail." He nods to his colleague. "Inspector..."

Inspector Saunders takes handcuffs from his jacket and walks forward. For an instant, the now-disgraced Director of CSIS looks like he's going to resist but instead he takes a deep breath and presents his wrists.

I remember doing the same thing just five hours ago.

"Behind his back," I suggest.

His look of resignation cascades into a look of venom, but Inspector Saunders does as I request.

Then a thought hits me. "Let me ask you something. Did General Matherson know about the bomb in the aircraft?"

He doesn't answer but his face says it all. "He didn't did he? He thought he was taking us to some place where we could be disposed of. But you had other plans. Tina's story in the Daily News Hound dot com exposed the General. To you he was a knight to sacrifice, to take off the board together with the three pawns. Another terrorist attack for you to save the country from."

I look into Heath's eyes. We lock eyes for a long time.

Then I say, "I wouldn't want to live in the Canada you imagine you could mould. Nor would thirty-seven million other Canadians."

He glares at me but I just smile.

"We're better than that." I say.

49

CAL

Monday, eighteen days later

It feels odd walking through these doors. "Cal!" Adry yells as she leaps out from behind the reception desk and gives me a hug. I notice an odd smell but before I can comment, I hear Nick grumbling. "About bloody time," With a smile on my face, so big it hurts, I walk into the main office. "And don't expect a hug from me," he adds. But he can't suppress the grin. "How was your Christmas?"

"It was great. Tina and I went to Toronto together and she and Ellie got on like a house on fire. I didn't get to see Sam but that was probably for the best. How are you?"

He shrugs. "The doctors say I'll live to be a hundred. They just said I mustn't do any dancing."

"Tell him, Nick," Adry says.

"Tell him what?" he asks.

"Yooooou know."

"Oh. That. Yes. Well I'm seeing someone."

"That's great Nick. Who?"

"My nurse from St. Paul's. I kinda plucked up the courage to get chatting with him."

I nod and pat him on the shoulder.

"We saw you on the CBC News," Adry says.

"Yeah, you were good," Nick adds. "Did you see on the same newscast that the government made some people in the Iranian embassy *persona non grata* and sent their asses packing? Your guy, Majid Zarin, was one of them of course." He gives a big smile. "Since you snuck the name of the firm into the news, we've got a bunch of new cases. So you need to sit yourself down at that desk and let's do morning prayers. You too Adry." We do as he asks. "OK, let's get after it. First item: while you were vacationing in Ottawa, Adry did your job for you. She tracked down that missing rich kid and his dad coughed up the fee."

"Well done Adry." I give her a big thumbs up and Nick nods enthusiastically.

"Second item," he says. "Do you want to tell her what we were talking about on the phone before Christmas?"

"Sure," I say. "Adriana, we've decided to fire you as Office Manager. We want you to work on investigations full time. Your first job is to find us a new Office Manager."

Her eyes are like saucers. They brim up, "You guys!" she says. I feel her tears as she hugs me. "Thank you so, so much."

"OK." I say, "Your last duty as Office Manager is to give me the four hundred bucks from the bet that Nick and I had. Susan Grey was not cheating on her husband. I was right."

She does as I ask and I have the distinct pleasure of waving the notes at Nick.

He responds with, "Susan Grey came to see me in the hospital. She told her husband everything. Gave me the biggest bunch of flowers you've ever seen. And she also gave us the cheque from her husband."

I just grin and pocket the money. I have a plan for it tomorrow.

"Next item," he says. "Your friend Dougie never came to pick up his shopping cart full of junk. It's starting to smell up the office. Track him down Rogan and get him to haul it out of here. Next item..."

As he hands out assignments all I can think is: it's good to be back.

50

CAL

Tuesday

The last time I was at a funeral I was arrested. And I was holding Sam's hand at the time. Now I'm holding Tina's. The funeral previous to that, it was Ellie's hand I was holding. After several long phone calls, Sam has agreed not to make Ellie change her name for which I am grateful.

Father O'Higgins says the final words before the coffin is lowered into the ground. He said a Mass for the soul of Denis Lamarche and the only other attendee was Ghost. If he hadn't run into me on the streets of the downtown east side four weeks ago, Canada would be a different country today.

Father O'Higgins walks from the grave, shakes our hands and leaves.

We stand in the bitter cold.

"So that's the end of old Wily," Ghost says with a sigh.

"I was surprised that Tommy wasn't here," I say.

"He's in the hospital. He got in a fight with a guy twice his size. You know Tommy..." he chuckles.

It triggers a memory. "If you see Dougie Blake, would you tell him to come by my office and pick up his stuff."

"Din'tja hear?" he says. "Old Dougie froze to death on Christmas Day. He must'a had a drink too many and fell over. Right in Coal Harbour. People walking by and no one checks to see if he's OK."

I shake my head. Another victim of the streets. I wonder if Ghost will be next.

"Hey Ghost, it's December thirty-first, last day of the year. How about a New Year's Resolution? Why don't you get off the streets? I'll help you. I know a nice cheap place you could stay and I can cover the rent for you until you get back on your feet, give you a bit of spending money too."

He turns a sad face on me. "Thanks Rocky. You're a good man. But being on the streets is the only life I've ever really known." My thought, *Free will: the persistent illusion that we have any control over the choices we make*, is broken with, "Of course, a couple of bucks wouldn't go amiss."

I give him a smile. "I'll do you one better than that." I pull out my wallet and take out the four hundred bucks. "Two hundred for you and two hundred for Tommy." I hand over the cash and say, "Let's go and have a big meal and toast old Wily with a few beers. Give him a good send off."

His cheery optimism returns. "Well, like I always say..." he gives us a big grin... "Fuckin' A!"

We turn our backs on the grave and head off.

I look at Tina. She smiles and mouths three words.

"I love you."

AFTERWORD

Thank you for reading *Cabal*. Reviews are the life blood of an independent author. If you have a minute to do a review on Amazon, it would be *really* appreciated. Also, a review at Goodreads or Bookbub is always appreciated.

I invite you to read the other books in the series: *Junkie*, *Oboe*, *Lockstep*, *Three*, *Captive* and the latest book *Jailed*. All are available in paperback from Amazon.

ABOUT THE AUTHOR

Hi. I am a former software developer, turned actor, turned author. The Cal Rogan mysteries are set in Vancouver Canada and, I hope, reflect the best and worst of the city. If you would like to know more about my views on the drug scene, publishing and writing, or would like to contact me:

My website: robertpfrench.com.

Facebook: facebook.com/robertpfrenchauthor